M000096665

MARKED BY DARKNESS

THE DARK FAE TRILOGY BOOK 2

SAMANTHA BRITT

Marked by Darkness © 2020 Samantha Britt
ISBN: 9781659154979
Cover Design by Covers by Christian

Copyright notice:
All rights reserved under the International and Pan-American Copyright
Conventions. No part of this book may be reproduced or transmitted in any form
or by any means, electronic or mechanical, including photocopying, recording, or
by any information storage and retrieval system, without permission in writing
from the publisher.
This is a work of fiction. Names, places, characters and incidents are either the
product of the author's imagination or are used fictitiously, and any resemblance
to any actual persons, living or dead, organizations, events or locales is entirely
coincidental.

CHAPTER ONE

THE GREEN EMBROIDERED CURTAINS ARE DRAWN CLOSED IN THE healing suite. I consider opening them but decide against it. Jordan's bed is placed in the center of the room, and the incoming sun shines directly on her this early in the day. As a fellow redhead, I know all too well how easy it is for our skin to burn. Even if Jordan's skin tone is darker than mine, I don't want to risk it.

So, I stay in my chair beside the bed. Jordan, the only girl who'd bothered to show me any kindness when I arrived in Seelie, still rests in a magically induced coma. It's been one week since she was stabbed in the back. Seven days since a knife punctured several vital organs and her life's been on the line.

The castle healers swear my friend will be healed, but their Fae powers have limits. Jordan's healing will take time. I've pressed them for a date when they think she'll be healed enough to at least wake up, but not one of the five healers on rotation will give me an estimate. Their avoidance frustrates me, and I'm ashamed to admit I lost my temper yesterday.

I'd arrived for my daily visit and ran into one of the gentler healers while she used magic to clean Jordan's body. As usual, I'd questioned when my friend would be able to wake up. I longed to see her kind, brown eyes and see for myself that she made it out of Queen Aria's demented contest with her life.

But when the healer gave me the same run-around excuse as always, I couldn't stop myself from yelling. Now, there's no healer here during my visit, and I have the feeling none will show up until I leave.

"Your Majesty," a rough voice calls from near the door.

I sigh and meet Vagar's red, reptilian-like eyes. "I've asked you not to call me that."

Vagar, the creature I met when I ventured into the cavern at the peak of the Cursed Mountains, doesn't so much as blink. No matter how many times I ask him not to address me like a queen, he never listens.

"The welcoming ceremony is due to begin in a quarter turn of the clock. His Highness will be expecting you." My intimidating guard's speech has come a long way since our first conversation in the cavern. Lord knows how many years Vagar spent alone in that cave. With no one to talk to, his speech suffered. But after only one week back in society, Vagar sounds nothing like the hissing or stuttering creature I first met. Though, I'm pretty much the only person he talks to. He prefers to grunt and mumble at everyone else.

Again, I sigh, mourning the fact my week-long reprieve has ended. I'd known I wouldn't be able to hide myself from Seelie Court society forever, but I hadn't expected Camden to insist I abandon my self-imposed isolation so soon. After the hell I experienced in the contest, I'd hoped I would be left alone for at least a month. But people want to see their winner. They want to see their next princess.

"You're right." I pick up the skirt of my long, golden gown so I don't trip when I stand. I give Jordan's hand one last squeeze before I move away.

I'm approaching Vagar and the door beside him, when a new figure steps inside the room. I release a surprised yelp while Vagar's hands blur with speed. He produces a knife and swiftly presses it against the newcomer's neck.

"Whoa! Don't kill me. I'm just bringing her flowers." The tall, blond sentry throws his hands in the air both in surprise and fright. One hand is empty while the other holds a luscious bouquet of flowers. They look like they've come from the castle gardens located outside my room. I've spent countless hours staring at the inner courtyard from my third-floor window, admiring the unique and stunning floral arrangements while I avoided interacting with citizens of Seelie Court.

"Morty," I greet the familiar sentry.

Vagar retracts his knife, but he twists his body to place himself in between us.

"Lady Serafina." The color slowly returns to his blanched face. He swallows thickly, avoiding Vagar's stare. "How is she today?"

"The same." I'm unable to hide my disappointment.

Morty jerks his head, careful to keep his feelings from his face. He takes four rigid steps into the healing suite. He removes the basically fresh flowers from the vase on Jordan's bedside table, replacing them with the new, vibrant bouquet.

I watch my friend's lover reach out and stroke a strand of hair off her forehead.

When Jordan first told me about her relationship with the sentry, I'd been against it. She's only twenty-two. I couldn't understand how she'd been so willing to give up her life in the Human Realm to be with someone she'd just met.

Not to mention the fact the couple could never get married. Unions between Fae and humans are against the law in Seelie. Their relationship seemed like a foolish mistake, but then I saw how much Morty cares for Jordan…

Every day, the sentry visits the healing suite and brings my friend fresh flowers. He stays by her side for hours, talking to her in his low, soothing voice, until he is forced to leave to fulfill his duties.

I hadn't believed Jordan when she said Morty loved her, but seeing his affection with my own eyes forced me to accept his love is real and true.

And it's loyal.

Morty continues to gaze at Jordan with undying adoration, and I know it's time for me to go.

I pull my eyes from the private moment and clear my throat. "Good day, Morty."

"Good day, my lady," his farewell follows me into the corridor as I walk out.

Behind me, Vagar's heavy steps follow. "The prince waits for you in his parlor."

I say nothing, but I turn right at the next hallway, knowing it will take me where I need to go.

We reach the central staircase and climb to the third floor. I ignore the quick curtsies and bows as I pass castle servants. I don't think I could get use to their deference even if I wanted to.

Once in the royal wing, I relax. The servants will have finished their morning tasks in this area of the castle, so I won't run into any more of them.

I pass the entrance to my rooms and continue toward the heavy wood doors at the end of the hall. Camden's personal guard blocks the entrance to the prince's chambers. Frederick, or Rick as I like to call him, watches my approach without making a sound. He waits until I stop in front of the doors and lift my brow before he turns.

Frederick cracks the door open. "Your Highness," he calls into the room. "Lady Serafina is here."

I hear the prince's muffled reply, "Let her in."

Frederick pushes the door open, and I step inside. The door closes quickly behind me, keeping Vagar in the hall. There's no need for my guard to follow me in. The prince's rooms are the most secure in the castle. No danger will find me here. At least, not the violent sort of danger.

My eyes widen in shock as I take in the naked torso facing me. Camden's tunic is stuck over his head, and I see one bright green eye peer at me through the neck hole.

"Serafina. Good morning. Will you help me?" He moves his arms in demonstration, looking helpless.

I choke back the drool that threatens to drip from my open mouth, pressing my lips closed. Who knew the prince's loose tunics hide such muscles? Seriously, Camden's ripped. I count all eight abs as I make my way over to him.

Slowly, I lift my hands and grab onto the end of his formal tunic. The fabric is bunched and sticking to his damp skin. I inhale the scent of soap. He must've just gotten out of the shower.

Careful to touch as little skin as possible, I tug the material down. Camden shimmies, helping the process along. Soon enough, his torso is covered. I'm relieved and a little disappointed.

I swallow and take a healthy step back.

Camden rolls his shoulder. His hair stands on end as he shoots me a sheepish grin. "Sorry about that. My valet usually helps me dress."

"Where is he?" I glance around the room and confirm we're

alone, thankful for the opportunity to pull my attention off the handsome prince.

"Polishing my boots, I think." Camden runs a hand over his messy hair when he sees himself in the mirror on the wall. "Lyr noticed a scuff on the left boot when he pulled it out of the wardrobe. I tried to tell him we were on a timeline, but he wouldn't hear it. He's very dedicated to his work."

"Ah." I nod like having a valet to run errands for you is a totally normal, and not at all an extravagant, thing to have. I, myself, have a lady's maid, but I rarely let her in my rooms to do her job. Like I said, I've spent the last week in my rooms. I've had no need to be primped and prepared for royal events. Not until today.

Camden clears his throat, and his eyes trail the length of me. "Forgive me for not saying anything sooner, Sera," he takes a step closer. "You look lovely this morning."

I can't help the blush. "Thank you."

His lips lift, and his eyes shine. "You're welcome."

I shift awkwardly. I'd expected to arrive, meet Camden, then immediately make our way to the throne room. The prince and I haven't been alone in the week since the contest ended, and we certainly haven't been alone in his private rooms. I'm not sure what to do. Should I sit? Or is that too casual? Should I make small talk? But what would I talk about?

Camden approaches the table beside the mirror, not seeming to notice my awkwardness. He slides a royal green sash across his body, then pins several medallions to the fabric. I watch him, thinking he looks like a fairytale prince. I guess that's really not that far from the truth.

The door opens and a frazzled servant rushes into the room. Lyr, Camden's valet, holds out shining black boots for the prince's inspection.

"Apologies for my tardiness, Your Highness," he pants. He'd obviously run to the room.

"No apologies necessary, Lyr," Camden says kindly. "Thank you." He takes the boots, leans against the table, and pulls them on.

Lyr bows low, then quickly backs out of the room. Before the door closes behind him, Vagar's eyes meet mine, silently searching for any signs of distress. He dips his chin when he confirms I'm unharmed. He's a diligent guard.

"There." Camden draws my gaze back to him.

He's turned away from the mirror and bestows the brunt of his perfect smile on me. "All done. How do I look?"

My heart skips a beat. "You look handsome," I admit. "Like always."

Now, it's Camden's turn for his cheeks to color. The blush only makes him more attractive. "Thank you, Sera." His voice is low and full of promise. He reaches out and grabs my hand.

Before he can close the distance between us, I blurt out, "Should we be going?" In the distance, I hear the sound of a clock strike the top of the hour. Thank the lord for impeccable timing.

Some of the heat fades from Camden's eyes, but not all of it. "Of course," his fingers lace through mine. "Let's go."

My gut twists, and I let him lead me out of the room without pulling away. I ignore Frederick's pointed look at our hands when we step into the hallway. I try not to care what anyone thinks about the intimate gesture. I have bigger things to worry about. Like my first official event as Lady Serafina Richards, unwilling fiancée to Prince Camden of Seelie, and future princess of a realm she knows next to nothing about.

Yeah… this is going to be a great day.

CHAPTER TWO

The throne room is a glittering masterpiece, highlighting the wealth and opulence of the Seelie Court. Gilded lotus blossoms adorn the floor; the surface flares bright when the clouds outside part and the sun, once again, shines into the room. Marble pillars support the cathedral ceiling, and magnificent portraits depicting scenery found all across Seelie land decorate the wall, spaced between the tall windows and the billowing white and green curtains.

Growing up, I knew magical creatures existed. I'd seen the trolls living under the bridge in my local park, and I'd watched nymphs bounce through the trees and dive into lakes. As a teenager, fear had plagued me when I witnessed their otherworldly power and grace, but sometimes I'd like to imagine I was one of them.

I could be graceful and charming, twirling around the fresh cut grass in my backyard. I could enchant people with my magical voice and lure them to do whatever I wished. But of all the fantastical imaginings I had as a kid, never did I imagine I'd find myself here... in Seelie... engaged to marry their next king.

I stand on the royal dais at the front of the room, watching all types of Fae arrive. Brownies wear pristine white aprons over their plain green dresses. Waif-like nymphs glide with incomparable grace in fine silk gowns that barely cover the most intimate parts of their bodies. Satyrs have donned fine sashes to cover their naked torsos. A group of them stand in the back corner. Their curling horns have been shined for the occasion, and their hooves polished.

Never before have I seen so many different types of creatures assembled in one room. I've learned all the creatures I've seen in my life are different types of Common Fae. They are natural citizens of the Fae Realm, but they do not possess as much magical power or ability as those known as High Fae, the ones who look human except for their incredibly good looks and pointed ears.

I've also learned Common Fae are known to mingle with their own kind, integrating with others only when necessary, and hardly ever for social occasions. They may share residence in Seelie, but that does not make them friendly neighbors.

My heart beats like a herd of wild horses, and I'm certain there are at least a few species of Fae who can detect my anxiety. It's nothing short of unsettling to consider that *I* am the reason so many Fae have come together today.

Beside me, Prince Camden stands with his head held high and a regal lift of his chin. He watches the Common Fae file into the throne room with a well-practiced smile. It's not too wide, but not too small. He knows how to work the crowd; Camden was born and bred for this. Whereas I spent my childhood watching cartoons and binge-eating junk food with Uncle Eric and Aunt Julie, Camden learned royal etiquette, political strategy, and the vast history of the Fae Realm.

As the nephew to the king of Seelie, Camden was born as the heir-apparent, but no one had expected him to inherit the throne. The king and queen had been married for many years at the time of Camden's birth, but Seelie Fae believed their monarchs would produce their own heir in time. But after centuries of an unfruitful union, their thoughts began to turn.

I observe the handsome male at my side. When I first met Camden, he'd been dressed as an ordinary archer. I hadn't known him as the Seelie Prince. There'd been nothing regal about him aside from his well-spoken words and authoritative air. Now, I realize what a fool I'd been.

Camden must feel my attention. He turns and lowers his chin to meet my eye. His practiced smile shifts with genuine affection. The sight makes my stomach twist, either with dread or excitement. I can't really tell which one.

"Sera? Is everything all right?"

Hardly.

"It's a lot of people."

My arm is tucked into the crook of Camden's elbow. He places his free hand on top of my fingers. "The moment you need a break, just tell me."

"Are you sure?" Queen Aria, Camden's aunt and the current ruler of Seelie, spent the previous evening lecturing me about how important it is to greet every well-wisher who's traveled to the castle. Common Fae rarely get the chance to interact with royalty, and they expect to have the opportunity to meet the prince's future bride. I'm expected to smile and wave like the dutiful, happy fiancée all of Seelie expects me to be until the masses are satisfied.

"I'm sure." Fondness shines in his gaze. "I know things have been challenging since the competition ended. I don't want to overwhelm you."

Challenging is an understatement. Surviving Queen Aria's horrendous competition was, itself, enough to crack even the most emotionally-stable person.

I'd watched girls die. My closest friend in the competition is still unconscious from injuries she sustained, and I have the unfortunate burden of being declared the victor. A mystical diadem is stuck on my head, and I'm trapped in Seelie as the prince's future bride.

But the competition and subsequent engagement aren't responsible for the majority of my distress. No, that honor lies with a particularly haughty Unseelie king who's been lying to me my entire life.

I don't know what expression I wear as the thoughts race through my mind, but Camden's smile falters.

"Thank you." I force the negative thoughts away and school my features. I'm about to be introduced to countless Fae, and first impressions matter. I haven't given up hope of getting out of this engagement, but part of that half-formed plan includes going about my days like nothing is wrong. As far as Camden and all of Seelie know, I'm a willing fiancée. "I'll tell you if I start to feel overwhelmed."

Camden's smile returns, and it's breathtaking. I wish it was enough to erase my toubles, but no matter how handsome or attentive the Seelie prince is, I can't forget all of this is happening against my will.

He removes his hand and faces forward, straightening his back and sharing his smile with the crowd. I swear, I hear both feminine and masculine sighs of appreciation.

The room continues to fill up until there's only a narrow path from the back of the room to the royal dais where we stand. Queen Aria is not here, but I don't expect her to be. This event is designed to celebrate me and Camden—the future monarchs. The queen will stay away so her presence doesn't interfere, but I would prefer her to be here. I don't particularly like the queen, but at least her presence would take some of the attention off of me.

A trumpet-like instrument blasts in the back corner of the throne room, signaling the start of the ceremony.

The instrument grows silent, and Camden's voice reverberates through the air, captivating the entire room with very little effort.

"Citizens of Seelie, thank you for honoring us with your presence. As you know, I have recently become engaged."

Several Fae clap and hoot their excitement.

"Serafina Richards bravely entered the queen's competition with twenty-three other young women, each one determined to claim victory." Camden gazes down at me. Happiness and affection are displayed for the entire room to see. "But from the first moment I laid eyes on Sera, I knew there was something special about her. She may have won the contest, but I'm the true winner in this room. I cannot imagine promising myself to another, and I'm forever grateful she is the one I get the honor of sharing my life with."

Now, the entire room erupts with cheers. And despite my best effort, I feel my cheeks heat. Camden means every word, and that makes everything so much worse.

I never wanted to win the contest. I only wanted to survive. If Jordan hadn't been bleeding out on top of the Cursed Mountains, I never would've touched that diadem—the cursed reason Queen Aria had started the competition in the first place. So many young women died trying to get the object, and now I'm stuck with the reminder of all that bloodshed.

Camden holds up a hand, and the crowd quiets. "I look forward to introducing each of you to your future queen. Let the welcoming ceremony begin." Once again, an instrument blares in the back of the throne room, but it's accompanied by excited chatter and eager applause.

The Common Fae begin to arrange themselves in a line. They will approach us one by one. I will smile and make small talk.

It's going to be hell.

I tear my gaze from the bustling crowd and see one group of Fae who aren't trying to get a favorable position in line.

Seelie nobles stand along the left side of the room, elevated on a modest dais. The richest and most powerful High Fae have met me on several occasions. This event isn't for them, but their attendance is encouraged. Nobles oversee most of the land in Seelie and act as landlords to Common Fae, and mingling with them helps keep relations between the two smooth.

But the nobles' smug expressions make me wish they'd declined Camden's invitation to attend the event. I never liked the way the wealthy males looked at me and my fellow contestants during the competition, and I like how they look at me now even less.

Several of the High Fae meet my eye as I observe their group, and their haughty smirks and flirtatious winks make me wish I was back in the training yard, wielding my trusty wooden staff. Let's see them look at me like a piece of meat when I have a weapon in my hands.

A small male approaches the royal dais, drawing my attention from the disconcerting nobles. The Fae's skin is pale blue, and his eyes are a similar color. His stature resembles a sprite, but his coloring isn't the usual green or brown hue. I'm not sure what species of Fae he is. Having grown up in the human world, I hadn't learned about all of the creatures residing in Seelie.

The Fae bows low, sweeping back his velvet cloak in a grand gesture. "Your Highness, Prince Camden, I am Ike from the

Wetlands of the pixies." He straightens, but keeps his head humbly tilted down. "It's an honor to stand in your presence."

A pixie? I observe the Fae with renewed interest. My best friend, Pascale, is a pixie, but she is not as small as this male. She'd told me most pixies lived in Unseelie. Clearly, I'm meeting one who doesn't.

Camden clears his throat. "Welcome to the castle, Ike from the Wetlands. Please allow me to introduce my future bride, Serafina Richards, from the human world."

Ike bows. "My lady. It is an honor."

I don't think I will ever get used to being treated with such respect. It just feels wrong. I've done nothing to deserve it.

"The honor is mine, Ike from the Wetlands," I recite the phrase Queen Aria had drilled into me the previous evening. "Thank you for traveling all this way. We hope you'll stay and enjoy the night's festivities with us."

Ike smiles, revealing four sharp canine teeth. "It will be my pleasure."

A royal sentry takes a step forward, signaling to Ike that his time has ended. The pixie departs, replaced by a pair of Brownies wearing their best servant garb. Our exchange proceeds pretty much the same as with Ike, except I find myself more distracted.

Brownies, like humans, are treated like second class citizens in Seelie, except they are actually paid. They work in the castle and noble houses, often leading the household staff and over-seeing the other servants. I wonder what possesses them to will-ingly subject themselves to those types of jobs. Brownies are exceptionally meticulous and clean, but surely they have other talents they'd like to pursue. Why do they willingly subject themselves to the ridicule of their fellow Fae by only working in lower servant positions?

The Brownies leave, and two sea-nymphs glide forward.

Throughout the room, I hear males, and some females, murmur their appreciation. The nymphs wear see-through gowns, dampened by their journey through the sea. Their skin is surprisingly tan considering they spend most of their days in the depths of the dark ocean, and their hair falls in delicate waves past their waist. Gorgeous, pale purple eyes gaze at the prince, and I'm reminded of another Fae who has similar eyes. Though, King Sebastian's are a deeper, more vibrant violet. The nymphs' eyes look like they've been washed out by salty water.

"Prince Camden," the two nymphs speak as one and dip low into graceful curtsies. Their cleavage is on full display.

"Ladies," Camden returns, wearing the same cordial and welcoming smile he's given everyone. He's unaffected by the nymphs' beauty, unlike most of the males in the room. I find myself wondering if it's an act, and also wondering why I care. It's not like we're a real couple. "Thank you for journeying to the castle."

"It is we who are thankful, Your Highness." The nymphs rise. They are so in sync that it's a little unsettling. They're stunning faces turn towards me, and I brace myself for another round of insincere conversation.

"You reign over The Darkness." Their voices adopt a low, monotone cadence. I almost look over my shoulder to confirm they aren't speaking to someone else, but their attention rests on me. Or, more accurately, the diadem adorning my head.

No one speaks. One glance confirms Camden's smile has dimmed. I watch the nymphs, trying to determine the motive behind their words.

Queen Aria never told anyone she wanted the diadem for herself, but that became obvious the day I returned from the Cursed Mountain with the jewel stuck to my head.

Queen Aria is only queen because her husband is ill and

unable to reign. Obtaining the ancient diadem would've given her the ability to control Darkness plaguing the Fae Realm. In possession of the diadem, Queen Aria could've wielded power to defend Seelie against Darkness, convincing the people to keep her on the throne.

Or she could've used the power to destroy those who opposed her reign. As far as I'm concerned, the cruel queen was just as likely to do the latter than the former.

But now that Camden has a bride and the diadem has chosen to literally stick to me, Queen Aria has no way to deter the nobles from moving forward with his coronation. She's only weeks away from losing her position of power. I hear she prowls through the castle like a wounded animal, striking out at any and every perceived offense. I regret that I've made an enemy of her, but I can't help but think it's worth it as long as it means someone so crazed doesn't obtain the mysterious power contained in Queen Lani's diadem. There's no telling what harm she would cause.

"Indeed," I reply after too many seconds have passed. Tension has descended on the throne room, and the crowd eagerly listens. I need to proceed carefully. This conversation will be reported back to Queen Aria, and she still has the power to enact retribution if she desires.

The nymphs' lips part into wide, adoring smiles. I'm taken aback. The expressions are so different from their earlier, ominous tones. "You will bring peace to our realm."

I give Camden a pleading look. I have no idea how to respond.

Yes, the people know I wear the diadem linked to controlling The Darkness, but the castle has been adamant about not hyping that particular fact. The political strategy is to focus on our upcoming wedding and the prince's coronation. Hopefully, not in that order. All discussion of the diadem and my supposed abilities have been shoved to the back of the royals' metaphorical to-do list.

Camden sees my expression. "The hope is for our realm to maintain the prosperity and peace achieved by my dear uncle, King Uri." He elevates the last part of his sentence and looks out into the crowd, drawing them to clap and nod approvingly. As far as I can tell, Common Fae love King Uri. His wife? Not so much.

I smile and clap politely, hoping the nymphs will take Camden's words for what they're intended to be—a dismissal.

I'm not so lucky.

The nymph on the left, the one with slightly darker hair, takes a step forward. I sense the sentry at my side stiffen. Camden senses it too. He holds up a staying hand to keep the guard back.

If the nymph notices the sentry, she doesn't show it. Water from her gown drips onto the floor. She continues to smile at me in an eerily admiring way. "Our king is rather fond of you."

Camden's arm flexes under my fingers. "Your king?"

For a moment, I believe she's talking about King Uri. But that isn't possible. I've yet to meet the bedridden monarch.

The second nymph follows her friend's lead and draws closer. "Yes, King Sebastian is quite smitten with the young prince's bride."

Bass?

I eye the two nymphs. Are they Unseelie? If so, what are they doing here? This event is strictly for Seelie Fae.

Camden's face is hard as stone as he lowers his arm and takes an ominous step forward, leaving me to stand alone.

"You're Unseelie?" He must already know the answer, but he's giving the nymphs a chance to explain their intrusion by asking.

The nymphs grin mischievously, and I know without a doubt they came her to cause trouble. "We are."

"You have crossed Seelie borders and attended this event without invitation. Explain your purpose here before I have you arrested."

My eyes widen. That seems a little harsh. I know Seelie and Unseelie aren't exactly best friends, but the nymphs haven't done anything more than crash a party—a very boring party.

"We simply wished to see the future queen." Again, the nymphs speak in unison.

"Very well, you've seen her. Now, leave my lands and return to your own."

"Shouldn't the girl come with us?" The darker-haired Fae surprises the room with the odd question. Camden doesn't speak right away. No doubt, he's just as confused as the rest of us.

I try to figure out what game the nymphs are playing, and I wonder if Bass put them up to it.

I haven't seen the Unseelie King in a week, not since he warned me to keep the truth of my half-Fae heritage a secret. My eyes travel down to my palm where the faded outline of a crescent moon and stars had swirled in a silvery-blue background.

I hate to admit it, but I've been hurt by Bass's absence. I mean... he's supposed to be one of my best friends. I know I'd acted like I hated his guts, and I still resent the lies he'd spun around me for years, but he's one of the few people I actually trust. I could use his help to try and figure out a way to end this engagement, and also how to handle the whole "Queen of the Dark" thing.

But Bass hasn't shown up since we last spoke. I feel abandoned, and it hurts.

"Why would Serafina go with you?" Camden finally asks what the entire room is wondering.

The nymphs share a cunning, maniacal glance.

My heart jumps in my chest. Could Bass have sent these girls to try and take me to Unseelie?

No.

No way.

I'm in the throne room in the freaking Seelie castle. Two nymphs wouldn't be able to get me out of here without a fight, and there are at least three dozen royal sentries lining the room.

"Don't you know?" They finally reply together.

Camden takes the bait. "Know what?"

A crazed, gleeful light fills both of their pale-purple eyes. "Why, because she's his chosen mate, of course."

CHAPTER THREE

"THIS IS AN OUTRAGE!" CAMDEN PACES THE SITTING ROOM, fuming as he wears down the plush carpet. I sit on the couch—the same one I'd once lied on when recovering from a particularly nasty head injury. It's strange to consider all that's happened since that first day of training. Never could I have imagined I'd wind up back in this sitting room as the prince's fiancée. Whatever deity is in charge of this world definitely has a strange sense of humor.

"I won't let him get away with this insult. He will answer for his insolence."

It doesn't take a genius to know Camden is ranting about Bass. The prince had handled the nymphs' inciting words reasonably well, quickly dismissing them with a laugh. It'd been forced, but the crowd had joined in, belittling the nymphs claims as nothing more than ridiculous lies.

Except... Fae can't lie.

The nymphs told the truth. Or, at least, what they believed to be the truth. That's the funny thing about Fae. They can't lie, but they're the ones who distinguish truth from lies in their own mind. There's no universal power regulating their speech.

One of the ways Fae circumvent their limitation is with a cunning mind and a silver tongue. They can manipulate words like no one I've ever heard. It's unnerving to have conversations with Fae. You must be extra diligent to discern hidden meaning or carefully omitted words. It's hard work, and it's enough to make your head hurt.

But I don't think the nymphs intentionally twisted their words. They'd been blunt with no distracting, flowery language. Which means there's a scandalous rumor running through Unseelie, claiming I'm their king's mate.

Camden might think Bass is responsible for the rumor, but the more I think about it, the more I don't think that's the case. He'd have to know the trouble the gossip would cause me. We might not be speaking at the moment, but I don't think Bass is capable of knowingly causing me more distress than he already has.

Frederick stands on the other side of the room. His arms are crossed and his gaze narrows as he watches his godson stalk towards the far window and back again.

Hours spent greeting the rest of the Common Fae hadn't curbed the intensity of the prince's anger. Camden's jaw is clenched and his hands form fists at his side. He's furious, and until he calms down, I don't see myself taking that nap any time soon.

I clasp my hands together and lay them on my gown-covered lap. We'd only escaped the welcoming ceremony five minutes ago. It's been a long, exhausting day. I've been looking forward to changing into shorts and a t-shirt to take a nap, but Camden has other plans.

"Do neither of you have anything to say?" Camden pivots and walks back towards us with wild eyes.

"What do you wish for me to say, Your Highness?" Frederick's tone is professional. He doesn't lead the prince one way or the other. I eye the broad sentry. I know for a fact he doesn't like the Unseelie king, and he knows Camden doesn't favor Bass either. I would've expected Frederick to take this opportunity to widen the divide between the prince and king.

"That bastard is trying to claim Sera as his mate." Camden scoffs derisively. "Can you imagine? What does he take me for? A fool?"

My lips are pressed together. I definitely can't imagine being Bass's mate. My life is complicated enough without throwing that absurdity into the mix. But there's no proof Bass is behind the nymphs' claim.

But I can't say that to Camden—not without taking the risk of revealing the truth of how Bass and I know each other. That's not something I'm prepared to share. Not for the foreseeable future, anyway.

"Forgive me, Your Highness, but there's no proof King Sebastian is behind the stunt." Unlike me, Frederick has no reason not to stir the pot.

Camden stops pacing. "I'm not sure I heard you correctly, Frederick. Are you honestly trying to convince me my rival was not behind this?"

Rival?

Interesting word choice considering the two Fae courts have been playing nice. Unseelie Fae once scoured the edges of Seelie, taunting Queen Aria to make a move against them. But as far as I know, that behavior ceased just before the latest competition began.

"I'm urging you not to let your emotions dictate rash behavior. All we know for certain is the nymphs are citizens of Unseelie, and they made an outrageous claim about their monarch and your future bride. We mustn't speculate without more evidence."

Camden scowls. "Do you seriously believe Sebastian wasn't involved in this?"

"I don't know what to believe," Frederick replies. "As I said, we need more information."

"What about you?" Camden whirls to face me.

I stare up at him. "What about me?"

"What do you make of that deplorable scene? Do you think the Unseelie king is responsible?"

I flounder for a response. "I agree with Frederick. I need more information before I can make that call."

Camden throws his hands in the air and resumes pacing. "Is no one on my side?"

"What would King Sebastian have to gain?" I shake my head, willing Camden to calm down and think about this rationally. "To disrupt the welcoming ceremony. But why? It's such an innocuous event. I don't understand what he would gain by interrupting it, even for a moment."

"To undermine my future reign."

My forehead creases. "How?"

"What is the one thing my aunt has been using to delay my coronation?" Camden asks with a leading tone.

"Your marriage," Frederick answers.

"Exactly." Camden takes a breath. "By claiming you are the king's chosen mate, the legitimacy of our betrothal is diminished. Therefore, my ascension to the throne has the potential to be delayed."

I chew my bottom lip, secretly pleased to hear there might be a reason to postpone our wedding, but troubled to hear it could delay Camden's coronation. I understand Camden's position, but I still don't believe Bass would orchestrate this situation in order to keep Camden from becoming king. There's no love lost between Bass and Queen Aria, despite how the two hang all over each other at public events. He wouldn't prefer her on the throne to Camden. Of that, I'm sure.

Camden sees my skeptical expression. "You don't agree?"

I choose my words carefully. "I don't know the king well enough to know his motives." I've never been so thankful I can lie. Being half-human has its benefits.

"But?"

"But," I continue, not surprised he knew there was something I held back. Camden's good at reading me. "I don't think he likes Queen Aria very much."

"That's true," Frederick backs me up. "There's tension between the monarchs, especially after the contest ended."

He means the day Bass stepped up and acknowledged me as the Queen of the Dark.

Yeah… to say that pissed the queen off would be an under-statement. If the two had been friends before, which I don't think they were, they certainly weren't friends any more.

"Right," I nod. "Why would the king want Queen Aria to remain on the throne?"

Camden scowls. "To irritate me."

"That doesn't seem like King Sebastian's style." Bass is upfront and not afraid of confrontation. He's not the kind of guy who goes behind people's backs to manipulate them.

Except for me…

"I thought you said you don't know him well enough to know his motives," Frederick states with thinly-veiled accusation.

I lift my chin but say nothing. The guard and I stare at one another. Ever since I won the contest, Frederick's been more suspicious around me. He questions almost everything I say, and his eyes watch everything I do.

Clearly, he's concerned about his prince's mysterious, half-human bride. I try not to let the extra scrutiny bother me. He and Camden are the only Seelie Fae who've witnessed my powers, revealing me as not entirely human, but I have yet to tell either of them the truth about my half-Fae heritage. Not to mention, I'm hiding the fact Bass and I have been friends for years.

As much as I hate to admit it, Frederick definitely has cause to be suspicious.

"Sebastian will be at the banquet this evening," Camden speaks, interrupting our stare down. "I will confront him there."

"Are you sure that's wise?" Frederick questions. "If the king is behind the rumor, then confronting him might be what he wants."

"I agree." The last thing I want is for Camden to cause a scene, placing me in the center of it.

Camden runs a hand through his hair, agitated. "Fine, I won't say anything. But I swear to all the Fae gods, if King Sebastian so much as looks at me or Sera in a taunting or insinuating way, I won't hold my tongue. I won't be disrespected in front of my future subjects again."

CHAPTER FOUR

As expected, I don't have time for a much-needed nap. I'm sitting in my private suite, staring at my reflection in the mirror. Pascale stands behind me, curling my hair with the curling iron she'd smuggled into Seelie from the Human Realm.

"Why the long face?" Pascale catches my eye in the mirror as she carefully pins a tight curl to the base of my head. The diadem gleams in the candlelight, and the reminder of my burdens sours my mood even more.

My best friend had moved into the castle with me shortly after I won the competition. Our reunion had been bittersweet. I was grateful to learn she hadn't been fatally injured by the Seelie sentries sent to abduct me from the bar I worked at, but I'd been devastated to learn she'd known the truth of my half-Fae, half-human heritage. Not only that, she also knew Bass, the enigmatic and broody guitarist I met when I was sixteen, was actually the Unseelie King—her sovereign.

The betrayal stings, but after days of wallowing, I'm finally able to acknowledge my friend's need for secrecy. I truly believe everything Pascale kept from me was done with my best intentions in mind, and it feels right to have her at my side as I try to figure out a way *not* to become the next Seelie princess. It's definitely better than being alone.

Pascale patiently waits for my answer, picking up another strand of hair and wrapping it around the metal barrel. I've barely spoken since arriving in my luxurious rooms and finding her here. I'd thought maybe she'd attribute my silence to exhaustion, but now I'm not so sure.

"Have you heard about the Unseelie nymphs?"

Pascale doesn't miss a beat. "Yeah. It's all Common Fae could talk about after they left the throne room."

I groan, not surprised in the least. Now I know why my best friend hasn't been pestering me about being so quiet.

"Do you think Bass had anything to do with it?" I know what I think, but I value Pascale's opinion.

I barely feel her fingers twitch as she picks up another section of my hair. "Do *you* think he had anything to do with it?"

"I asked you first."

"And I asked you second," she replies with a smirk. If she wasn't holding a hot curling iron to my head, I would spin around and level her with my most irritated glare. As it is, I have to be satisfied with glaring at her reflection.

"Don't be annoying," I say.

Pascale snorts. "I'm annoying? I'm not the one brooding over a silly rumor."

"So, it *is* just a rumor?"

She lifts her eyes and raises a brow. "Don't you want it to be a rumor?" There's a knowing glint in her eye, and I hate myself for not hiding my emotions better. It's been a really long day. I need to get it together before I'm forced to go out and mingle with Common Fae again.

"Duh." I straighten my back and put on a blank expression. "Why would you even ask that?"

"My bad." A smirk pulls Pascale's lips, and I know she's not convinced.

Whatever. I don't have the energy to argue.

I change the subject. "Are you still planning to come to the feast with me?"

"That depends, is lizard boy going to be there?" Pascale gestures to the corner of the room where Vagar, my trusty body-guard, stands. His slitted eyes shift over to us, but he doesn't say a word.

"Don't be rude," I chastise her.

"Me? Tell that to him. He's the one who looks like he's ready to rip my head off if I accidentally burn you with the curling iron."

A low growl comes from the corner.

Pascale takes a step back and holds up her hands. "It was a figure of speech, scary monster Fae. Lighten up."

Vagar eyes Pascale with obvious distrust before finally looking away. Pascale mumbles something about creepy guards under her breath, and I have to stifle my laugh.

"Vagar's just protective." Sure, his scaly skin, sharp horns, and bright red eyes are frightening to look at, but he's loyal. The only time I truly feel safe in Seelie is when he's around. Just his presence is enough to deter would-be assailants.

"He's definitely dedicated. I'll give him that." With one more cautious glance over her shoulder, Pascale moves closer and resumes styling my hair. I'm thankful Camden listened to me when I said I didn't need my lady's maid to help me with my hair and makeup this evening. It's strange to have people wait on me hand and foot, and I wasn't up for it after such a long day.

"So, are you coming with me?" I ask again, watching her reflection.

"I don't know if that's a good idea," she finally says. She's careful to avoid my gaze, pretending to focus on my hair even though we both know it's nearly done. All that's left is to curl the baby hairs.

"Why not?"

Pascale walks in front of me and carefully curls the short hair around my left ear. "I don't think your darling fiancé would want me there."

I scowl, waiting until she moves the hot metal away from my face to say, "Why would you say that?"

"Um... hello? I'm Unseelie." She curls the hair around my right ear.

"So?" I challenge as she clicks off the curler.

Pascale crosses her arms and leans back against the vanity, looking down with raised brows. "Seriously, Sera? Your prince was just insulted by Unseelie nymphs in front of hundreds of his future subjects. How do you think he will react to seeing an Unseelie pixie at your side?"

Instead of arguing against her, I find myself mumbling, "He's not *my* prince."

She rolls her eyes. "Whatever. You know I'm right. Or was Prince Camden *not* in a pissy mood after the welcoming ceremony?"

"That doesn't mean he'll be rude to you." Camden's probably the nicest guy I've ever met. It's amazing, considering he grew up a royal prince who had everything handed to him. I can't imagine him being rude to Pascale just because she's Unseelie.

"Please, we both know the only reason he tolerates me living in the castle is because I'm your best friend." Pascale shakes her head. "The guy's got it bad, but I don't think his feelings are going to stop him from losing it if he sees me at the feast tonight. I think it's best not to poke the beast until he has more than a few hours to calm down."

She's speaking like Camden is some short-tempered frat guy who just had his manhood insulted.

"He's not like that," I say. "I'm telling you. Nothing will happen."

Pascale sighs and shoves off the vanity, walking to the center of the room. She throws herself onto the bed, bouncing up and down several times before she's comfortable. I stand up and follow her, sitting on the edge of the mattress.

She sees my pouty face and gives another heavy sigh. "Sera… come on. You know I'm right about this."

But I don't. I honestly don't think Camden will do or say anything about my friend if she showed up tonight. But seeing her strained expression makes me admit I have no desire to force her to do anything she's not comfortable with.

Still, I give it one last try. "Bass will be there."

"I know. If you ask me, that makes it even worse."

On that, we agree.

I close my eyes and take a deep breath. "I know."

"I don't suppose you can skip this shindig with me?" Pascale asks in a semi-joking voice. We both know there's no way I can get out of the feast. I'm the one everyone is there to see.

"I wish." I open my eyes. "I already can't wait for it to be over."

"Hey." Pascale reaches out and gives my hand a squeeze. "Don't worry. It's just one feast. It'll be over before you know it, then you and I can go back to spending our nights binge-watching T.V. and eating junk food."

The memory of how we used to spend evenings in our apartment makes me smile. "I don't think there's T.V. in Seelie."

"Psh. Not a problem. I can smuggle in a T.V."

"But how will we stream shows without internet?"

"Hello?" Pascale wiggles her fingers in front of my face. "Magic."

I laugh, not sure if she's serious. "That seems like a silly use of magic."

Pascale narrows her eyes in mock annoyance. "Do you want to Netflix and chill, or what?"

Still smiling, I hold up my hands in surrender. "You're right. I'm sorry."

"That's better." Pascale sits up and gracefully leaps off the bed. "Now, let's get you dressed so you can go perform your fiancée duties. The sooner you get to the feast, the sooner it will be over, and the sooner we can pig-out on some potato chips and chocolate bars while watching the latest serial killer documentary." She waggles her eyebrows like her genre of choice is the most exciting and binge-worthy option out there.

I get off the bed and follow her over to the changing screen positioned in the left side of the room. Vagar doesn't strike me as the type to ogle a girl as she undresses, but I still want privacy when I change. I slip behind the screen and retrieve the forest-green gown from its hanger.

I remove my silk robe, tossing it over the changing screen, then slip on the gown. It's flowy on top, but tightens around my hips to form a sleek skirt all the way to my feet. Walking won't be easy, but at least tonight's event is just a feast and not a ball. I doubt I'd be very graceful dancing with the tight fabric wrapped around my legs.

I step out from behind the screen with my back turned to Pascale. Her small fingers make quick work of the delicate buttons. She steps back and admires me with a bright smile. "You're gorgeous, Sera."

"Thanks." I sit down to put on the golden heels she'd put out to match the dress. Pascale is definitely more of a fashionista than I am.

I stand, prepared to walk out the door and face the daunting evening, when Pascale holds out a thin, gold bracelet to me.

My throat goes dry, and I'm unable to do more than stare at the offending piece of jewelry.

Pascale's eyes soften with understanding. "I know you don't want to wear it, but it's expected."

I shake my head. "No one mentioned it during the welcoming ceremony."

"That's because you were wearing long sleeves," she counters, holding the bracelet higher. "People will notice if you aren't wearing the engagement band at the feast. You don't want Camden to get suspicious, right?"

Pascale knows I don't plan to go through with the marriage. She also knows I'm trying to act normal so Camden doesn't figure that out.

I sigh and, against my will, hold out my wrist. "Fine."

Pascale slides the stunning diamond-encrusted bracelet onto my wrist, then squeezes my fingers before she pulls back.

"Don't worry, Sera. This won't be forever."

I'm only mildly reassured. Like I said, Fae can't knowingly lie, but that doesn't mean everything they say is true.

CHAPTER FIVE

"I MUST SAY, LADY SERAFINA, THERE IS SOMETHING ODDLY familiar about you."

I lift my head and meet the gaze of the kind-eyed Brownie sitting across from me. Her name is Valeria. Her voluminous black hair is tied in a neat bun, and a pair of tiny horns stick out of her head just above her ears. I'm pretty sure I've seen her before. I think she works in the castle, but we've never spoken. The purpose of the feast is to give Common Fae the chance to meet and converse freely with their monarchs—or future monarchs, in my and Camden's case.

Part of me had wondered if Common Fae would feel comfortable speaking with me. Normally, the royals are so far removed that I'd expect there to be some hesitation on their part.

But I was mistaken. The feast is currently in its third course, and the Fae seated around me have had no trouble drawing me in to conversation. The two sprites, one gnome, and Valeria have been nothing but friendly and cordial. I'm surprised to admit it, but I'm actually enjoying myself. Perhaps it's because the setting is more casual than I'd expected.

Not all Common Fae who've travelled to the castle are able to dine with us in the banquet hall. There simply isn't enough room. So, a lottery had been played to see which fifty Common Fae would have a seat at the table with me and Camden while the rest of the guests are enjoying the feast in smaller dining rooms throughout the castle. This arrangement is much more palatable to my socially-awkward self.

"I feel the same," I tell Valeria, spearing my fork through a vegetable which tastes similar to carrots, but is an off-green color. "Don't you work in the castle?"

"I do, but that's not what I mean." Valeria leans forward, gazing at me intently. I resist the urge to shift in my seat as I swallow the partially chewed food in my mouth.

"You've probably seen many redheaded women from all the queen's contests." The words taste like bile and nearly stick in my throat. I've yet to learn why Queen Aria insisted all of the competition's contestants be young, attractive redheads. I know the belief is her magical orb selects the human contestants from the human world. Once identified, Seelie sentries were sent to abduct the queen's contestants. But that just doesn't seem believable to me.

There'd been four other contests before mine, and every single one of the young women chosen to compete had died. Mine wasn't only the first to have a victor, but also the first to have survivors. All except Jordan and I were returned to the Human Realm. Pascale told me the others had been glamoured to forget about their experience in Seelie and the horrible contest.

Part of me envied their cleared mind. They could go on and live normal lives while mine is destined to be entwined with the Fae Realm for the foreseeable future.

Valeria purses her lips. Doubt swims in her eyes, but she says, "Yes, perhaps that's it."

I manage to give her an awkward smile, then feel the brush of someone's gaze on me. I follow the sensation, turning my neck until I'm looking at Camden. He sits on the other end of the table.

An enthusiastic sprite is waving his hands in the air, clearly excited about whatever he's saying to the prince. Camden's lips move in response, but his attention stays on me. His lips curl up and his eyes brighten as we stare at one another. My traitorous stomach decides to twist, and my heart gives a tiny flutter. My body hasn't caught up with my mind about the fact I don't intend to pursue a real relationship with the Seelie prince.

"Our prince is smitten," the gnome, Henrik, comments. His words distract me, and I'm able to pull my eyes from Camden. My cheeks heat.

"And so is our lady, it seems," Valeria teases good-naturedly.

I pick up my water goblet and take a healthy swallow. The four Fae closest to me watch with amused grins.

I dart a quick glance back at Camden. He's turned to speak with the excited sprite, but a smile lingers on his lips.

"His Highness is very handsome," Valeria says.

"Yes. He is." I take another drink, praying for the color to leave my cheeks.

"Have you two decided on a wedding date?"

I almost choke on the water. Forcing the liquid down, I have to cough several times before I'm able to speak. The noise, unfortunately, draws extra attention to my end of the long table.

At last, I say, "Not yet."

Valeria gives me a knowing look. "Does my lady have a case of cold feet?" she asks the question kindly without any judgment.

The listening Fae wait for my answer. They, too, seem curious, but not judgmental.

"Please, just call me Sera," I say without thought. "And yes... I guess I'm a little nervous about getting married."

Valeria grins. "That's perfectly normal, *Sera*." She emphasizes my name, clearly thrilled to be given permission to address me so casually. If I had my way, all Fae would drop the title Queen Aria has decided to bestow upon me. It's just for show, anyway. I'm not actually the lady of anything in Seelie.

Henrik clears his throat. "If you don't mind me asking, how old are you?"

"Nineteen."

A murmur of surprise flitters among those who've heard me.

"That is very young to think of marriage," Henrik remarks. He furrows his wide forehead and crinkles his protruding nose.

"Perhaps not for a human?" Valeria supplies, tilting her head in question.

"No, it's young for humans too." At nineteen, I barely feel like an adult.

When I'm not trapped in the Fae Realm, forced to compete in a dangerous contest and be engaged to a handsome prince, I work and go to school. Other than making sure I can pay rent and make good grades, I pretty much don't have any real responsibilities.

I've never really considered getting married—it's not like I had guys lining up at the door to take me on dates—but if I had to guess, I would assume I'd at least be in my late-twenties before I even considered tying the knot. It's a huge step in life, and one I'm not at all ready for, especially if it comes with the title of princess.

"Well, I'm sure most humans don't find themselves matched

up so well at a young age." The female sprite, Juria, says. "You are a very lucky young woman."

I force a smile. "Thank you."

Juria's bright teeth gleam as she smiles. My fingers tremble. I tuck them into my lap, under the table. I still have a pile of vegetables and shredded meat on my plate, but I won't be finishing them.

Henrik begins discussing unusual weather patterns he's noticed in his home region. Valeria engages him with prompting questions like when did it all begin, and how severe is the damage to the region's crops. I pretend to listen, but much of what they say goes over my head. I really need to commit a map of Seelie to memory and learn more about the different parts of the court.

Why? Do you plan to stay in Seelie forever?

I sit back in my chair with a frown. I try to convince myself I only wish to learn more about Seelie because it's the best way to keep Camden unaware of my true plans. He won't think I'm trying to get out of this engagement if I'm going out of my way to learn more about his lands. That's all this is. Nothing more.

The sound of silver tapping glass chimes across the table. Everyone looks to the source of the sound. A well-built and handsome High Fae is standing in the center of the table. He isn't a noble, but he looks just like the others who roam around the castle. With his strong jawline and impressive posture, he could easily pass for a noble if you didn't notice the subtle wear of his dinner jacket and trousers. No hoity-toity noble would be caught dead wearing a piece of clothing with so much as a loose stitch.

Beside me, I hear Valeria sigh, "Oh my... he's lovely."

I smirk and give her a wink. "*Very* lovely."

It's Valeria's turn to blush, and my smile widens. She hadn't intended for anyone to hear her.

"Master Rynn," Camden calls out in greeting from the other end of the table.

"Your Highness." The Fae, Master Rynn, lifts a glass of wine in the air. "I would like to propose a toast to you," he swings his eyes to me, "and your bride to be. I believe I speak for all of Seelie when I say we are *very* much looking forward to the prosperity of your future reign."

Is that a dig at Queen Aria? If so, I'm impressed.

It takes guts to openly speak against Queen Aria in the castle, even in such a subtle way.

Rynn holds out the glass. "To Prince Camden and Lady Serafina, may their union be fruitful and their rule benevolent."

Everyone at the table except Camden and I stand and lift their glasses. "To Prince Camden and Lady Serafina," they chant, motioning towards Camden and me. Then, everyone takes a healthy sip of their drink before breaking out into polite applause.

I tilt my head in humble acceptance. I've done nothing to deserve their well-wishes, and I'm genuinely touched by it.

Camden surprises the table when he pushes back his chair and gets to his feet. He lifts his glass toward me. "To the young woman who has made all of my wildest dreams come true, your future queen, Lady Serafina."

Once again, the room chants the toast. Only, this time, everyone finishes the contents of their drinks in boisterous celebration. Including Camden.

He tilts back the crystal goblet and chugs the sweet red elixir.

When Camden lowers his head, I see a trail of red liquid dripping down the corner of his mouth. In that moment, he looks so undeniably happy that I feel my heart clench with affection.

I may not want to marry him, but Camden has been nothing but kind to me since the moment we met. What Rynn says is true: Camden's future reign is sure to be prosperous and benevolent. Seelie deserves someone like him, and Camden deserves someone to help him reach his destiny. Someone better than me.

The Fae chat with one another. Everyone is invigorated by the impromptu toasts and the general feeling of levity all around the table. I smile as I watch the Common Fae, and I find myself thankful for the opportunity to meet and interact with them. These Fae are more relatable, and much less daunting, than the Seelie nobles who watch my every move, waiting to see me fail. I can actually see myself being friends with these Fae.

We are all so caught up in the moment that no one notices the shadowy figures gathering outside the windows along the east side of the banquet hall. Not until they glass shatters and shadows leap into the hall.

Surprised shouts fill the space.

In the next moment, I hear a sharper cry. It came from Valeria.

Her face is white with horror as she stares at something over my shoulder. I turn and gasp when I see an arrow sticking out of Rynn's neck.

Blood gushes from the fatal wound, creating a river of blood trailing down his throat. I scramble to my feet and my eyes immediately search for the archer responsible for his death.

The world blurs and time slows. My eyes land on the massive, black-scaled creature standing just inside the doors leading to the balcony. A black bow is drawn back, ready to fire a sharpened arrow.

And it's pointed at me.

CHAPTER SIX

ONE MOMENT, I'M STARING DEATH IN THE FACE—THERE'S NO other way to describe the menacing monster or his intentions as his weapon centers on my chest. But before the arrow is released and I meet my end, I'm tackled from the side. Air rushes out of my lungs. I hear the whistle of the arrow fly overhead just before it embeds in the tapestry hanging on the wall behind me.

My hip flares with pain as my side collides with the hardwood floor. I hiss and try to roll off the rapidly bruising flesh, but a heavy body is sprawled on top of me, holding me in place. I twist my neck and identify my savior.

"Vagar," I pant and try to wiggle free, but it is no use. He's too heavy. "Get off me."

"Stay down, my queen," he commands. "It's not safe."

Glasses and plates crash to the floor. I hear Common Fae scream. The fearful sound of steel clashing against steel reaches me. I can only pray the castle sentries have joined the fight and are protecting the unarmed citizens. Whoever the intruders are, it's obvious their purpose here isn't peaceful. If it weren't for my dedicated guard, I would be dead right now.

"Sera!" A distant voice shouts above the sounds of the attack.

I lift my head to see who is calling for me, but I see nothing except overturned chairs and Vagar's scaled flesh.

"SERA!"

I grow still and suck in a breath. I recognize the owner of the voice.

Could it be?

Freshly polished black shoes rush into view. The newcomer kneels down and lowers his head to meet my gaze. I'm rendered speechless by the unexpected sight of familiar violet eyes.

"Sera? Are you hurt?" Bass stares at me, not bothering to hide his concern. I see a flimsy purple film shimmering in the air behind him. He's constructed a protective barrier around us. Vagar realizes it too. My protector lifts himself off me, and I'm finally able to take a full breath.

Though, Vagar doesn't go far. His massive torso is hunched over me. He's ready to dive on top of me again should the need arise.

For a moment, all I can do is stare. I'd noted Bass's absence at the beginning of the feast. I'd scanned the length of the table and only saw Seelie Fae.

I'd assumed he'd decided not to attend the event in order to avoid a contentious interaction with Camden. But here he is, looking at me with such concern that it makes my heart ache with longing.

"Sera?" Bass cups my head with his left hand. His touch sends shivers down my spine. "Can you hear me?"

"Yes." I push myself off the floor. I'm sitting in a safe bubble while the rest of the room is still in chaos. I'm relieved when I see the sentries seem to have the situation under control. The few dark, scaly monsters in the hall are surrounded, and the sentries are currently detaining them with binding magic. The monsters gnash their teeth and hiss as the Seelie power burns their flesh. There are far less monsters than I'd seen break through the windows. I wonder if the others are dead or if they've escaped.

"Where's Camden?" I look between Bass and Vagar. The latter is expressionless and unresponsive. I'm his only concern. He continues to survey the room, assessing it for any lingering threats. I move my attention to Bass.

The Unseelie king frowns, eyeing me up and down. "You're hurt."

His words cause Vagar to growl and roughly pull me back onto my butt to look me over. I swat his massive hand away and scramble back into a sitting position. "Stop it. I'm fine."

Neither Vagar nor Bass seem to hear me. Vagar's attention finds the source of Bass's concern and he gives another frustrated growl. I glance down and see where a shard of glass has sliced the back of my forearm. All things considered, I'm lucky it isn't worse.

I tell them as much. "Seriously, I'm fine. It's just a little cut. It could be worse."

"I'm pretty sure the plan *was* for it to be worse." Bass sits back on his heels but makes no move to leave my side.

"How do you know?" As far as I can tell, Bass wasn't in the banquet hall when the attack began.

Bass opens his mouth to speak before deciding against it. He jerks his chin towards the balcony doors and says, "The prince killed the archer. I have a feeling he wouldn't do that except for a particularly good reason."

My stomach churns. I turn and confirm the monster who'd fired the arrow at me is dead. Black char marks show where Seelie power burned his torso, but his wounds don't stop there.

The monster's eyes are black as charcoal, having been inciner-ated along with all of his internal organs. Off to the side, the Seelie prince is listening, stone-faced, as a sentry interrogates a captured creature.

I choke down the bile threatening to crawl out my throat. "C-Camden did that?" It doesn't seem like something he's capable of. But another glance at his face reveals the prince isn't his normal self.

"Yes." Bass rises. He holds out a hand. "And you shouldn't be surprised. Fae males are notoriously protective of their part-ners." Some deep emotion flares in his purple eyes, but I choose to ignore it. I take his hand, and he helps me to my feet.

I pull back before I have my balance, and I stumble a step before Bass and Vagar help steady me with two, strong hands on my upper arms.

"I'm good." I shrug them off. I gesture to the shimmering barrier separating us from the rest of the room. "Shouldn't we get rid of this?"

"Not yet," Vagar growls. "Not until all of the intruders are taken care of."

I'm pretty sure 'taken care of' means something different to me than my guard. I scan the room and confirm all of the assailants are in the sentries' custody. "I think we're good." I gesture to the detained creatures. When the barrier remains, I give Bass a pointed look.

He scowls. "Fine. I'll drop the barrier, but only if you agree to stay close to Vagar. It's obvious at least one of the intruders wanted you dead." I don't need to follow his gaze to know he looks at the burned monster.

"Agreed." I roll my shoulders back, trying to act brave and unaffected by my close call with death. "Let's go figure out what this was all about."

True to his word, Bass drops the barrier. I hadn't realized it muted some of the banquet hall's sound. Noise assaults my eardrums the moment the barrier disappears, and I wince.

Now, I hear Camden barking questions at the contained monster. "I will only ask you once more, what was the purpose of your attack? Tell me now, or I will end you and turn my attention to one of your more agreeable comrades."

Bass strides towards the interrogation. I nearly trip over my skirt when I follow. Once again, Vagar's swift hand steadies me. He releases me the moment he knows I won't fall, but he stays close as I make my way to Camden.

Bass's furious expression is a match for the prince's as both Fae stare down the attacker. The monster's blood red eyes and black, scaly skin are a stark reminder of my guard's features. I glance between him and Vagar, confirming the similarities. I've never asked Vagar what type of Fae he is, but it might be time to do so.

The monster's glare is full of hatred and disgust. He spits on the ground, barely missing the prince's boots. The sentry behind the captive steps forward and jams the hilt of his sword into the monster's lower back. He howls and curls inward.

"Speak," Camden barks. "Or my sentries will end your life on this blood-stained floor."

"My life means nothing," the monster's voice cracks, and his glare levels on Camden.

The sentry strikes the monster again. This time, he strikes right where a person's kidney would be. I have no idea if the creature's anatomy is similar to a human's, but the monster releases another howl of pain when he's hit.

Power flickers beneath Camden's hands, and his voice drops to a dangerously low volume as he leans down, putting himself in the monster's line of sight. "Why did you attack my feast? What was your goal?"

The monster doesn't speak.

Camden snaps his fingers and a sharp bolt of golden power flies into the monster's eye. His scream is fierce, and I have to hold my breath to avoid inhaling the smell of burnt tissue.

"Death is not the worst we can do to you," Camden threatens coldly. "Tell us what we want to know, and your end will be painless."

I brace myself for the monster's inevitable rejection. I will leave the throne room if Camden continues to torture him for information. I understand the necessity, but it's not something I want to watch.

No one speaks as we wait for the monster's reply. His one eye watches Camden with suspicion, but also resignation. Finally, he says, "Our fight is not with you, but the girl."

All at once, Bass and Camden turn to look at me. The sentry keeps his attention on the captive, but he spares me curious glance. Vagar doesn't so much as blink. He's focused on the monster whose comrade tried to kill me.

I meet the monster's one-eyed stare, ignoring everyone else. "Are you talking about me?"

The monster's lips curl back in a horrendous sneer. I'll take that as a yes.

I breathe in through my nose, giving myself a moment to get my thoughts in order before I ask, "What have I done to you?"

His gaze shifts to something over my head. Or, more accurately, something *on top* of my head.

"Is it the diadem?" I lift my fingers and brush them against the headpiece. A familiar zip travels down my arm when I touch the delicate metal. I remove my fingers and the unsettling sensation disappears.

The monster bares his sharpened teeth. "It does not belong to you."

"The diadem has chosen her," Vagar interrupts, taking a threatening step forward, as if to defend my honor or something. "She is the rightful queen."

The monster turns its sneer on my guard. "I refuse to listen to the words of a traitor."

I blink and glance between the two massive, black-scaled bodies. Could they know each other?

Vagar doesn't let the monster's insult stop him. "A traitor is one who fights against the crown they are sworn to serve. From where I stand, that makes you the traitor."

Neither Camden nor Bass say a word. They are content to sit back and watch the conversation unfold. I wonder if they understand the dynamic between my guard and the captive, or if they're just as lost as me.

"The Darkness belongs to us," the monster hisses. "Not them." He jerks his chin toward me, Bass, and Camden. "High Fae will always be our enemy. Darkness cannot thrive in their light."

"You want the diadem?" Bass asks the monster, finally breaking his bout of silence.

"I want to free The Darkness."

"Why?" Bass persists.

Once again, the monster's eye lands on me. "Queen Lani is gone. The time for us to rule ourselves has come. The Darkness is ours."

The diadem buzzes on my head. I don't know if it's a warning or just a weird coincidence.

I lift my chin, determined not to show fear. "I'm not your enemy." I don't know the history behind the attackers and their link to the diadem, but I didn't ask for it to glue itself to my head.

"You're wrong." The monster leans forward. The sentry's hand digs into his shoulder, keeping him seated. "As long as the diadem rests on your pretty little head, you will always be our enemy. Until the day you draw your last breath, my people will not stop hunting you. We've gone too long without the power of our Darkness, and we won't stop until we get it back."

CHAPTER SEVEN

MY KNEE BOUNCES UP AND DOWN WITH AGITATION. I SIT IN A meeting room in the royal wing of the castle, waiting for Camden and Queen Aria to arrive.

Three nobles I don't know sit at the table. They're Seelie—I can tell from the medallions adoring their forest-green tunics and their fair hair—but I don't believe I've ever seen them at the castle. Something about their demeanor strikes me as honorable. I find myself wondering if I haven't met these Fae before because they keep themselves separate from the soulless politics which run Seelie Court.

Bass stands in the back of the room with arms crossed over his chest, and Vagar is positioned just behind my left shoulder. Other than them, I'm alone.

My restless mind replays the violent scene in the banquet hall. I shudder like I'm standing amongst the bloodshed and seeing it for the first time. At least ten Common Fae lost their lives, and I doubt I'll ever be free of the guilt I feel for their deaths.

After the captive's ominous speech, Camden had ordered Vagar to escort me out of the banquet hall. I'd left without protest —too taken aback by the discovery of my latest enemy to do anything else. My guard and I had just stepped outside the hall when I heard a quick cry for mercy before the thump of a decapitated head hit the floor. Don't ask me how I knew that's what the heavy noise was... I just did.

Vagar escorted me to my rooms, but I'd been there less than five minutes before Frederick arrived. He didn't say much, only that he'd been ordered to bring me to this meeting room.

So, here I am, waiting to learn what the hell is going on and, more importantly, how we can make sure nothing like this ever happens again.

"Sera?"

I look up and see Bass looking pointedly at my bouncing leg. I press my heel into the floor. "I'm fine."

His lips turn down skeptically. "You must have questions." I know he's trying to distract me, but I can't find it in me to care. I go along with it, ignoring the fact we have an audience.

"What type of Fae were they?" I don't need to specify. Bass knows who I'm asking about.

"Dark Fae."

I lift an eyebrow. "Dark Fae?" That's a thing?

"Yes. They're ancient—almost as old as the first recorded king and queen of the Fae realm. No one has seen their kind for several centuries."

"How's that possible?" The Fae Realm can't be *that* big.

"Dark Fae are reclusive. They dwell among the shadows deep in the earth, mostly in the Dark Forest and Cursed Mountains." He addresses the two places my contest had taken place. I shudder to remember the evil dwelling in those bleak, fearful regions. I find it hard to believe that is where Queen Lani ruled. Who would want to live in such a place?

Bass continues, "While most Fae live in the light, they live in the dark. Our realm is precariously designed to balance between the two domains. And, as I'm sure you know, the scales of fate have recently tilted out of our favor."

"Are you talking about The Darkness?"

"Yes."

I shake my head. Bass speaks with confidence, but I can't help but feel like his explanation is too incredible to believe. Queen Aria has been searching for the diadem to control The Darkness for years, but she only did so for selfish, power-hungry reasons. She hadn't been concerned with Darkness spreading across her land. Not really.

I look at Vagar. My formidable guard meets my eye. "Are you Dark Fae?"

He dips his chin. "I am."

"But you protected me from them. Are you estranged from the others?"

"I vowed my life to the service of Queen Lani many years ago."

There's something he's not saying. "What happened to her?"

Bass and the three Seelie nobles watch Vagar, just as eager for his story as I am. My guard had caused quite a stir when he first showed up at the castle, and now I know why.

"Her Majesty was different from the Dark Fae," Vagar begins. "She grew up a High Fae in the light, but she ruled over The Darkness, maintaining the balance between Light and Dark for centuries. Under her rule, Dark Fae were treated fairly and our society benefited from her reign.

"But prosperity breeds complacency and greed," Vagar growls. "Dark Fae rose up against Her Majesty, intent on taking the throne and placing a Dark Fae in power. When Queen Lani learned of the plot, she spelled herself into the recesses of the Cursed Mountain, taking her diadem with her. With the control of The Darkness locked away, the Dark Fae had nothing to do but wait for the moment to strike."

"If the Dark Fae wanted the diadem, why didn't they get it from the Cursed Mountains before I did?"

"Only one worthy of becoming the future queen could retrieve the diadem," Bass answers for Vagar. Vagar nods, confirming the Unseelie king's words.

Ugh... not again. I don't want to become the Seelie princess, and I definitely don't want to be the Queen of Darkness.

"So, these Dark Fae were waiting in the wings for someone to risk their life and retrieve the diadem." I bet Queen Aria had no idea her plans to secure the diadem for herself played right into an enemy's hands.

"Then what? The Dark Fae kill me and steal the diadem from my corpse?" The words come out harsher than I intend, but I don't try to take them back or soften their blow. If it's true, then this mess just got a whole lot worse.

"No harm will come to you, Sera, I swear it." Camden's voice precedes his entrance. He still wears formal attire from the feast, but his hair is no longer disheveled, and his shirt isn't untucked from fighting.

The nobles quickly rise and bow as the prince joins us at the table. Bass remains upright against the wall, and Vagar doesn't so much as blink. I stay seated, watching Camden with curious eyes.

"Where's the queen?"

"My aunt has left this matter for me to solve."

I frown. That's unlike Queen Aria. She isn't one to shy away from opportunities to display her power or authority. I'd expected her to be chomping at the bit to play queen and formulate a plan to combat this unanticipated foe and keep her diadem safe.

Warning bells chime in the back of my mind. Something's going on, but I haven't the slightest idea what it could be.

"Aria doesn't plan to join us?" Bass sounds just as suspicious as I feel.

"No." Camden pulls back the chair and sits beside me, avoiding the incredulous looks he's getting from the entire room. The prince leans close until I can feel his breath caress my cheek. "How are you feeling?"

"I've been better." I'm surprised when my voice comes out a little breathy. I clear my throat and say, more evenly, "I've learned a little about our attackers. I didn't know Dark Fae existed."

Camden sits back with a frown. "Even knowing they exist did not spare me the shock I felt when I saw them attacking the feast. Dark Fae haven't interacted with the rest of us for several hundred years."

And they've finally decided to come out of their creepy dark caverns in order to kill me... how nice.

"We must discuss a strategy to keep Lady Serafina safe," the noble sitting in the middle of the group says. His face is worn, betraying the truth of his advanced age. I cannot even begin to guess how old he must be to have wrinkles on his face. Hundred-year-old Fae barely look older than thirty.

"I agree, Lord Gentsworth." Camden places his elbows on the chair's armrests and steeples his fingers under his chin. "The Dark Fae betrayed the purpose of their attack, but they didn't seem bothered by their capture. If I had to guess, the attackers knew there was a high chance of failure. Whoever orchestrated the attack must have a backup plan to see the job done."

I choke back the saliva building in my throat. It's definitely unnerving to hear someone talk about your planned murder so casually. I know Camden doesn't intend to sound callous, but seriously, would it kill him to sound a little more concerned?

"Additional sentries should be posted along the castle borders," a different noble says. This one looks younger, his face free of age lines or blemishes. But that really doesn't tell me anything about his true age.

"Already done, Lord Faines." Camden's hands fold in his lap. "Security at the palace and in the neighboring villages will be heightened for the foreseeable future. Until Sera is my wife and crowned a Seelie princess, we must be extra vigilant to ensure no harm comes to her."

"What about that title makes her safe from the Dark Fae?" Bass challenges, and he doesn't bother to sound diplomatic.

Camden's eyes harden as he meets the king's glare. "As a royal princess, Dark Fae will know harming her will start a war."

Bass scoffs. "I don't think they are averse to causing conflict, Your Highness. They did, after all, attack a feast where you, yourself, could have been injured."

Bass has a point. Why would Camden think I'd have more protection as his wife than his fiancée?

"What do you propose we do then," Camden grinds out, unable to hide his annoyance. If I had to guess, I'd say some-one's still angry about the whole Unseelie nymph debacle.

"I propose you offer a more realistic and effective solution to ensure Serafina's safety, rather than wishfully thinking she will be immune to harm once she holds the title of princess."

The two males glare at one another with enough hatred to fuel one thousand suns. I've never seen either of them look so out of control, and I don't know what to expect.

A noble Fae clears his throat. It's Lord Faines. "Perhaps Lady

Serafina should leave the castle." When he sees Camden scowl, he quickly adds, "At least until we can come up with a solid way to protect her from the Dark Fae's threat."

Lord Gentsworth and the other noble murmur their approval. Vagar huffs, and I can't tell if he agrees or disagrees with the idea. As for Bass and Camden, neither gives a reaction one way or the other.

Then, Camden asks, "What do you propose?"

"Somewhere the Dark Fae would never think to look for her," Lord Faines answers. "The Human Realm, perhaps?"

Hope flares in my chest, but it's quickly stomped out when Camden says, "No. Dark Fae will know she's human. If she's not here, that will be one of the first places they'll look."

I hate to admit it, but he's right. While I want to go back home, I know I can't take this threat lightly. Until the Dark Fae aren't a problem for me, I can't return to Earth. I can't risk leading them to my loved ones.

"What about a lesser noble's house?" Lord Gentsworth suggests.

Camden shakes his head. "The amount of protection Sera needs will draw attention to any noble's house, making her an easier target."

I consider suggesting they send me to a house without my own personal army, but I'm not in the mood to argue with a protective and stubborn Fae male. Not about this. I don't want to die.

The room quiets as everyone considers their options.

"What if Sera goes to Unseelie?"

My head snaps up.

Surprisingly, it's not Bass who'd voiced the suggestion. The third noble, the one I've yet to learn his name, is looking around the table, somewhat uncomfortable with the extra attention.

"Lord Dane," Camden addresses him. His voice is cold and a little threatening. "Are you actually recommending we send my betrothed to live in the home of our rival court." The prince gives Bass a harsh glance. "No offense, Your Majesty."

"None taken." Bass wears an indifferent expression, but I see through the façade. He's intrigued by Lord Dane's suggestion, maybe even pleased with it.

Bass wants to keep me safe, and that will be easier for him to do if I'm in Unseelie. But he has to play it cool. He can't seem too eager to have me move to his court, or else Camden will be sure to not agree.

It sucks, but the relationship between the two courts is so formal, that it's not up to me to agree to go to Unseelie. Camden must also sanction the plan, or there is no telling what kind of backlash will ripple through the Fae Realm.

Lord Dane coughs. "Your Highness, we cannot know when the Dark Fae will strike again, but we can be certain they will. Lady Serafina must be moved to a secret location as soon as possible. As the future Seelie princess, the Dark Fae will never suspect she's in Unseelie. At least, not right away. Moving the lady will give us more time to formulate a strategy to neutralize the threat without needing to worry about her imminent safety."

For such a quiet and nervous Fae, Lord Dane certainly knows how to present an argument. The other two nobles nod their heads in agreement, even Vagar grumbles a somewhat approving sound. The prince, however, is not so easily swayed.

"Her presence in Unseelie will hardly go unnoticed," Camden protests. "Surely, both Seelie and Unseelie Fae know I've found my bride. News of her new location will spread as fast as wildfire in a dry forrest, and the Dark Fae will learn where she is."

"I do not wish to interrupt—"

"Then don't," Camden growls at Bass.

"Camden," I murmur. He turns my way.

I lower my voice, even though the Fae in the room will easily be able to hear me with their enhanced hearing. "Can you just hear him out? I'd like to hear any plan that might keep me alive."

Some might say it's low to play on a person's emotions, but I need Camden to calm down. He's letting anger cloud his judgement, and the only way I know how to make him focus is to remind him that my life is on the line. He can have his pissing contest with Bass at another time and, preferably, not about me.

Some of the anger fades from Camden's eyes, but not all. Still, he exhales, "Very well."

I offer him a smile and reach out to squeeze his arm. "Thank you." When I try to pull back, Camden's hand lands firmly on top of mine, holding it there.

Then, he looks at Bass.

Bass smirks. His eyes land briefly on our hands before he continues, "I agree with you, Camden. Eventually, word of Serafina's presence in Unseelie will spread, but we can take precautions to delay that for as long as possible."

Camden doesn't look happy to be listening to his rival's advice, but he plays along. "How?"

"Seelie Fae must think Serafina is still in the castle. I've heard she rarely leaves her private rooms, so that shouldn't be too hard to manage."

I don't even need to wonder how Bass knows I like to stay in my rooms. Pascale is, undoubtedly, his source. But Camden doesn't know that.

"Despite the information your *spies* have shared, Serafina does, in fact, leave her room and show herself around the castle. Nobles and servants will notice if she disappears."

"Then you enlist someone to act as Sera in her place," Bass

replies swiftly. He rubs his chin, as if thinking. "You can glamour someone to look like her. One of the surviving contestants, perhaps?"

"That's not a bad idea," Lord Gentsworth offers.

"I agree. The only Fae not susceptible to a glamour placed by the prince is Queen Aria, and she will not reveal the ruse once she knows its purpose."

"I don't think so," Camden states.

Five pairs of surprised eyes land on Camden. Vagar also looks at the prince, but his reaction is not as easy to read.

None of us is sure what his last objection is about.

"Your Highness?" Lord Dane subtly asks for an explanation.

"Queen Aria will not be privy to this council's decision," Camden states without a moment's hesitation.

The nobles shift in their seats. It's obvious they aren't comfortable with the idea, but they are not so bold as to openly object.

"Um," I interrupt, lifting a hand. It's not necessary. I easily catch the room's attention.

Again, Camden's expression softens when he looks at me. "Sera?"

I drop my hand. "Is that a good idea? Shouldn't the queen know where I am?"

I can already imagine how pissed she'll be if I leave Seelie. Not because she cares about me, but because of the beloved diadem still stuck to my head. There is no way she will approve of the plan, and she's likely to freak out when she realizes I'm gone.

"Queen Aria has decided not to join us this evening, and she has placed all of the responsibility of Serafina's safety on my shoulders. Whatever decision we reach, the queen will not know the extent of it, if only for the sake of maintaining the utmost secrecy."

I hear Camden's excuse, and it sounds believable. But I know there's something the prince isn't saying. Could it be he and his aunt have become so estranged that now they keep secrets?

They've never been exceptionally close, but there was a façade of familial respect between them. It seems that precarious wall has crumbled.

"Are you saying you agree with my plan?" Bass asks. I'm grateful he doesn't come off as arrogant. Otherwise, there's no way Camden would be considering the option like he is.

The prince lifts his chin. His finger brushes against the back of my hand. He's torn, but I refrain from trying to sway him one way or the other. I trust he will see the merit of the idea on his own.

When Camden doesn't speak, Lord Gentsworth fills in the silence. "It is a good plan, Your Highness. Everyone in this room can swear an oath of secrecy. Lady Serafina can go to Unseelie until the Dark Fae have been dealt with, and no one will be the wiser."

I blink, surprised by their willingness to take such a vow. When Fae swear an oath, it's binding. Any attempt to break it is a painful experience, and often ends in the death of the oath taker. Hence, Fae don't offer oaths lightly.

Camden mumbles something unintelligible under his breath, then faces me. "What do you think?"

I press my lips together, trying to figure out what I'm feeling.

Do I want to stay in Seelie? Not really.

I'd feel like a sitting duck, waiting for a hunter to come by with their loaded rifle and shoot me in falsely calm waters.

But do I want to go to Unseelie where I will have to face Bass every single day? I'm not so sure.

By living at his court, I'll be faced with the reminder of his deception every minute of the day. It sounds like torture.

But the alternative is death.

I take a deep breath. Meeting Camden's stunning green irises, I murmur, "What choice do we have? I can't stay here. It's not safe."

Camden closes his eyes and exhales. When he opens them, resigned acceptance swirls in his stare, mixed with concern motivated by deep affection. "Very well, Sera. Unseelie, it is."

CHAPTER EIGHT

"I CANNOT BELIEVE EVERYTHING WORKED OUT SO PERFECTLY! Not that you almost being murdered is perfect, but you have to admit the end result is definitely convenient!" Pascale dances across my bedroom, throwing different items of clothing into a massive suitcase on the floor.

Why she bothers? I don't know. I'm pretty sure Camden or Bass can use magic to move my stuff between the courts, but I don't point it out. My pixie friend is on a roll, and it takes a formidable force to stop her when she gets going. I know from personal experience.

"Convenient for who?" I mumble under my breath.

Pascale, of course, hears me. "Convenient for you and me, duh. Or are you seriously telling me you aren't ecstatic to have a way out of this engagement like you've been planning this past week?"

"I'm leaving Seelie, not calling off the engagement."

Pascale pauses over the suitcase, holding an armful of delicate nightgowns. "Do you not want to end the engagement anymore?" Her wide eyes grow even wider as she stares at me, and it's like she's trying to peer into my head to read my mind.

I sigh. "Of course I want to end the engagement, but it's not that easy."

"Sure it is. We go to Unseelie, Bass finds a way to get that tiara off your head, and then we go back to New York City and continue going to school. Sounds easy enough to me."

"It's… complicated." How do I explain the feeling of obligation I feel to Camden? Not obligation to marry him, but at least the obligation to explain why I can't. I'm half-Fae. My mom was once a slave in the Seelie Court. The secrets I keep weigh heavy, and Camden's done nothing but look out for me since we met. I can't just disappear. He deserves more.

Pascale raises a skeptical brow. "Sure… *complicated*. Whatever you say. Are you trying to tell me you're changing your mind about going to Unseelie? Because I'm seriously going to question if you've been compelled to stay if you tell me that."

I'm saved from answering by a knock at the door. Vagar detaches himself from his shadowy post against the wall and goes to answer. Seriously, sometimes I forget he's even in the room.

My guard steps aside when he identifies the newcomer. It's Camden.

Pascale, well-practiced in Fae etiquette, dips into a graceful curtsy. I can't help but smirk. The elegant action is so at odds with her bright pink hair and worn blue jeans. She looks a little ridiculous.

"Your Highness," she greets. "I was just helping Sera pack…"

Camden waves his hand in the air. "Yes, I can see that. Would you be so kind as to give us a moment alone?" His gaze shifts to Vagar. "Both of you?"

Pascale shoots me a questioning glance. I dip my head, and she nods.

"Of course." She strides across the bedroom and jerks her head at Vagar. "Come on, big guy. Let's leave the lovebirds alone."

The urge to grab the nearest pillow and chuck it at Pascale's head is strong.

Pascale is almost out the door when she realizes Vagar hasn't budged.

Pascale rolls her eyes. "Seriously? Sera, tell your soldier to stand down or else he won't leave."

I give her a glare, then tell Vagar, "It's okay. Please give us a minute. You can stand guard outside."

Vagar huffs, but he honors my request and follows Pascale out of the room. My best friend waggles her eyebrows at me just before she pulls the door closed behind her. My lips twitch with a scowl, but knowing Camden is watching, I control myself.

The prince and I are alone. This is the first time Camden has insisted on speaking in private. Not even when he gifted me my gold engagement bracelet had we been alone. I brace myself for the uncomfortable conversation he clearly wants to have.

"You're almost packed?"

I follow his gaze to the messy pile of clothes on top of the suitcase, blushing when I see the skimpy nightgowns and underwear are in plain sight. "Yeah. Almost."

I'm not sure what to do. I think about sitting on the bed, but reconsider when I realize social politeness would have me invite Camden to sit on the bed with me. With anyone else, I wouldn't think it's a big deal, but I don't want to give Camden the wrong idea. Standing it is.

Camden walks across the room and looks out the window to the inner courtyard. We both know he's not admiring the scenery.

Finally, he sighs. "I don't want you to go." He shifts his sad green eyes my direction for a split second, then he's back to looking outside.

"I know." I don't know what else to say. I can't say I don't want to go. Just because I can lie doesn't mean I want to.

"I thought we would have more time together. My aunt has been filling my schedule with meeting after meeting. Now, I wish I would've told her no more often." His sadness tugs on my heartstrings.

I might not want to marry the guy, but I'm not heartless. It's touching to know how much he cares, even if I don't understand how he feels the way he does. I mean... we barely know each other. Camden's feelings for me seem more duty-bound than romantic, but maybe he doesn't know the difference.

I cross the space and join him, looking out the window. Common Fae meander through the courtyard, enjoying their time at the castle. They must be the Fae who weren't in the banquet hall. I can't imagine the survivors of the attack would feel like walking around in the open after what they'd experienced.

"The Fae who witnessed the attack have been sworn to secrecy," Camden tells me.

I lift an eyebrow. "Really?"

He nods. "Our position is precarious. We don't want to cause Seelie citizens to panic. The potential fallout might be exactly what the Dark Fae want."

I give a humorless scoff. "I'm pretty sure we know what they want."

Camden turns, and his eyes move to the top of my head. "I know the diadem is powerful, but if I'm being honest, I'd gladly give the cursed thing to the Dark Fae if it meant keeping you safe." His tone deepens with intensity. He actually means it.

Camden would discard the powerful token to save me from danger.

He's so honorable… I don't deserve it.

"I'm sure Queen Aria would object to that plan," I mutter.

The queen hadn't balked when her first group of contestants perished while trying to retrieve the diadem. She'd hosted several more events, all to get access to the item on my head. Queen Aria won't condone Camden handing her precious diadem to anyone but her.

"The queen has no say," Camden growls.

I blink. That's the second time he's let his composure slip when talking about his aunt. "Is everything okay with you and the queen?"

The muscle in his jaw ticks with annoyance. "Our relationship is much the same. She continues to act as if she's training me ascend the throne, but I can't shake the feeling it is all an act. She is planning something, but I can't figure out what it might be."

I chew my bottom lip. "Maybe it's nothing. I know you two aren't close, but we have enough problems without fighting among ourselves."

Queen Aria might want to hold the throne, but Seelie is against her. Camden had heeded her request to wait until he found a bride to step up as king, even going along with accepting a bride from her contests. He's held his end of the deal. Now, it's time for her to hold hers.

But my words don't have their intended effect. Camden's eyes brighten, and his nostrils flare ever so slightly. In a husky, emotion-filled voice, he says, "*We?*"

His intensity is disconcerting, and my heart stutters in my chest. I clear my throat. "What?"

He takes a small step towards me. "You said '*we*' have enough problems."

I laugh awkwardly. "Is that a bad thing?"

"Not at all." Camden takes another step. "Quite the opposite, actually. It's nice to hear you speak about us like we're a team."

Oh crap.

This is what I've been trying to avoid.

Camden reaches out and takes my hand. The look on his face tells me exactly what he wants to do right now.

He hasn't kissed me since I won the contest. Part of giving me time to adjust included no public displays of affection, but we're not in public at the moment. My head is spinning. I try to find a way to keep him from making his move, but I draw a blank.

"Well..." I fumble for a response. "We kind of are a team."

He laces his fingers through mine. "Yes... we are." Heat flares. I need to deescalate this situation and *fast*. His emotions zip between us, and they are robbing me of all rational thought.

With a gentle tug, I fall against Camden's chest. At five-six, I'm not short, but pressed up against his taller frame, I feel petite. My head tilts back to meet his gaze, and my free hand lies flat over his heart. It's beating a mile a minute, just like mine.

Camden stares at me like I'm a precious gem in the royal treasury. "Gods," his eyes flicker between mine. "You're so beautiful." His admiration is limitless, and my guilt grows.

Camden doesn't know me... not the real me.

"Thank you." Hopelessly, I try to step away from his distracting, muscular torso. Camden won't have any of it. His arm snakes around my waist, holding me to him.

"Camden, I—"

"Don't." He shakes his head. "Don't say anything. I already know what you want to say."

I seriously doubt that. If he did, I wouldn't still be pressed against him.

"It's just that this… everything that's going on… it's too—"

"It's a lot. I know." Once again, Camden cuts me off. "I know all the reasons why you should run out of this castle and not look back, but I wanted to see you before you go so I can try to give you a reason to return."

Intrigued, I find myself replying, "Oh?"

"Yes." His feelings are right there in his eyes. He drops my hand and cups my cheek, still holding me against him with the other arm. "I want you to come back to me, Serafina. Not because you will be the future queen, and not because you feel like you have to. I want you to come back because I've never felt this way before, and I think there is something wonderful between us. Be it day or night, you're always on my mind. I can't stop thinking about you even when I try. I don't know how you perceive this relationship, but I need to tell you this isn't just a convenience for me."

My heart pounds against my sternum. I never thought I would ever inspire such feeling in another person. Stuff like this only happens in the movies. How can this be my life?

"I want you, Sera. Body and soul. I will sacrifice anything to keep you safe." The hand around my waist disappears, but I only mourn its loss for a second before it joins its pair, cupping my other cheek. "All I ask is that you come back to me. Give me a chance to steal your heart, just like you've stolen mine."

What in the world is a girl supposed to say to that?

My head tells me to discourage his affection. I can't afford to develop feelings for the Seelie prince. My plan is to leave him and return to my normal life. But my traitorous heart and every sentimental bone in my body has other ideas.

"Okay," I breathe.

Camden's responding smile is nearly my undoing. Part of me wants to throw myself at him and say screw it to all my previous plans. This guy adores me. It's not love, but it has the potential to get there. If I decide to give it the chance.

Then, Camden kisses me.

Passion, desperation and longing fill every press of his lips, and I find myself returning the sensations with equal fervor. And I know, even before the kiss ends, that I'm so screwed.

CHAPTER NINE

MY DEPARTURE RECEIVES NO FANFARE. THAT'S INTENTIONAL. WE can't make a scene if we want castle residents to believe I'm still in Seelie.

Camden holds my hand in the carriage. The wheels bounce along uneven ground, causing our shoulders to bump against one another with the uneven rhythm. Pascale and Frederick are in another coach a few miles behind us, along with two suitcases filled with my Fae-gifted belongings.

We've been riding for the better part of an hour. The driver, a young human man named Zach, is taking us well past the borders of the village nearest the castle. When I'd asked why Bass couldn't simply use magic to transport us to Unseelie, I'd learned Seelie castle is warded against such arrivals and departures. That's not to say it's prevented, only that any such transportation across royal grounds leaves a detectable mark in the air. Anyone who wants to can read the signature and deduce who traveled from the castle, as well as their destination. To keep my location safe, we have to leave castle grounds. Hence, the carriage ride.

I'm just surprised that we've had to travel so far. But I suppose it's better to be safe than sorry and to make sure no one witnesses my secret departure.

Camden stares out the window, looking just as out of focus as he had in my bedroom.

Our kiss had ended almost as soon as it started, but its impact hangs heavy over my head. The feel of his lips against mine plays in my mind, making my toes curl. I thank god Camden had put an end to the kiss before it went to another level. I'm not entirely sure I would've tried to stop it, and that admission has me reeling.

I can't believe I'd been stupid enough to promise Camden the chance to steal my heart. It's hard to admit, but I'm pretty sure I have a little crush on the Seelie prince.

Which is totally absurd. I can't afford to let my feelings get in the way. Camden wants me to marry him and be his queen, but I have absolutely no intention of going along with his plans. Once he figures that out, I'm sure he will toss me aside like the half-human abomination I am. I can't afford to let my guard down for that inevitable hurt. I just can't.

"We're getting close." Camden looks away from the window. His attention focuses on my face.

I dip my chin. "Good." The sooner I get to Unseelie, the sooner I can put Camden and these unsettling feelings behind me.

His eyes roam my features as if trying to commit them to memory. "We won't have much time once we reach the glen," he says, identifying the location where we are to meet Bass. "I want you to know, I will work tirelessly to destroy the monsters responsible for your turmoil. I'll think about you every day you are away, and I'll try my best to find a way to visit without revealing our secret." His fingers tighten just before he lifts my hand. Closing his eyes, he presses his lips against my knuckles. The raw emotion when he reopens his eyes is nearly enough to make me want to kiss him again.

"Everything will be okay," I reassure him. "Please... don't worry about me."

He laughs weakly. "That's like telling me not to breathe."

How can such a corny sentiment sound so genuine? I didn't think it was possible—not until my paths crossed with the male next to me.

Caught in the moment, I say, "Thank you for everything you've done to help me, Camden." I'm thinking about our extra training sessions, and his help in preparing for his aunt's dangerous contest. "I would not have made it off the Cursed Mountain without you."

Or Bass's magical assistance.

Camden doesn't know my thoughts have switched to his rival. His eyes soften, and he cups my cheek. "Oh, I don't know about that. Queen Lani's diadem is a powerful relic. It wouldn't reveal itself to just anyone."

I bite my tongue to stop myself from correcting him. Aside from Vagar, no one knows I didn't just find the diadem lying on a rock in the cavern. At least... that's not the end of it.

The moment my fingers touched the humming headpiece, Queen Lani, herself—or at least a magical projection of her— drew me into a glamour and spoke with me. We discussed her diadem, and I even mentioned Queen Aria and her competition.

The Dark queen had roared with laughter, enjoying Queen Aria's mistake. Unbeknownst to the Seelie queen, I'm half-Fae, and only a worthy Fae could've retrieved the precious diadem.

My conversation with Queen Lani had felt so real. I'd been disoriented and confused when it ended, finding myself back in the dark, damp cavern with no evidence of the stunning queen.

Bass found me shortly after, and we'd both been shocked to realize I'd regained the memories Pascale had erased just before Seelie sentries dragged me through the portal to the Fae Realm.

I hadn't had the time to tell Bass what really happened with the diadem and the former queen. I'd been too busy being angry and worrying about getting back to Jordan before she bled to death.

But it's been a little more than a week, and I can't say why I haven't confessed the truth of what happened to anyone. I guess part of me feels like it's too hard to explain. I'll sound crazy if I say I spoke with a queen who's been dead for who knows how many years. I'm not sure sharing the story will change my fate anyway.

It's not like admitting an ancient, powerful queen gave you her diadem would convince anyone that having the diadem is a mistake. It'll only solidify the idea I'm destined to master the power it takes to rule The Darkness... whatever the heck that entails.

Camden's thumb brushes my cheek. "Do you want to know one of the most endearing things about you?" he asks after I don't respond to his remark.

I jerk my head slightly.

His lips quirk. "You're modest. I can't tell you how refreshing it is to be around a woman who isn't constantly trying to be the center of attention."

I frown. "You like me because I'm a wall flower?"

"I don't know the meaning of that phrase," Camden shakes his head, "but I can tell from your tone it isn't a good thing. Trust me, I'm trying to pay you a compliment. You're strong without feeling the need to be abrasive. You're intelligent without feeling the need to brag. And you're so beautiful without feeling the need to use your looks to motivate people to give you what you want. You're an anomaly, Sera. I know I've said it dozens of times, but I am so unbelievably happy that it's you who is at my side."

Now I know why I've appreciated the distance between us this past week. My soft, half-mortal heart can't handle his sweet declarations. They're messing with my head. I've got to get out of here.

I swallow and turn to look out the window. That's when I feel the carriage begin to slow down. Talk about perfect timing.

Once we stop, Camden hops out and offers a hand to help me out of the carriage. Normally, I wouldn't need assistance, but my long travel cloak is a tripping hazard if I ever saw one. The moment we reach Unseelie, I'm going to ask Bass to change into shorts. Or pants. Whatever is more appropriate for the weather in the unfamiliar court.

Across the bright green glen, I see Bass standing with two formidable Fae by his side. They wear black trousers and midnight blue tunics, and their dark hair and pale skin is a direct contrast to the tan, blond Seelie around me.

Camden sees the trio and immediately lifts his chin, as if to show he's not intimidated by them at all.

The second carriage arrives. Frederick steps out, followed shortly by Pascale. My best friend shoots me a wink, then snaps her fingers. The tarp on the back of the carriage deflates as magic removes the suitcases it'd covered. I follow Pascale's gaze back toward Bass and his guards. The suitcases have appeared behind them. One of the massive Fae's fingers begin to glow, the warm blue color surrounding my personal items, and then the suitcases vanish.

Totally cool.

"Your Highness?" Frederick steps next to Camden. "It's best you stay on this side of the glen."

Surprise has me asking, "Why?"

The sentry's eyes dart to mine. "The border between Seelie and Unseelie is located in the middle of the valley. Part of a Seelie monarch's power is knowing when Seelie subjects leave our land. Queen Aria will be able to sense if Prince Camden crosses into Unseelie territory the next time they speak."

Camden's jaw muscle ticks. Before he can devolve into another bout of angry frustration, I reach out and cup my hand around his palm.

"Hey. Remember, we're doing this to keep my location a secret. The longer it takes for people to realize I'm not in Seelie, the more time you will be able to make a plan to stop the Dark Fae, and I can come back."

The last words taste like ash on my tongue, and I can barely choke them out.

If I have my way, my next move will be to go back to the New York. I haven't spoken to Uncle Eric since I was abducted, but Pascale swears he knows I'm all right. I didn't have the heart to ask what lie she fed to him or the rest of my family to make them not worry. I hate that they're being manipulated, but there's nothing else to be done. Not while I'm still stuck in the Fae Realm. Knowing the truth will only stress them out.

But as soon as I'm able, you can bet I'll be taking the train back to Connecticut. Uncle Eric had asked me to visit during Thanksgiving. My dates are a little off, but I think the food-gorging holiday hasn't passed yet. Who knows? Maybe this move to Unseelie will allow me the freedom to go home, if only for a day. I can't risk more time. Not while Dark Fae are hunting me.

Camden squeezes my fingers, then lifts my hand to his lips. His eyes close with his kiss. When they open, acceptance stares back at me. "Stay safe, Sera."

"I will." I draw my hand out of his grasp. Pascale appears beside me, and Frederick is positioned behind the prince.

"See you later, Rick."

He gives me a bored stare, but I swear his lips twitch with the hint of a smile. "Goodbye, my lady."

I give Camden another farewell glance, then turn around and cross the glen.

Pascale keeps up with me. As we draw closer to Bass and his guards, I notice just how massive the two Unseelie Fae are. Their height is only slightly taller than the Seelie sentries I've met, but the breadth of their shoulders and width of their thighs is staggering. I've never seen anyone packing that kind of muscle. Bass has some serious talent on his payroll.

I stop a few feet in front of Bass and lift my chin. "Hey."

He grins, and it's so different from the broody demeanor he adopts as the Unseelie king. I'm taken back to all the late nights we spent at the diner, laughing and joking at anything and everything. I'm reminded of my second best friend.

"Hello, Sera." He tilts his forehead. "Pascale."

"Bass," Pascale greets with a smile even wider than his. I look at the guards to gauge their reaction to her informal behavior, but their attention is focused across the glen. I don't need to turn to know Camden and Frederick are watching us. The hair on my neck tickles with Camden's stare.

I take a breath. "Should we go?" The need to escape this scrutiny builds with every second.

Another look at the guards reveals they are armed to the teeth. Several daggers and a sword sit on the weapons belt at their waist. They came prepared for a fight. Or maybe that's just how Unseelie guards arm themselves around their king.

"Yes." Bass nods, then lifts a hand to one the guard on his left. "Varth, please escort Pascale."

"I don't need an escort." Pascale puts her hands on her hips. "I can transport directly into Unseelie just like any Fae."

"But not into His Majesty's palace," the guard, Varth, contradicts.

My eyebrows lift. "Palace? I thought the plan was for me to be inconspicuous." Strutting around the center of Unseelie society hardly seems like the best way to keep my presence a secret.

"It is," Bass confirms, but he doesn't elaborate.

I cross my arms and narrow my gaze. "So, what's the plan? We go to your massive, populated house and then what? You disguise me as a maid or something?" I know we have an audience across the glen, but I'll be damned if I don't ask him what the heck he's thinking.

This time, the guards exchange a look, taken aback by my abrasive tone and obviously displeased by it.

Whatever.

I don't care what they think, and Bass isn't going to let them do anything to me.

Bass sighs. "This is a conversation for another time." He glances pointedly over my shoulder.

I press my lips together, wanting nothing more than to insist he explain himself before dragging me to his court, but I resist. Despite the betrayal and secrets, I *do* trust Bass. He wants to keep me safe. But he and I are going to need to talk about how he makes these decisions. I'm not going to sit back and let him run my life. Not anymore.

My hands fall to my side. "Fine. But we're talking about this the moment we get there." My tone brooks no argument.

"Agreed," Bass replies. He waves Varth forward.

The guard holds out a hand to Pascale. My friend steps forward and takes his hand, shooting me an encouraging smile just before a faint blue light engulfs the pair and they disappear from sight.

The wind blows through the tall grass, creating the only sound in the glen.

Then, Bass clears his throat and offers me his arm. "Ready?"

I eye his impressive bicep and feel the undeniable urge to be just a little bit petty. I move forward, but instead of grasping onto Bass's arm, I wrap my fingers around the second guard's elbow. He stiffens, but he doesn't pull away.

"Ready," I say with a sickly-sweet smile.

The guard looks between me and the king with nothing short of discomfort. "Y-your Majesty, I—"

"It's all right Ivan," Bass smirks. "Please transport Lady Serafina to my palace." Then, he disappears. His transportation occurs much more quickly than his guard's. I guess that shows how powerful he is.

I shake my head. I still can't believe the guy who'd been my friend and adolescent crush is the freaking king of Unseelie Fae. My life had absolutely no chance of being normal, did it?

A throat clears, and my eyes move up to the uncomfortable guard.

He swallows one more time, then manages to ask, "Shall we?"

I look back over my shoulder. Camden still stands across the glen. Frederick's hand is on his shoulder, holding him in place.

I lift my fingers in a final goodbye, wondering if I will ever see the prince again.

Wondering if I even want to.

Wondering if I should.

Camden's a good person, and he did what he could to help the women forced to enter his aunt's murderous competition.

He'll be a better ruler than the queen, and part of me wants to see the kind of king he will become—the kind of Seelie he will create. But the other part of me thinks its best if we never meet again.

Camden is charming, handsome, and kind. It will be too easy for me to fall for him.

So, I take a breath, feeling grateful for this divinely orchestrated distance and say, "Yeah. Let's go."

CHAPTER TEN

THE UNSEELIE PALACE IS UNLIKE ANYTHING I'VE EVER SEEN. Don't get me wrong, the Seelie castle is stunning, but even the bright court's opulence has nothing on the elegant and classical beauty of their opposite's home.

Ivan and I had appeared in a quaint sitting room. One look out the window revealed we were on the highest floor of the building, overlooking a vast and magnificent city. The homes and buildings ranged in style, color, and height, but they all blended together to create a view that was warm, welcoming, and breathtaking.

Bass had to call my name three times before I'd given him my attention. He'd worn a knowing smile. He knew just how wonderful his home is.

Now, Bass and I stand in the library with a cathedral dome ceiling. He holds out a book to me.

"You want me to read that?" I eye the offering skeptically. The volume is four inches wide—bigger than my college textbooks.

"If you don't want to blow your cover and reveal to everyone you aren't really Unseelie, then yes."

I groan, tucking a strand of my recently dyed hair behind my ear. "Isn't my disguise enough?"

Pascale did the dirty work, but Bass was the one who oversaw my transition. He'd chosen the inky black hair color, as well as my ensemble. Not that I dislike the loose blouse and black leggings, I'm just itching for some shorts or jeans. Something familiar. The Fae clothes are comfortable and pretty, but their style isn't human. It's just another reminder that I'm not where I want to be… and I'm not who I thought I was.

Bass eyes me from head to toe with a neutral expression, only focusing on the diadem for one second. He's glamoured the powerful relic so no Unseelie can see it, but its weight still feels heavy on my head.

"The disguise is effective, but your knowledge, or should I say lack of knowledge, of Fae relations and history are a dead giveaway that you weren't raised in Unseelie."

"So? Is that really so uncommon?" I never saw Fae moseying around the Human Realm, but that didn't mean they weren't there. Surely, some Fae live among humans and raise their kids on Earth.

Bass sighs and drops the book on the table between us, tired of holding it. "Yes, it really is uncommon. But even if it weren't, the goal here is for you to blend it. Your looks make that nearly impossible to begin with, let's not add your human mannerisms to the mix."

I frown and look at the shelf behind him, trying my best not to reveal how his remark affects me.

My heart is ready to beat out of my chest anytime Bass so much as looks my way. I tell myself he hadn't been trying to call me pretty or anything. He was just commenting that I don't look like normal Unseelie Fae.

I really need to get this stupid crush under control. I have more important things to worry about. For instance, not getting murdered by Dark Fae.

"I don't see why I can't just stay in my room like in Seelie." It's not like the space is small. Bass gave me and Pascale an entire suite to ourselves, including a dining room, parlor, kitchen, and study. Our rooms are ten times the size of our shoebox apartment in New York City. It even has a terrace garden. Confining myself there won't be difficult at all.

But Bass is one hundred percent against the idea.

"Once Dark Fae realize you aren't in Seelie, they'll search here. We have time to establish you as an ordinary Unseelie Fae who won't draw any attention whenever they start looking at our court."

I shake my head. It's Bass's fault I'm in his court. I could be hiding in an obscure cottage somewhere in the Unseelie countryside, but Bass wouldn't agree. He thinks I'm safest out in the open, which kind of makes sense, but my desire to argue against almost everything he says is strong.

"They will only start looking for me if my replacement gets found out," I remind him. I have to believe Camden will select someone reliable to pretend to be me, giving us as much time as possible to figure out a way to defeat Dark Fae.

"Haven't you heard?"

"Heard what?"

Bass blinks, then frowns. Clearly, he's not looking forward to telling me whatever it is he thought I already knew. "Your fellow contestant, Jordan, has agreed to act as your replacement."

"What?" I practically shout, drawing several curious glances from the Unseelie citizens in the library. They've been looking at their king the entire time we've been here, but now my outburst has shifted their attention to me. Curiosity and intrigue illuminate their stares. I ignore them.

"What do you mean? Jordan's barely recovered from her injuries!"

The morning of my departure, Morty had dropped by my rooms and told me his beloved had finally awakened from the induced coma.

Every fiber of my soul had wanted to go see Jordan, but Vagar and Frederick had refused to let me delay. We had a precise schedule to keep if we wanted to leave the castle without Queen Aria or any other nobles noticing, and we couldn't afford any setbacks.

Reluctantly, I'd relented to their decision and hadn't gone to visit my friend. But I had no idea Jordan decided step up and pretend to be me inn order to help keep my departure a secret. My eyes water as I think of how lucky I am to have befriended someone as selfless and giving as Jordan. My fate in Seelie could have been very different without her by my side.

Bass sees my emotion and his gaze softens. "She volunteered for the position," he tells me, as if that will make me feel better.

I shake my head, trying to clear away the image of anything happening to Jordan. She's already done so much for me.

I shift the conversation back to where it started. "Jordan is smart. She won't be found out and Dark Fae won't search for me here. There's no reason for me to establish myself at Court."

"And when the Dark Fae launch their second attack?" Bass asks. "If they manage to get close enough to realize Jordan's not you but only a well-constructed glamour designed to trick them? What then?"

I suck in a breath. "That won't happen." I know I sound naïve. "Camden is securing Seelie, especially the castle. Jordan will be safe." Plus, Morty will look out for her. He won't let anything happen to my friend.

"Until she isn't." Bass shakes his head. "Listen, Sera. I don't want to argue. I hope you're right and this preparation is overkill. But just humor me. This isn't meant to be a punishment. I only want you to do everything you can to make sure you're safe. Being at court, in the public eye, will make you stand out less than if you were a random woman in some obscure village in my land. Please, trust me. I know from experience." Pain flickers in his gaze as if reliving a raw experience.

How can I argue with that?

"Fine." I slide into a plush leather chair and reach out to drag the book towards me.

I look at the title and frown. "This isn't in English."

Bass waves a hand over the book. The air shimmers with purple magic and the golden letters morph into a recognizable alphabet.

"Is there anything your powers can't do?" I ask, only slightly joking. It's surreal to think about how much power Bass possesses. It seems limitless.

"Unfortunately, there are many things I cannot do." There's a dark, ominous implication in the broody words. I press my lips together, deciding against digging for an explanation. Part of me thinks Bass hadn't intended to say the words in the first place.

I shift my attention to the newly translated cover, and my eyebrows lift. "History of Unseelie? Isn't that a little... bland?" For such an impressive looking book, the title doesn't seem to fit.

Bass smirks. "It sounds more impressive in the Fae tongue."

Uh huh.

Instead of engaging, I open the cover. The first page reiterates the same boring title. I flip through and stop once I reach a table of contents.

The First Days, The Great War, The Divide, The Winter Wars...

I scan the long list, only stopping when I see "The Darkness". Eagerly, I flip to the page listed. Flowery script adorns the top of the section, and smoky ink scrolls out the title.

Bass makes himself comfortable in the chair across from mine. He kicks up his tall leather boots and places them on the table. I spare him a glance. A book has manifested in his hands, and he reads intently. I return my attention to the history book.

I'm not a very fast reader. At least, I'm normally not. But I find myself devouring the five long pages describing exactly what the mysterious "Darkness" is. I reread the section several times. My forehead creases as my confusion grows.

The book states The Darkness developed as the Fae Realm came into existence. I kind of already knew that. The Darkness is nature's balance to the Light of Fae and their magic. But the book doesn't make Darkness sound like the ominous, dangerous entity everyone makes it out to be. In fact, Darkness is described as an entity to be admired and revered. Without The Darkness, The Light cannot thrive. Without The Darkness, life in the Fae Realm would sputter out into oblivion.

So when did The Darkness stop being a necessary element of life and become a source of evil and fear?

"Penny for your thoughts?"

I meet Bass's gaze. He's lowered the book to rest against his chest. His expression is, once again, carefully neutral.

"I'm thinking about The Darkness."

Curiosity sparks in his eye. "Oh? What about it?"

I put the book on the table and slide it his way. "This describes The Darkness as something exceptional—something that isn't fearful or destructive."

Bass pulls the book to him and scans the section. "Indeed."

I wait for him to say something else. When he doesn't, I exhale. "That doesn't make sense. Dark Fae are evil. That comes from The Darkness. Right?"

"Not necessarily." Bass looks up. "Dark Fae were once ordinary Fae, like Seelie and Unseelie. Sourcing their power from The Darkness may have altered their appearance and abilities, but the choice to commit evil acts was entirely by choice."

I sit back, completely confused. "But Queen Aria wanted to harness The Darkness's power... to stop it from spreading across Seelie land." I think about the bad weather events Henrik, the gnome, had described to Valeria at the welcoming banquet. I may not know exactly what the Seelie queen wanted to use the power for, but her people did complain about unusual events occurring around their homes.

"Again, that's a personal choice. The previous owner of your diadem harnessed the same power, but Queen Lani wasn't evil, nor did she use The Darkness for her own benefit as I believe Aria would've, had she been given the chance."

I picture the stunning queen from the illusion in the cavern. She hadn't seemed evil, and she'd given me the diadem to prevent Queen Aria from getting ahold of it, but does that mean she never committed evil acts with the dark power? I want to believe it, but I don't know.

After a lengthy bout of silence, I finally ask, "Did you know her?"

"Who?" Bass had resumed reading the text while I was lost in my thoughts.

"Queen Lani. Did you know her?"

He laughs.

"What?" I ask, not entirely sure what's so funny.

His eyes glitter with amusement. "How old do you think I am?"

I sputter for a response. "I-I don't know, but you're definitely not twenty-five like I thought."

Bass ignores the subtle jab, still chuckling. "Fair enough. Just so you know, I'm relatively young for a Fae. Queen Lani disappeared hundreds of years ago. I've never met her."

"Then how do you know she wasn't evil?" I avoid asking for his real age. Logically, I know it shouldn't matter, but I don't want to learn the guy I crushed on for years is really some eighty-year-old.

"My father." Some of the levity fades from his voice. "He and Queen Lani were acquainted."

His father must've been ancient...

"What did he tell you?"

"The same thing written in this book," Bass pushes the text back to me. "Along with some personal stories. But the gist is the same. Queen Lani was set to inherit the throne as the first female monarch, but she abdicated her seat to her younger brother in order to reign over Dark Fae and control The Darkness instead."

I frown. "Why would she give up the Unseelie throne for the other?"

"It wasn't the Unseelie throne," Bass tells me. "This happened before The Divide."

I blink, connecting the dots. "Are you saying Seelie and Unseelie used to be united?"

"Yes. And this is exactly why you need to read that book. All Fae know this history."

"It's not my fault."

"I'm not saying it is, but the fact remains we must get you caught up on Fae history and modern affairs if you have any chance of blending in."

I don't argue with him this time. I retrieve the book, pull my legs up onto the chair, and prop the book against my thighs.

This time, though, I'm unable to focus. I reread the same paragraph four times before closing the book with a sigh.

"Done for the day?"

I meet Bass's eye. "I'd like to be."

"You don't need my permission."

"Really?" I lift an eyebrow. He's been acting like his permission is exactly what I need. I hadn't wanted to come to the library in the first place. Bass hadn't dragged me here or anything, but he'd pressed the issue until I was so annoyed that I finally gave in.

"And here I thought you were the king of Unseelie."

"Being a king doesn't mean I'm a dictator." Bass kicks his feet off the table and plants them on the ground. He stands and lifts his arms to stretch his back. I try not to stare at his rippling abs as his shirt's fabric presses against his skin.

Bass drops his arms, then holds out a hand to me. "Come on. I think I know something else you'll find more enjoyable than studying."

I eye his hand for one questioning second, then decide there's no harm in humoring him. Not if it means I get out of reading the book for now.

I place my hand in his, ignoring how my skin tingles as his fingers tighten around mine. I expect Bass to let go once I'm on my feet, but he continues to hold my hand as he leads me out of the library.

Two Unseelie see us, and they share a pointed look after seeing our linked hands. Self-conscious, I try to pull away. But Bass doesn't release me. He dips his head, acknowledging the Fae, as if it is no big deal that he's walking through his palace, holding hands with a strange Fae. This definitely doesn't seem like the way to keep me out of the spot light.

We head to the stairs that lead to the top floor. I find my voice. "Are we going back to my rooms?"

Bass shoots me a sly grin. "Yes."

"Why?"

"Patience."

Normally, I'd keep pestering him until I got an answer. Bass always liked to be vague, finding it amusing to make me and Pascale wait for him to tell a good story or share a piece of gossip about one of his bandmates.

Suddenly, I wonder if all of those stories had been real. Was Bass in a real band? I know he played shows, but what about the tour he allegedly went on last year? Was it all an act? Or had there been some truth to his disappearance?

For the sake of my mortification, I hope so. Otherwise, Bass's departure can undoubtedly be linked to the foolish moment when I thought it would be a good idea to reveal how I felt about him. Needless to say, that'd been a huge mistake—one I've wished I could take back times than I can count.

We arrive outside of the rooms Pascale and I share. Not bothering to knock, Bass opens the door, but he doesn't walk inside. He drops my hand, and I tilt my head. A question in my eye.

Bass waves a hand toward the door. "After you." Mischief shimmers in his gaze. I watch him, trying to decide if I should go along with whatever antic he's orchestrated, when I decide I don't have the energy to try and figure out what he's doing.

So, I shrug and walk inside, and I'm instantly bombarded by a group of familiar and semi-familiar faces.

"Surprise!"

CHAPTER ELEVEN

MY MOUTH FALLS OPEN. PASCALE STANDS IN THE CENTER OF THE room, smiling broadly.

"Surprise!" She shouts again, spinning around and gesturing to the small crowd behind her. I recognize the friends I met at The Dark Horse on the night of my abduction. Tonk, Richie, and Aerie have removed the glamour used in the Human Realm. Now, their otherworldliness is on full display.

But they aren't the ones who've shocked me.

Standing amongst them are two of Bass's bandmates. At least, that's how I knew them. But even standing in the bright and luxurious room, there's no missing the telling glow around them. George and Henry are Fae.

I'm an idiot.

How could I have missed the truth for so long?

If there was one thing I should've been good at, it was seeing supernaturals in the Human Realm. But I'd been around the guys dozens of times, and I'd never suspected they were anything other than human. Both George and Henry sport the good looks characteristic of all Fae, but now that they've removed whatever magic masked their true identity, their race is obvious.

Henry, the fair-haired band member, is the first to break the silence. "Long time, no see, Sera."

George lifts a hand in greeting. An auburn strand falls over his forehead, and he brushes it away.

I'm at a loss for words.

Pascale steps forward. "And you remember my friends; Richie, Tonk, and Aerie."

Given his cue, Tonk glides forward. If his blue hair didn't mark him as a pixie, the shimmering wings protruding from his back do. Just like the first time we met, he takes my hand and kisses my knuckles, lingering for an uncomfortable second before releasing me. I wonder if he's just smelled me like he had at our first meeting.

"It's good to see you alive and well." Tonk's expression is sincere, and I notice a faint scar bisecting the skin above and below his left eye. "We feared the worse when we found Pascale in Central Park."

I try to shove away the memory of my bleeding friend. She'd tried to save me from my abduction, but the Seelie sentries proved too resourceful. Despite Pascale and her friends' best efforts, I'd been taken to Seelie and forced to compete in Queen Aria's deplorable contest.

"Thank you." I don't know what else to say. My gaze shifts over Tonk's shoulder as he backs away. Aerie, the stunning siren, looks bored while Richie is stoic. I can't get a read on him.

Bass clears his throat, immediately capturing the room's attention. Just like a king.

"Pascale and her friends will be helping you acclimate to life in Unseelie, as will George and Henry."

"Oh?" How can they help?

"Yes," Bass confirms, then gestures to one of his bandmates. "George fancies himself a historian, though he works as one of my personal guards when his nose isn't in the books."

Ah, so that's why George was a member of the band. He had to stay close to his king to keep him safe.

"And I'll be taking over your combat training," Henry, the more flirtatious one, says with a quick wink. "I can't wait to see what moves you learned in Seelie."

I look between the two Fae. They don't address the elephant in the room. They don't explain their deceit. And that makes me mad.

Before I can express my anger, Pascale chimes in with her bubbly, distracting attitude, "And the four of us will be taking you out into the city!"

For one moment, hope flares as I think she's talking about New York City. But logic returns and I realize she's referring to the city surrounding the palace.

"Why take me out in the city?" I'm not supposed to draw attention to myself.

"To mingle of course," Pascale replies. "It'll help you blend in."

It's a different tactic then I would take, but I don't have it in me to argue anymore. It'd gotten me nowhere with Bass.

"Okay." I turn to Bass. "And what are you going to do?"

He gives a roguish grin. I ignore the way it makes my stomach clench. "I'll oversee your trainers and provide supplemental training when needed."

Part of me is disappointed Bass passed my training off to others, but what should I expect? He's a king. No doubt, he has more pressing matters to attend to. Helping me adjust to life in his realm is hardly worth a king's attention.

I try not to feel bitter about it.

The palm of my hand tingles, as if empathizing with my emotions. I glance down at the pale outline of the crescent moon and swirling stars. I'd received the mark after I'd accepted Bass's help during the competition. And thank goodness I had. He'd saved me and my friends more than once, all because he'd been able to sense when I needed help.

I wonder what's going to happen when winter comes. In exchange for Bass's magical assistance, I'd agreed to spend the season in Unseelie, but that was before I knew he was really my friend, not just the Unseelie king. Is he going to enforce the bargain now that I'm here, or am I free to come and go as I please?

Not that I'm looking to leave Unseelie anytime soon. Dark Fae are after me. Or, more accurately, the diadem currently concealed with a powerful glamour. I won't be going anywhere until the enemy is taken care of.

But when that happens, will I still be obligated to remain in Unseelie if it's winter? King Sebastian, the powerful and formidable ruler would enforce our deal, but would Bass? Logically, I know they're one and the same, but it doesn't *feel* that way.

Bass clears his throat, pulling me from my thoughts.

I look at him and see the book from the library is in his hands, but his attention isn't on me. He holds the book out to George. "For her studies."

George accepts the text with a respectful dip of his head.

The door to the apartment opens. Vagar enters. I'm surprised to realize he hadn't been concealed in the room's shadows this entire time. In Seelie, he rarely lets me out of his sight, but I haven't seen him since this morning. What has he been doing all this time?

"Gods!" Henry exclaims. I see Tonk and Richie flinch out of

the corner of my eye. Aerie eyes my guard with intrigue but doesn't move while George's face is blank.

Vagar pays them no mind. He crosses the room until he stands just behind my right shoulder. I give him a greeting smile, and the corner of his lip curls in return. It looks more like a snarl than a grin, but I know the intention behind the gesture.

"Uh…Sebastian," Henry mock whispers. "There's a Dark Fae in your palace." He aims to joke, but his neck muscles are tense. He's ready to jump to action.

"This is Vagar," Bass says calmly. "He's Sera's personal guard."

"I thought the plan was to keep Dark Fae away from the queen."

My head jerks up at Henry's words. "I'm not a queen." I don't care if there's a powerful diadem magically glued to my head; I refuse to be addressed as the queen of anything. The only Fae who can get away with it is Vagar. The Dark Fae will not stop addressing me with his late mistress's title, and I've grown tired of trying to convince him otherwise. Vagar is stubborn.

Awkwardness descends until Henry dispels it with a charming grin. "Apologies. Let me rephrase. I thought the plan was to keep Dark Fae away from the *lady*."

I'm still not thrilled with the title, but it's better than the alternative.

"It is," Bass confirms. "But Vagar is a loyal servant of the diadem. He protects whoever wears it."

Behind me, Vagar grumbles, "I'm loyal to the queen." It seems my dark, brooding guard doesn't like being tied to an inanimate object.

The Fae, pixies, and siren all blink, surprised to hear Vagar speak.

Then, Henry huffs in mock annoyance, continuing to break the tension. "So he can call you queen but I can't?"

I eye the drummer up and down. "He's more intimidating than you."

The room chuckles. Even Bass smirks. Henry places a hand against his chest, pretending to be injured.

I ignore his antics. "I trust Vagar. He's been with me since the cavern."

"Ah." Henry's eyes twinkle with interest. "Yes, the infamous cavern. I knew you were made of tough stuff, Sera, but I was surprised to hear about your success. Everyone in the Fae Realm knows how futile all of the false queen's competitions have been."

He means everyone knows how all of the contestants died.

Anger flares deep in my chest. "And did none of you ever think to stop Queen Aria from hosting her cruel contests?"

I picture my fellow contestants. Amanda, Hannah, Trish, Brittany, Jordan... all the beautiful red-haired women whose lives had been unapologetically interrupted by a selfish queen and her power-hungry desires. My stare lands on the Unseelie, shifting to Pascale and her friends.

My best friend grimaces, but she sounds strong when she says, "That's not fair, Sera. We're members of Unseelie Court. We have no say over what happens in Seelie."

"But did any of you even discuss it? Did you ever consider how horrible it was for the queen's sentries to kidnap innocent humans and force them down the road which eventually ended in their death?" Sorrow, frustration, and pain churn in my stomach, threatening to explode out of me in a fit of tears or screams. I'm not sure which. "Did you even care what she was doing before it was *me* she kidnapped?" My eyes sweep the room.

Henry and George avoid my gaze, instead looking at Bass.

But Pascale returns my stare. Her eyes are wide and pleading. She knows why I'm upset, but she doesn't want me to be upset with her. I don't blame her for any of this. Not really. But my emotions are getting the better of me. For weeks, I kept them at bay in Seelie. I made sure not to draw attention to myself. I would've been happy isolated in my rooms until I figured out a way to get back home.

But the time for hiding my emotions has passed. They are bubbling to the surface, and I'm unable to reason through all I'm feeling. Not at this moment. Right now, I'm at their mercy and my words are subject to their whim.

"Of course we cared—"

I cut Pascale off with a slice of my hand. "Not enough to stop her. Not enough to save me from what I had to endure."

"We fought for you," Richie speaks up, allying himself with Pascale. I don't miss how close he stands to my friend. "When those sentries entered the bar, we fought to help you escape. Tonk nearly lost his eye in from the sword that sliced his face."

My eyes find the pixie. Now I know where he got the faint scar.

Normally, Fae heal quickly. There must've been some magic in the sword to prevent his magical healing.

I'd seen Tonk and the others fight to save me, but I'd never considered what might've happened to them when the sentries eventually found me near Bethesda fountain.

"I'm sorry," I tell him.

Tonk's lips lift slightly. "Let me buy you a drink and I will forgive you."

And just like that, the tension building inside me escapes in a disbelieving laugh. Is he seriously flirting with me right now? With an audience?

Richie's hand shoots out and smacks Tonk on the back of the head. Pascale laughs awkwardly, but Henry howls with genuine laughter. George and Aerie are content to watch on, both wearing subtle grins.

Tonk glares at his friend, then turns back to me with a raised brow, waiting for my response.

I open my mouth to reply, but I'm beaten to it when Bass says, "While I'm sure Sera would love to have a drink with you, might I suggest you not put her in danger by going on your excursion alone?"

Tonk flushes and immediately bobs his head, as if realizing he's made a huge faux pas. "O-of course, Your Majesty. I wouldn't risk her safety by leaving the palace on our own."

"Good." Bass shifts his feet, and it brings him a little closer to me. "Now, if you'll excuse us, I'd like to have a word with Sera before you all leave the palace."

My eyebrows lift. "We're leaving the palace. Today?"

Pascale smiles, all evidence of her earlier guilt disappearing, "We thought we'd show you the market." She motions to her group of friends. "And then maybe have dinner at a restaurant."

It all sounds so... normal. I'd expected all of my meals to take place in a fancy banquet hall. Going out into a city and grabbing a bite to eat sounds too human to happen in the Fae Realm.

Misreading my expression, Pascale is quick to say, "Unless you want to stay at the palace. If so, that's fine. There's plenty of stuff we can do around here to get you seen. Maybe we can interact with some of the Court residence—"

"No," I cut off her rambling. "Going to the city sounds... fun." Can I even have fun anymore? I haven't tried since the Cursed Mountain. Perhaps it's time I start.

Pascale beams. George and Henry have already walked out

the door. My friend and her posse follow. Even Vagar steps into the hallway.

I raise my brow at the move. Vagar sees and, I swear to god, he shrugs at me. Then, he disappears from sight, closing the door behind him.

I gape after the Dark Fae. Then, feeling Bass's gaze, I turn and ask, "What have you done to my guard?"

His lips pull down, confused. "What do you mean?"

"Vagar just left me in a room with you, and he left me alone all morning. Did you threaten him to stay away from me or something?"

"Maybe he trusts me."

Maybe. "But… why?"

Bass crosses his arms. "You do know I'm the Unseelie King, right? What reason would Vagar have *not* to trust me?"

"He doesn't know you."

"He knows enough. He knows I'm powerful and I can protect you."

"But Camden's powerful," I counter. "And Vagar would've never willingly left me alone with him."

The scowl morphs into a delighted grin. "Really? Your trusty guard doesn't trust the princeling to keep you safe? I have to say, Vagar's instincts are rising in my esteem with each passing day."

I roll my eyes. "Seriously, are you still going to try and act like you're better than Camden? He's not here. He can't hear your insults."

"It's not an act. I *am* better than him."

I throw my hands up. "Okay. Sure. Whatever. I don't care. What did you want to talk to me about?" We'd had plenty of time alone this morning. Why hadn't he just said whatever he wanted to say earlier?

Amusement fades. "We need to talk about your anger."

Um… no we don't.

"I'm not angry."

"Not at the moment," he says, "but are you really going to deny the anger you felt when you attacked Pascale?"

I balk. "I didn't attack her!"

"Oh, so was that you being friendly?"

It's my turn to cross my arms. I avoid his gaze, letting my silence speak for itself.

I'm not going to have this conversation with Bass. I acted like a jerk. I get that. But I'm not going to sit here and dissect my feelings. Especially not with him.

"Look, I understand there's some lingering resentment from what you were forced to experience, but you shouldn't take it out on Pascale. She's not responsible, and she was devastated when you were taken."

Guilt pricks my chest, but I refuse to let it show. This conversation has reignited my anger. It's not a blazing fire like before, but it still burns.

"Who should I take it out on then?" I snap. "You?"

He shrugs, as if the thought of me hating him doesn't bother him in the slightest. "If that will make you feel better, then sure."

"Fine. Consider it done," I say, even though I know hating Bass won't make me feel better. The truth is, I'm tired of resenting my friends for the secrets they've kept, and I'm tired of reliving the horrors of the contest anytime I close my eyes. I want to find a way to get over this, but I don't know how.

When neither of us speaks, I clear my throat. "Can I go now?"

Bass shakes his head. "There's one more thing. I've wanted to tell you this for a while now, but I didn't want to mention the contest and risk upsetting you." My muscles tense, and I frantically start to wonder what on earth Bass had delayed telling me.

What could be worse than anything I've already heard or experienced?

"Your fellow contestants," he begins, "and the ones before you, haven't you wondered why they were chosen? Why *you* were chosen?"

I don't know where he's going with this. "Queen Aria saw us in her orb," I tell him what Jordan once told me. I would've thought he knew this. "Then the queen sent her sentries to get us."

"Yes, but have you ever wondered why the orb showed you to the queen? Have you questioned why all of the young women in the contest were attractive redheads in their prime?"

I give him a pointed look. Of course, I have. "What does this have to do with anything?"

"Just answer the question." His expression is serious, and I know there's a point to this conversation, even if I can't figure out what it is.

"Yes, I thought it was weird that we were all redheads," I tell him.

"Any ideas why?"

"No."

"Not one?" Bass pushes. He tilts his head. "Come on, Sera. You're smart. Think. Why would Queen Aria only select redheaded young women from the orb?"

"I honestly don't know."

"Okay," Bass nods. "How about a different question. Did you notice Queen Aria seemed to have a special dislike for you? More so than the other contestants?"

"I guess." Queen Aria glared at me every chance she got, but I wasn't observant enough to know if she treated the other girls the same way.

"What if I told you it's because you look like someone—someone Aria hates with every fiber of her being."

Questions and thoughts race through my head, but I still can't make sense of what he's trying to get me to realize. "Who do I look like?"

Bass takes a deep breath, then says in a low, loaded voice, "Your mother."

CHAPTER TWELVE

MY EARS RING. I STARE AT BASS WITH MY JAW POPPED OPEN. HIS face is calm and patient as he waits for me to digest what he's said.

Finally, I find my voice. "You... you know what my mother looked like?"

"I do—I did."

I'm floored by the admission. I've never met either of my parents, and Uncle Eric rarely spoke about my mother when I was growing up. Anytime I would ask questions, he'd always seem so sad, but that didn't stop him from telling me things about her.

I know turkey was my mother's favorite sandwich, and that she loved soda. I know she was kind and hardworking. Uncle Eric even showed me pictures of her from when she was pregnant with me. But as I got older, I stopped asking so many questions.

My mother's gone. She died shortly after my birth. Things could've gone so bad for me, but I wasn't raised without a parent. Uncle Eric was there for me. So was Aunt Julie. My life could've been a whole lot worse without them. And for that, I'll always be grateful.

So how is it that Bass knew my mother?

Does he also know the identity of my father?

In the cavern, Queen Lani revealed my mother had been a servant. That means my father was likely Seelie, not Unseelie, but maybe my mother told Bass my father's name.

My heart beats erratically in my chest. I reconsider Bass's earlier questions, taking into account the new information he's provided. "You think Queen Aria hates me because I look like my mother?"

"I'm not sure Aria is cognizant enough to know that's why she dislikes you. Trust me, if she truly thought you were your mother's daughter, she would've done more than throw insults your way or sneer at you."

I shake my head in disbelief. Does Bass really think this is the best way to reveal that he knows information about my parents—information that he kept from me for weeks? Or, rather, *years*?

"Why are you telling me this now?"

"Because I incorrectly assumed you needed time to adjust to life here before I shared this information," he says evenly, but there's a bite in the words. "But seeing as you still can't seem to process or control your emotions, I figured it'd be best to, as humans say, lay all the cards on the table."

I'm both terrified and intrigued. I don't know if I want to hear more of what Bass has to say—not if he wants me to go into the city with Pascale and her friends once we're done talking. If the news is as bad as he makes it seem, I doubt I'll be pleasant company once I hear it.

My legs begin to shake. I move and sit on the couch to avoid the embarrassment of collapsing into an emotional heap.

Bass watches my move without saying a word. Once I settle on the plush cushion, he walks and sits in the chair to my left. He angles his torso to face me. With a steadying breath, I do the same.

He takes his time to formulate his words. For being the one to bring up the subject, Bass seems lost with how to actually say what he wants to say. Then, he just gets right to it. "Your mother's name was Kristianna Roberts."

That's the first I've heard of her last name. I'd always assumed it was Richards, like mine. I voice my concern. "Not Richards?"

"No. Eric gave you his last name once Kristianna... once your mother was gone."

I nod, and my already pounding heart kicks up another notch. "How did you know her?"

Bass runs a hand down his face, looking worn and tired. "I met her in Seelie." He pauses. No doubt, waiting for me to react to the news my mother was once in the Fae Realm. Except... I already knew that.

His purple irises widen, understanding my lack of surprise. "You knew?"

"Yes."

"How?"

I swallow the lump threatening to lodge in my throat. "Queen Lani told me."

Bass leans back. "Queen Lani?"

I nod.

"When?"

When does he think?

"In the cavern," I answer, then finally share the truth of what happened to me on top of the Cursed Mountain. "I found the diadem. When I touched it, I was transported into Queen Lani's study."

Bass looks like he can't believe what I'm saying, but his eyes are bright with excitement. "And Queen Lani was there. In the flesh?"

"Yes. Well... I think so. She seemed real to me. But I think it must've been some kind of enchantment. She said she'd locked herself and her power in the diadem to keep greedy Fae from accessing it, but she knew about Queen Aria and her contests. Queen Lani knew the queen was after her power."

"She bound her soul to the diadem to keep it safe," Bass mutters under his breath, shaking his head. Strands of black hair fall in his eyes, and he pushes them back. "And she actually told you this? In person?"

"Yes."

"Gods," Bass exhales. "And she willingly gave you the diadem?"

I shrug, not minding the repetitive nature of his questions. I get it. He's shocked.

"I guess you can say that. In the vision, she wore the diadem, but the diadem was on my head once it ended."

Bass releases an incredulous laugh and closes his eyes briefly. It's like he's trying to picture the scene I've described. "This is... remarkable, Sera."

"I know," I sigh.

He opens his eyes and meets my stare. "But why didn't you say anything before?"

Again, I shrug and give a semi-lie. "I didn't really know if it was real." That, and I didn't know if anyone else would believe me.

I'd decided to focus on how to separate myself from the

diadem, get out of my engagement, and return home rather than tell everyone the fantastical story. I didn't want anyone to think I was crazy. It's been my fear my entire life.

Bass continues to look as shocked as I'd been when I found myself in that study, face-to-face with a queen I'd thought had been dead for years. "So, Queen Lani was privy to today's current events?"

"Yes."

"That's amazing." Bass leans onto the right armrest and strokes his chin. "The enchantment must've been powerful to keep her aware of what transpired outside of the cavern, all while keeping her power safely stowed away. I knew she held great power, but I had no idea its limits reached so far."

"I guess we know why Queen Aria wanted the diadem so bad," I offer with a false laugh.

"Yes, I suppose we do." Suddenly, Bass locks down all emotion. His face is stony when he asks, "What else did Queen Lani tell you?"

My forehead furrows. Does he sound nervous?

"Just that my mom was a human slave. Since Unseelie don't force humans to work, I'd assumed she was in Seelie." I'm unable to hide the bitterness from my tone. I still can't believe a race of beings actually condone forcing humans to work against their will.

"That's it?" Bass seems mildly relieved.

My eyebrows turn down. "Isn't that enough?"

"Of course." Bass composes himself, once again adopting an emotionless expression.

"So, is it true?" I ask when he says nothing. "My mother was a slave in Seelie?"

"I'm afraid so."

I release a heavy sigh. "That... sucks."

"Yes," Bass confirms.

"What else do you know about her?"

The hand stroking his chin falls away. He sighs. "Not much. She left the Fae Realm shortly after we met, but I learned she was taken to Seelie when she was ten years old. She started her servitude working for a seamstress in the village outside of the Seelie castle."

"A seamstress?"

"Yes. Jinny's her name."

I gasp. "As in... Mistress Jinny?"

Bass says, "Yes, I believe that's what she's called. Why?"

"I-I'm pretty sure she's the seamstress who oversaw the contestants' gowns for the banquet," I tell him. "She... she called my Kristy."

Bass nods, not at all surprised. "As I said, your resemblance to your mother is strong. It's nothing short of a miracle Queen Aria didn't recognize you."

"But why would the queen recognize the daughter of a servant?" There are dozens upon dozens of young human women working in the Seelie castle, and none of them directly serve Her Majesty. Only nobles act as the queen's ladies maids. "And why would she hate her?"

"Why does Aria hate anyone?" Bass asks with a tired sigh. "Jealousy. Envy. Misplaced anger. Take your pick."

"Why would the queen be jealous of my mother?"

Bass levels me with a telling look. "Why do you think?"

I narrow my eyes, then it dawns on me. I rear back like he slapped me in the face. My stomach twists with disgust and horror.

"A-are you..." I can barely get the words out. I squeeze my eyes shut and finish the question, "Are you my father?"

"What?!"

My eyes fly open. Bass stares at me like I've grown two heads. His jaw has dropped, and his eyes are wide with shock. He snaps his mouth closed then asks, "What in the world would make you think that?"

Embarrassment heats my cheeks. His reaction makes me feel foolish, but I try to explain, "Queen Aria flirts with you all the time. I figured there was something going on between the two of you. Or maybe that she wanted there to be something going on between you. If you and my mother were a thing… that would give the queen reason to hate her."

It seems like a reasonable guess in my mind, but seeing Bass's face as I say it out loud makes me feel like it's totally ridiculous.

"Nothing has happened between me and Queen Aria. *Ever.*"

"Ever?"

"Ever," he confirms with a growl.

I swallow back my embarrassment. "And… you're not my father."

"Of course not!" Bass exclaims. "Do you honestly believe I would keep something like that from you?"

My gaze narrows. "You're pretty good at keeping secrets."

Bass sees my glare and sighs, letting his indignation fade away. "Fair enough."

He doesn't try to defend his previous deceit, and I appreciate it. More than he can know.

"So, Queen Aria hated my mother, and you think she subconsciously hates me because I look like her," I summarize our conversation, getting us back on track.

"Yes."

"And that's why she selects redheads?" The question leaves my mouth the moment the thought enters my head.

Is Queen Aria so sick that she picks young women who resemble the human servant she hated?

And if so, what did my mother ever do to earn such hatred? Jealousy? But what would a queen have to be jealous of a servant for?

Compassion seeps into Bass's gaze. "I can think of no other reason why Aria would specifically select red-haired contestants."

"That's..." I'm at a loss. "Insane."

"Agreed." Bass laces his fingers together and watches me, waiting for my next question. There are so many things I want to know.

But a knock at the door interrupts. Bass purses his lips, debating whether to answer the door or tell them to leave.

I make the decision for him.

We maintain eye contact as I get to my feet, and Bass's head tilts in silent question.

"They're waiting for me." I motion toward the door. And, if I'm being honest, I've had enough mind-blowing realizations for one day. I could use the distraction Pascale and her crew will provide. There will be time to ask Bass questions when we return. It's not like Dark Fae will be defeated in a day. I'm stuck in Unseelie for the foreseeable future.

Bass says nothing.

Another knock sounds.

I press my lips together, then ask, "Can we talk later? About... everything?"

Bass shakes his head, clearing his thoughts, then stands. "Of course." He waves a hand. "I hope you enjoy the city." He tucks his hands behind his back, waiting for my departure.

"Do you want to come with us?" I don't know what possesses me to ask. I guess it's just what a friend would do.

The corner of his mouth twitches, but he withholds a smile. "Thank you, but I have matters to see to here. Running a court isn't an easy job."

And, once again, I'm reminded of just how different Bass is from who I thought he was.

"Right. Totally." I blurt the words, shifting my feet, unsure why I feel so awkward. "Well… I guess I'll see you later."

He dips his chin, his eyes glittering with unnameable emotion. I half expect him to ask me to stay, but I'm disappointed when he says, "Bye, Sera."

Swallowing down my disappointment, I walk out of the room, using every ounce of strength I possess to not look back.

CHAPTER THIRTEEN

"To the west is the gallery district. You'll find all sorts of artisan boutiques and shops. It's a great place to spend an afternoon. To the east is the theatre and dance district. And in front of us, the food quarter." Pascale beams as she shares information about the city's layout, obviously taken with the Unseelie city and all of the treasures it possesses.

It took us twenty minutes of leisurely walking to travel from the palace border to the city center. In that time, I'd learned the city is called Vyneris, and its existed for a little more than four hundred years. Bass's father, the late King Mardrek, commissioned the city to be built to help accommodate the growing population in his court.

I'd been stunned to learn Seelie and Unseelie aren't the only Fae Courts to exist. I shouldn't have been surprised, considering Dark Fae are a thing, but I was. I hadn't heard one word about Summer, Winter, Spring, or Autumn Fae in the weeks I'd spend in Seelie, but apparently seasonal courts also existed in the Fae

Realm. Their lands are located on a separate land mass and inter-action between the two continents rarely occur nowadays.

But throughout the centuries, citizens of all the different courts migrated to live in Unseelie after hearing of its fair and just treatment of its citizens. Unfortunately, travel between the seasonal courts ceased some time ago.

When I asked why, Richie had explained living conditions in the seasonal courts had improved drastically, meaning their citi-zens no longer felt the need to move homes in order to seek a better life. The news had filled me with hope. Fae might be an old and powerful race, but they're still capable of change. Perhaps Seelie will abandon its practice of kidnapping humans for forced labor one day.

So, with the rapid influx of Fae, King Mardrek had created a city reminiscent of ancient cities in Europe, only... prettier. Stone and brick buildings no higher than four stories are pressed together, separated by clean alleyways every so often. Smooth, stone roads create pristine walking and driving paths throughout Vyneris. Pedestrians stroll along the edges, while horses and other types of beasts carry their passengers in the middle of the road.

Unlit, elegant gas lamps adorn every corner street, and I wonder if they are more for decoration than utility. The shops I'd passed so far had electricity, and that seemed the more efficient lighting option if given the choice.

Our group had stopped beside one of the pretty lamps as Pascale gave her speech. Fae of all types walk around us. Some have wings like my pixie companions: light and shimmering, almost invisible. While others have wings of solid black or blue, and they look much more daunting.

Then, there are those who don't have any wings. They look like the High Fae I met in Seelie, but they don't carry the same arrogance I've become accustomed to seeing. Their clothes are fine, but modest, blending in well with the other Unseelie citizens roaming the streets. If it weren't for the tipped ears, I would think the Fae were human. I've seen several of my race, too, and their demeanor is much more relaxed than the humans in Seelie.

Not your race anymore.

I shove away the thought. I identify as human, even with Fae blood running through my veins.

Pascale continues to ramble about the food quarter, describing the different types of restaurants and cafes we can find in the area. I'm only half listening. Most of my attention rests on the busy streets around me, observing and dissecting the Fae I see, looking for any sign of dissatisfaction. I find none.

I catch the eye of a young female Fae crossing the street. She looks like she's twelve or thirteen, but I have no idea if that's accurate. Fae age differently than humans, and I've never asked if childhood and adolescence progress the same as us.

Well... I did.

But my humanlike growth could've been due to the fact I'm half-human. I add that to the long list of things I don't know.

The young Fae continues to look at me. For a second, I worry she sees that I'm different—that I don't belong in Unseelie. Bass and Pascale had seemed confident my disguise would let me blend in, but what if they're wrong?

What if this girl has some special ability to see through such things? My ears are glamoured into points to make me look full-Fae, but what if she can tell they're fake. If she knows I'm human, who else can?

These thoughts race through my mind. I prepare to be called out when she draws closer, but all the young Fae does is offer me a tentative smile before bounding down an adjacent alleyway. As if nothing at all was amiss with the strange woman who'd stared at her as she crossed the street.

My shoulders droop with a sigh. I've become paranoid.

"Sera?" Pascale says my name. Based on her tone, it's not the first time she's tried to get my attention.

I look away from the alley and see Pascale, Richie, and Tonk all look at me. Aerie stares at her fingernails, looking bored.

I clear my throat. "Yeah?"

"Did you hear a word I said?"

"Yes." I nod. "You were talking about the restaurants."

"And did you hear me ask which one you'd like to try for dinner?"

I blink, and Pascale has her answer.

She huffs, "Do you want me to tell you about them again?"

"Please don't," Aerie mutters. Pascale glares at her.

"That's okay," I interject. "I'm open to trying anything."

Pascale looks back at me with a frown. "Are you sure? You're a little picky."

"I am not!"

My best friend rolls her eyes. "Please… yes you are. You can't even touch a hamburger if there's ketchup on it."

"Really?" Tonk gives me an incredulous look. "You don't like ketchup?"

"Only on hamburgers," I defend myself. "I'll eat it with fries and stuff."

"Wow," Tonk shakes his head. "Just, wow."

I plant my hands on my hips, playing the part of being offended when I'm really not. It feels good to banter like my life is normal—like I'm not some half-human, half-Fae freak who has a powerful object stuck on her head.

Tonk turns to Pascale. "Maybe we should just go back to the palace. I'm sure King Sebastian's renowned chef wouldn't mind making a plain grilled cheese sandwich, not once he learns she's his *special* guest."

I don't even bother asking what he means by "special guest". The implication's clear, as is his intention to rile me up.

"Look, I said I'd try anything. Someone just pick a place." I look at Richie and Aerie, hoping to rally them to my cause.

Richie's smiling, and faint amusement glints in Aerie's eyes.

"There's a tavern owned by Brownies," Aerie offers. "They have a varied menu."

I visibly start. "Brownies own businesses?"

Aerie lifts a brow. "Is that surprising?"

"I thought Brownies were normally maids and stuff..." Almost as soon as the words pass my lips, I regret them. I sound ignorant at best and prejudiced at worst. "What I mean is, I only saw Brownies working in household positions in Seelie."

Aerie crosses her arms. "In case you haven't noticed, you're not in Seelie anymore. Here, Fae can do whatever job they desire as long as they work for it." Her words are stern, but they aren't harsh. I'm lucky. I deserve a reprimand.

I can't let my experience in Seelie make me prejudiced to all of the Fae Realm. It's already obvious that life in Unseelie is different than what I've come to expect living in Seelie.

Richie clears his throat and saves me from needing to reply. "Shall we go? I don't know about you guys, but I'm starving."

"Me too," Tonk chimes in. Then, he grabs my hand and wraps it around his elbow, like he's a lord and I'm a lady about to enter a ballroom. "Lead the way, Aerie."

The siren looks at each of us. Hearing no objection, she turns and walks down the road, leading us into the food quarter. Pascale shoots me a grin and bounces after Aerie. Above us, the sun begins its descent across the sky, and I estimate we have about an hour before sunset.

The streets grow more crowded. The smell of freshly baked
bread and roasting meat fills the air, making my mouth water.
Tables and chairs appear outside the buildings. The outdoor
seating seems to be the preference of the Fae dining at the restaurants. I don't blame them. The weather is pleasant. It reminds me
of Fall.

The Fae Realm doesn't follow the Human Realm's weather
patterns. Seelie was unnaturally warm and sunny for the time of
year, but Unseelie is cool and crisp while still bright and sunny.
I'm glad I wear leggings. I'd be chilly in a dress.

My stomach growls. I press my free hand against the noise,
but it doesn't mask the sound.

Tonk grins and pats my hand. Then, he leans close and his
breath tickles my glamoured ear, "Don't worry, princess, we'll
get you food before you starve."

I'm about to tell him not to call me princess when Richie
interrupts.

"Careful, Tonk," he calls out behind us. "You know she's
spoken for."

He'd said something similar at The Dark Horse. Tonk had
been flirting shamelessly, and Richie had called me off limits.

I glance back at the Fae who's race I haven't been able to
identify yet. "What do you mean by that?"

"Pardon?" Richie tries to look calm, but he blinks repeatedly,
telling me he's somewhat nervous.

"What do you mean, 'I'm spoken for'?"

His hesitation is brief. "You're engaged." His eyes land on
the gold bracelet encircling my left wrist. Camden's engagement
band.

I stare at the jewelry in panic. What had I been thinking? I
should've removed the bracelet the moment I arrived in

Unseelie. It's an identifying mark—something Dark Fae could use to hunt me down.

Reading my expression, Richie's eyes soften. "I can hold it for you... if you want to take it off." He knows my leggings don't have pockets.

Tonk drops his arm, freeing mine. I glance at the gleaming metal, the setting sun shining against its surface. This bracelet isn't important to me. It's just something I had to wear to make Camden believe I accepted our engagement until I found a way to get out of it. So why do I hesitate?

I don't want to marry Camden. That fact remains. But I have to admit, I feel bad. At this moment, Camden is using all of the resources at his disposal to try and find the monsters who are after me. He cares. He really cares about me. He might even think he's in love with me, though I think the idea is completely ridiculous. He doesn't know me. Not the real me.

Camden knows the girl who had no choice but to fight for her life. He thinks I'm some tough, powerful creature. When, in reality, I'm just an ordinary girl with ordinary dreams. I'm not the woman he thinks I am, and the sooner he realizes that, the better for both of us.

Richie and Tonk watch me without speaking. I don't look to confirm, but I'm pretty sure Aerie and Pascale are looking at me, too. No doubt, they overheard Richie's remark and noticed my subsequent silence.

Get a grip, Sera. You didn't want to wear the bracelet in the first place.

But removing it... taking off the bracelet now that I'm in Unseelie... I can't deny it feels like a betrayal. I know it shouldn't, but it does.

I take a breath, ignoring my wary audience, and slip the bracelet off my arm.

Immediately, I feel the loss of its weight, and I tell myself that means nothing. I hold out the jewelry.

Richie takes the bracelet with a kind smile, tucking it safely in the front pocket on his very mortal-looking pair of jeans. Once again, Tonk loops my arm around his, and our group continues walking through Vyneris.

I follow along, pretending with the rest of them that I hadn't just severed my last tie to Prince Camden... likely for forever.

CHAPTER FOURTEEN

"OH MY, THAT IS ABSOLUTELY DELICIOUS!" AERIE'S EYES twinkle with more feeling than I've ever seen on the stoic siren. I blame the two goblets of wine. She's steadily working on her third while I've barely touched the one sitting in front of me. "I cannot believe nymphs crashed the Seelie Welcoming Ceremony. Tell me again how absolutely flabbergasted His Highness was when they showed up!"

I'd thought the group would've steered clear of any mention of Seelie or Camden after the situation with my bracelet, but after eating a delicious meal, we'd moved on to drinking. And the alcohol has definitely loosened the Fae's tongues, as well as lowered any reserve they might've felt about bringing the sensitive subject up.

Pascale's eyes are glassy, and her grin is silly and wide. "I wasn't there, but the rumors painted him as absolutely livid!"

I don't say a word. Camden had been angry, but he'd kept it together in front of the crowd. I'm sure some Common Fae exaggerated when sharing their story to make it seem more exciting.

"Did he have them arrested?" Tonk asks, sipping on ale.

"No." Pascale's pink hair sways as she shakes her head. "Which surprises me, considering what they said."

"What did they say?" Aerie and Tonk ask at the same time. Richie listens intently, but he's refrains from acting as enthusiastic as his friends.

Pascale's reply forms on her lips, but she hesitates. She shoots me a wary glance.

"It's fine." I wave a hand, pretending like my heart isn't racing. I hadn't thought about the nymphs taunting words since the day of the welcoming ceremony. The Dark Fae's attack had effectively distracted me.

Pascale hiccups, then turns her intoxicated gaze back to her friends, pitching her voice low like she's sharing a state secret. "The nymphs said she was a favorite of King Sebastian."

"No!" Aerie whisper-cries, though she looks delighted. "What else?"

Only Richie casts me a hesitant glance. I do my best to hide my emotion from my face. I must succeed, because he turns back to listen to Pascale.

"They said..." Pascale pauses and looks around the tavern dramatically, milking this moment for everything it's worth. "They said Sera is the king's chosen mate!"

Aerie gasps, so does Tonk. Even Richie rears back in shock.

"Are you serious?" Aerie probes. "They actually said that? Not only to a room full of Seelie, but in front of Prince Camden?"

"Yes," Pascale practically squeals.

"That's so..." Aerie can't think of the word, but Richie fills in for her.

"Ballsy." He sips his drink.

Again, his eyes find mine. I shrug, then follow his lead and take a healthy gulp of wine. The liquid burns the back of my throat, but the taste isn't unpleasant.

"Extremely ballsy," Tonk agrees. "What would possess the nymphs to do such a thing? You don't think the king put them up to it, do you?"

"Abssssolutely not," Pascale slurs. "Bass wouldn't do that. He's not sh-showy."

"Shh," Aerie hisses, leaning forward until her chin practically touches the table between us. "You know you can't call him that in public."

"Oops," Pascale slams a hand against her mouth. "I forgot."

My head swivels as I watch them talk back and forth. So, there is some kind of etiquette in Unseelie. Bass can be friendly with Common Fae, but they can't be so casual when others are around.

"What I want to know is why the nymphs would risk their necks like that," Tonk says over the rim of his glass. "They're very lucky the prince didn't do worse."

Richie hums his agreement.

"No kidding." Pascale shudders. "I didn't see him, but I heard he looked positively murderous when the nymphs delivered the insult."

That's it. I can't listen to this anymore without saying something.

"Camden isn't a monster." My words immediately capture the table's attention. "He's not going to freak out because someone tried to rile him up." I sound defensive, but I can't help it. Camden's a good guy. He's not going to arrest people for insulting him. That's something his crazed, power-hungry aunt would do. Camden's better than that.

Tonk and Richie share a glance while Pascale and Aerie

continue to watch me through bleary eyes, blinking as they try to think of something to say.

It's Richie's calm voice which breaks the silence. "No one here thinks Camden's a monster," he tells me. "But any Fae male, no matter his age or rank, would be absolutely livid to hear someone claim his companion is coveted by another."

"Heck," Tonk nods and adds, "even females get territorial over their partners. It's a Fae thing, Instinct, if you will."

I frown and take a sip of wine to buy myself time. "It was just a stupid prank," I finally say, refusing to think of Camden as territorial. That just sounds so... *barbaric.* It's so at odds with the level-headed and sincere male I'd come to know during my time in Seelie.

Still, the words remind me of the fury I'd seen in Camden's eyes when the nymphs uttered their taunting words. I remember how he paced across his room in an angry huff, unable to dispel the volatile emotions. Could his behavior be the result of some deep-seeded Fae instinct? The kind that makes him believe that, as his fiancée, I belong to him? My stomach twists unpleasantly with the thought.

I lower the goblet onto the table, and my hand trembles slightly. Some of the wine sloshes over the brim, spilling onto my fingers. I dry off the liquid with the cloth napkin tucked underneath my plate, hoping no one noticed the nervous gesture.

"I don't think it w-was a prank," Pascale hiccups.

I purse my lips. "What else could it be?"

"A taunt," Aerie provides with excited eyes. Clearly, the siren isn't one to shy away from conflict. "His Majesty probably employed the nymphs to attend the event to get under the prince's skin."

"I already t-told you," Pascale shakes her head. "Bass wouldn't do that."

"Why not?" Aerie challenges, not willing to have her idea dismissed so easily. "The prince is untested, and King Sebastian cares about the girl's wellbeing." She gestures to me like I'm an afterthought, then continues, "I'm sure it bothers the king to know the prince believes he has a claim on her. So why wouldn't he try to rile him up a bit?"

"Because His Majesty is not so foolish as to wish a reenactment of the Great War," Richie says in a tone that says, *all of you are absolutely ridiculous.*

Before anyone else can respond, two shadows appear at the edge of the table. I turn toward the newcomers, but I have to tilt my head back to see the tall males' faces. Two pairs of chocolate brown eyes meet mine, before shifting to take in the rest of the group.

Richie, the most sober of the bunch aside from me, clears his throat. "Hello, gentlemen. Can we help you?"

"Yeah," the Fae standing closest to me says. "We heard you talking about Seelie." His tone is not friendly. Warning bells go off in my head.

"You're mistaken," Richie says coolly. He can't outright lie to the Fae, but he can choose words which will make the males infer what he wants them to.

"I don't think we are," the other Fae says. His voice is deeper and more menacing. "What we want to know, is why Unseelie Fae are sitting in this tavern, talking about the Seelie prince like they know him."

"Because we do know him," Aerie replies, flipping her hair over her shoulder in a haughty gesture. "He's the prince of our rival court. Everyone knows him."

His eyes narrow. "That's not what I mean."

Why do I feel like we're about to get into a bar fight?

Why is this guy is so upset? It's not like we're sitting on

rooftops, shouting Camden's praises to all of Unseelie. This was a private conversation amongst a group of friends. This guy is out of line.

Maybe it's the few sips of wine, or maybe it's knowing I have Fae power coursing under my skin. Whatever it is, I grow a backbone. "Look, I don't know what your problem is, but maybe you shouldn't be eavesdropping on people's conversations."

The strangers' eyes snap to me. They'd written me off as unimportant. I don't blame them. I look meek compared to my companions. But not anymore.

The Fae closest to me leans forward and growls, "Maybe Seelie sympathizers shouldn't be in Unseelie territory."

My eyes widen ever so slightly. Is that this guy's problem?

Unhindered by Fae rules against lying, I lift my chin and say, "We aren't Seelie sympathizers."

"No? Then why did we hear you all speaking about the princeling. It seems like you know him personally."

"Is it a crime to know a prince?" I succeed when I try to sound bored. I lift my goblet, proud to notice my hands no longer tremble despite the adrenaline pumping through my veins.

Both Fae snort. "Loyalty to a court full of Fae and human rights violations should be a crime."

I hide my surprise behind my goblet. This isn't the sort of conflict I'm used to witnessing in a bar. Normally, fights break out of ridiculous or childish insults, or the perception of such insults. But these Fae... their problem is they think our group allies with the atrocities found in Seelie. They couldn't be more wrong, but it's not like I can easily explain why we were talking about Camden and his court in the first place.

I settle on saying, "No one said we were loyal to Seelie."

The Fae continue to assess me. Their eyes trail over my face, my dyed hair, all the way down to the tips of my finger tapping against the goblet. I don't show emotion, even though my pulse is racing. I hope they can't smell my fear.

To my left, Richie has gone rigid, and his eyes are hard. Tonk and Aerie look equally ready for a fight. I'm going to try and make sure it doesn't get to that point.

Pascale lifts her lips in a flirtatious smile, patting her eyelashes at the male closest to her. "I think we got off on the wrong foot. Why don't you both sit down and have a drink with us?"

The males share a look. Then, once again, their attention falls on me. "You'll have to forgive us. We don't share a table with a prince's whore."

Richie growls, and Tonk slaps the table out of anger. Pascale, still under the influence, is confused while Aerie hisses under her breath. I swear I see a storm brewing in the siren's sea-blue eyes.

As for me, I'm mortified. The Fae had practically yelled the insult, and now we've garnered the attention of the entire tavern.

Gradually, my embarrassment slides away and makes room for fury.

How *dare* he speak to me like that. He doesn't know me. He doesn't even know the truth of what we'd been talking about.

What kind of ass hole makes snap assumptions about someone and openly insults them like this? And here I'd though Unseelie were more civilized than Seelie. They're just as cruel, but they don't bother to try and hide it.

With a cold, dark voice I don't recognize, I say, "I think it's time for you to go."

My companions stiffen. No doubt, they hear the dangerous note in my words. They know of the untapped Darkness contained in the diadem on my head, and they don't know what will happen when I access the power. No one does.

The strangers, however, are unaware I'm a wolf in sheep's

clothing. Once again, they share a glance, and then they have the nerve to chuckle.

"Your suggestion is noted," one tells me, "but I don't take instructions from whores—"

Before he can close his mouth from the last word, my hand lifts as if by its own accord, and I snap my fingers.

Then, the tavern goes dark.

CHAPTER FIFTEEN

THE DARKNESS LINGERS IN THE TAVERN LIKE A HEAVY, WARM blanket. Wisps of power curl in my hair, kissing my cheeks, and tickling my ears with their adoring whispers and endless supplications.

I don't hear anything but The Darkness, lovingly telling me of how they've missed the world. Being locked in the diadem is lonely. They don't want to go back. They enjoy being free.

Please don't lock us away again.

Their touch is both dense and light—both sheer and solid. The power Queen Lani contained wasn't some inanimate source of magic. I can't see it, but I know, deep in my soul, that The Darkness is a living, breathing entity. It's different from the remnants of Fae magic I've experienced so far. It needs to be protected. Its whispers intensify, urging me to keep them safe. Begging me to let them remain free.

In the back of my mind, I know this isn't right. I shouldn't feel so comfortable. The room's devoid of all light. I can't even make out the shadows of my companions. The fact Darkness speaks to me should send me in a panic, but I can't deny how peaceful this moment feels. I haven't felt this serene since I was abducted from Central Park.

Then, I hear Pascale scream my name, and the peace shatters.

I gasp. On my inhale, The Darkness is sucked out of the room. I hear it cry out in protest before its presence is safely locked back in the diadem. Light returns to the tavern. I feel the weight of the diadem. I reach up and brush the invisible item, hissing and pulling back when the metal scorches my skin.

"Sera!" Pascale grabs my arm, shaking me. The lines around her eyes relax when my eyes meet hers. "Are you all right?"

I try to speak, but my throat is dry. I swallow several times, and I'm barely able to manage a strangled, "I'm fine."

She drops her hands and takes a step back. "What the hell just happened?"

I shake my head, unable to articulate what I'd experienced in those blissful moments. Movement over Pascale's shoulder draws my attention. Aerie and Tonk are huddled together, jumping apart when they see me looking their way. Richie stands next to him, wearing a grim expression. I follow his gaze and feel my blood run cold when I take in the state of the tavern.

Chairs and tables are overturned. I don't know if I'm responsible, or if The Darkness had run amuck without my knowledge. Either way, I suppose the damage is ultimately my fault.

I can't explain what happened. I just… lost it. Even now, I feel dark energy swimming beneath the surface, competing with my other Fae power for dominance. The Darkness has tasted freedom, and it won't willingly submit to its cage anymore.

In the corner nearest the exit, I see the two Fae who'd approached our table. One has slick blood trailing from his temple. The other lies flat on the ground, his eyes fluttering as he regains consciousness.

Oh my god.

I hurt them.

My anger unleashed The Darkness... and I actually hurt someone.

Any residual resentment flows out of me like a broken dam, replaced by guilt and fear. I shouldn't have snapped. Sure, the guys had been rude and insulting, but unleashing The Darkness was unnecessary.

Winning the diadem marked me as the next ruler over The Darkness, but I don't even want the job. And based on what just happened, I don't think I'm qualified to reign over the powerful entity. If the fate of the Fae Realm relies on me taming The Darkness, there's a bleak future ahead.

I've wanted to abdicate the title since the moment it was bestowed on me, and now I want to separate myself from it even more. I'm not strong enough. The Darkness will take my half-Fae blood and chew me up, then spit me out. It's a dominating force, and I'm nothing but its vessel to be unleashed.

My chest rises and falls in rapid succession. I'm hyperventilating.

"Sera, relax. It's okay. We'll clean up the mess." Pascale tries to console me, but she doesn't know the dark thoughts clouding my mind, intensifying my panic until the walls blur and I barely hear her.

She shakes me then shouts something to Richie.

The tall Fae approaches, watching me like I'm a wounded animal in danger of striking out without warning. The look stings, but I can't blame him for it. Not after what just happened.

Richie's lips move, but like Pascale, I barely hear his words.

I guess he figures that out, because the next thing he does is hold out a hand. I stare at his palm for several seconds, then realize what he wants. I put my hand in his, and Richie's chest lowers with his exhale.

The world blurs, and we faze out of the tavern.

I don't immediately recognize my new surroundings. The plush carpet and expensive artwork aren't familiar yet, but there is no missing the glare coming from the male leaning against the sturdy oak desk.

Bass's eyes are like purple ice, spearing me where I stand, disoriented, in the middle of the office. My hearing returns. The window behind Bass is open, and the sound of trees rustling in the breeze gives off a false sense of calm.

"Richie," Bass's voice is as cold as his glare. "Find Henry and take him to the tavern to clean up the mess."

Richie doesn't hesitate. He leaves me on my own, disappearing through the open door. It closes loudly behind him, and my heart rate spikes. I try to stay calm, having no desire to fall prey to panic again.

For several agonizing seconds, Bass says nothing. He simply stares at me, and a host of emotions plays across his face. None are positive.

Frustration, irritation, and disbelief war for dominance on his flawlessly handsome face. I hate that even when he's looking at me like I'm the dirt under his shoe, I still can't help but find him overwhelmingly attractive.

I shove down any and all thoughts of his looks, forcing myself to focus on the impending reprimand. I can practically see the seething words building behind his flaring irises. I brace for their impact, determined not to do anything as mortifying as crying. I feel bad as it is. I hurt two innocent Fae by losing my temper. I deserve what's coming, but I can maintain some dignity by not losing control of my emotions again.

I'm so hyped to take my verbal punishment, that I'm stunned when Bass says nothing more than, "What happened?"

I wait for him to say more. I wait for him to accuse me of weakness or behaving rashly—both are true. But no more words come from that side of the study. Bass waits patiently for my answer, though it's obvious anger simmers under the surface.

I breathe deeply, still trying to calm myself from my earlier episode.

At last, I'm able to speak. "I-I think I released some of The Darkness."

Bass isn't surprised. For a second, I wonder how he knows what's transpired in the first place. I'd just been at the tavern, and none of the patrons had left the premises. How could someone have already told him what happened?

My question is answered when Bass says, "I know. I felt it. What I want to know is what happened to cause you to unleash the power?"

My lips part in surprise. "You *felt* it?" How is that possible? The tavern is at least a mile from the palace.

"Not much goes on in this court without my knowledge," he replies coolly. "Now, what happened?"

Seeing no way to stall, nor having the desire to do so, I tell him the story. I describe the Fae strangers, and their aversion to us discussing Seelie and Prince Camden as if we were allies. I tell him how their insults grew uglier each time they opened their mouth until I snapped.

"And what did they say?" Bass prods when I stop speaking. "What was so awful that it made you unleash The Darkness?" His voice holds no inflection. He isn't accusing me of anything. He's just asking the question. I can't tell if it's an act, or if he's really not as angry as when I first started my story.

"It doesn't matter," I sigh. "I overreacted."

"It does matter," Bass counters. "What did they say?"

I *really* don't want to say it out loud. It's more than a little embarrassing. But Bass is unrelenting. I won't be able to avoid telling him.

So, I mutter with heating cheeks, "I told him to stop eavesdropping on our conversation. Then he called me a whore."

One beat, the silence is loaded and heavy. Then, it breaks in two. "*What?*"

I cringe away from his shout. Compared to the previous silence, it nearly knocks me off my feet.

Bass shoves off the desk and begins to prowl across the study, renewed fury fueling his steps.

For the life of me, I can't understand why the insult makes him so angry. Looking back, even I know my reaction was uncalled for. I don't know if The Darkness had heightened my anger with the intent of getting free, but it seems the most likely explanation for my ridiculous behavior.

So what's Bass's excuse?

The last I checked, he didn't have a powerful diadem magically fused to his head, whispering its desire be freed and inciting violence.

"Bass," I call hesitantly, "Calm down."

"Calm down?" His gaze snaps to mine. "A citizen of my court insults you, and you want me to calm down?"

This is *not* how I anticipated this going.

"They're just words." I tell him. "They hurt, but I'll get over it. I *am* over it."

Bass refuses to be consoled. "It doesn't matter. No one should treat you this way. I vowed to protect you. What kind of male am I if I can't even protect you in my realm?"

Ah. This stems from his own guilt.

I don't know when Bass promised himself he'd protect me,

but my money is it occurred sometime after I was abducted. To think, my friend conversed with me in Seelie like I was a total stranger. I know it was an act, not to mention I'd been deprived of my memories so I wouldn't have recognized him anyway, but I don't understand how he could be so good at pretending like I meant nothing to him. His current state screams that he cares, and a small part of me is thrilled by the display.

Get a grip.

I cannot afford to let any of my previous crush return to the surface. Bass and I are *so* beyond that.

But the way Bass is acting, and the heat in his eyes gives me pause. My breath catches in my throat when Bass locks his gaze on me. His nostrils flare right before his form blurs.

I stumble back a step when he reappears in front of me. My hair flies back as a gust of wind travels through the room. My heartbeat spikes for the one-hundredth time today. Bass follows my retreat, refusing to let space exist between us. He reaches out to brush the hair out of my face. My throat dries when his hand lingers, cupping my cheek.

Bass isn't one for physical touch. Sure, I'd seen King Sebastian caress Queen Aria's hands and whisper into her ear. He even made a show of holding my hand on his arm when he'd escorted me around as a contestant. But that'd all been an act.

Bass rarely hugged me in the Human Realm. Except for the one night when I'd thought we'd go further…

No.

My inner voice is harsh, demanding I not let my thoughts go there.

I appreciate her strength. Because at this moment, with Bass's eyes swirling with intense emotion and his thumb stroking my smooth skin, I feel weak. So weak.

I want to revert back to those innocent days… the ones where I held out hope Bass and I could one day be more than friends.

Stop it.

I squeeze my eyes closed. I can't look at him if I have any hope of maintaining my dignity. His touch sends every nerve firing. My chest aches with yearning, and I hate that I can't control this reaction.

"Sera?" His voice is so… caring. And throaty.

I can't do this.

I open my eyes and shake my head, displacing his hand. Then, I take several steps away until my back hits the bookshelf I hadn't seen behind me. I'd kissed Camden days ago. I told him I'd give him a chance to steal my heart. I can't ping back and forth between guys. Not if I don't want to deserve the insult spewed by the Fae in the tavern.

This time, Bass doesn't pursue me, but there's undeniable heat remains in his gaze.

"Sera?" He repeats. This time, his voice isn't so enticing, but it's still not totally normal. He's affected. By what? I don't dare think about it. "What's wrong?"

"Nothing." I force the word out.

A shadow crosses his face, but the heat in his eyes intensifies. For the first time since I was abducted, I wish I was wearing a stupid dress. The extra fabric would be able to hide how weak my legs have become. I lock my arms and grip the shelf at my hips, holding myself up before my lower limbs decide to give out on me.

A predatory smile tugs at Bass's lips, and my pulse skyrockets. He takes slow, purposeful steps, closing the distance between us. He doesn't stop until I have to tilt my head back to maintain eye contact. I'm hyperaware of his chest as he inhales and his shirt brushes against my chest.

What is happening right now?!

Bass, once again, lifts a hand to my face. He tucks a stray piece of hair behind my ear and licks his lips. Warmth flares low in my stomach, and my grip on the bookshelf tightens. I'm surprised the wood doesn't crack.

"You aren't acting like it's 'nothing'." His breath brushes my forehead, giving me goosebumps.

"W-what?" I stutter. My mind is muddled.

Instead of explaining, Bass says, "Your safety and comfort mean everything to me, Serafina Richards. I *loathe* the idea of anyone causing you pain, especially in my court." His admission is sincere, and it thrills me. This isn't the reserved guy I've known for years. Bass is so expressive... and alluring. I wonder if this is who he really is. Maybe the Bass I knew as a teenager wasn't real.

Overcome with the intensity of his stare and the emotions it elicits within me, I break away and glance down. My eyes land on my wrist, noticing the absence of my gold engagement band, and it's like a bucket of ice water is poured over me.

What am I doing?

I can't let Bass say this.

I can't *want* to hear him say this.

So much is happening. I just freaking hurt two Fae on accident, for goodness sake! All because The Darkness got the better of me and escaped in a moment of weakness.

My focus should be on remedying *that* situation. Then figuring out a way to honorably bow out of my engagement. I shouldn't be shaking with anticipation, noting how moist Bass's lips are. Or how easy it would be to lift onto my toes and press my lips against his.

Bass's eyes flare. I swear, it's like he's heard my thoughts.

Slowly, he begins to sway forward. His attention lies solely on my slightly parted mouth.

Every rational thought leaves me. Deep in my soul, I want this. And I'm not going to stop it.

I suck in a breath and wait for his lips to meet mine.

Just as Bass is a hairsbreadth away, the study's doorknob turns. Startled, I leap away from the bookshelf, putting a good four feet between us.

George steps into the study. His gaze zeroes in on us, and he sniffs. I cringe, wondering if he can smell the evidence of what almost happened. He glances from me to Bass. While I'm sure I look like a spooked colt, Bass is the image of composure.

He smiles an easy grin, and greets his friend, "George. Can we help you?"

To his credit, Bass's bandmate gets ahold of himself. He straightens and clears his throat, avoiding my gaze altogether. "Just... checking to make sure everything is all right. I got wind of what happened in the food quarter."

Shame floods my cheeks, as well as something else.

Rather than standing there and listening to Bass tell George what had happened, I quickly say, "I'm going to my rooms."

Then, without waiting for permission or any acknowledgement, I run out of the study.

It's not until I cross the threshold that I hear George state matter-of-factly, "Whatever that was... I don't think it went well."

Bass's responding growl makes my heart clench, and I pick up my pace.

CHAPTER SIXTEEN

"So, I heard you had a little outburst yesterday," Henry calls out in greeting, approaching me in the sunlit parlor where I sit facing the palace gardens through the foggy window. It's been raining all morning, which is a perfect reflection of my mood. I don't bother responding to his greeting, hoping it will encourage him to walk away and leave me to my self-loathing.

But I'm not so lucky.

Henry throws himself onto the plush chair across from mine and smiles at me like we're best friends. Or maybe secret lovers. I really can't tell if he's trying to flirt with me, or if he's just this over-the-top friendly with everyone.

Back when Pascale and I would go see Bass's band play, neither George nor Henry really spoke with us. Sure, we'd been introduced, and we'd exchange pleasantries when we saw each other, but we were never friendly. Knowing one another's names is all that made us more than complete strangers.

I watch Henry with dull, tired eyes. I'd been staring at the rain pelt the luxurious greenery for almost an hour, using the time to chastise myself for so many aspects of my behavior yesterday.

Pascale had found me later in the evening, and she'd assured me Henry had wiped the minds of all of the tavern's customers, including the two Fae who'd instigated the confrontation. It was kind of her to try and take the blame off me, but I have no disillusion that I'm the only one responsible for the situation reaching such a dangerous level.

Needless to say, I hadn't slept well.

"Don't worry," he continues cheerfully, totally ignoring my less-than-enthusiastic behavior. "I made sure none of the survivors will remember a thing. You're free and clear."

I cringe when he says survivors. "Were a lot of people injured?" I can still see the blood trickling down the Fae's temple and the destroyed furniture.

"Nothing that a little healing power couldn't fix," he tells me.

When I remain silent, his voice loses some of its teasing tone. "You know... you shouldn't feel bad. None of us knows how The Darkness works. Learning to control it will have a learning curve."

His compassion is almost worse than his humor.

I burrow deep into my chair and stare at the rain drops falling from the sky. "I don't want to learn to control it. I don't even want to have it."

A sleek, soothing voice murmurs in my ear, trying to coax away my sadness. That's another thing. It seems that the taste of freedom has enabled The Darkness to speak with me whenever it wants, even though it's contained in the diadem. It's a quiet sound; much quieter than the sound I'd heard while encased in the dark. But it's still unnerving.

I plan to tell Bass about the new voices, but I haven't seen him today. He might be avoiding me, but I try to keep those thoughts at bay. Bass is the Unseelie king. No doubt, a busy schedule is enough to keep him from meeting me at breakfast or checking on me around lunch. Sure, it's my first day in his court, but I don't need to be coddled.

Nope. I don't need to be coddled at all.

Henry crosses his arms. I feel his stare burning the side of my face. I try to ignore it, but between that, the whispering shadows, and the silence between us, I find myself giving in and turning his direction.

"What?"

He doesn't even blink? "What do you mean, what?"

"What do you want?" I ask.

A gleam sparkles in Henry's eyes. He's trying to get a rise out of me.

"Did you forget? I'm supposed to continue your combat training."

I did forget. The events of yesterday had wiped it from my mind.

"I don't need combat training," I counter. I'd been forced to fight in Seelie to prepare for the contest, but I don't plan on embarking on another life-threatening mission for as long as I live.

"I see. You plan to just let the Dark Fae kill you and steal the diadem."

I stiffen. "Of course not."

Henry lifts a brow. "Okay. So you plan to fight?"

I'm so not in the mood for this. "I have enough skill to fight off a Fae until help arrives." I'd become pretty good with a wooden staff. Plus, I have Fae powers.

"What if help isn't close by?" He counters. "What if a more experienced and talented Fae comes against you? How will you stop them?"

"That won't happen." As soon as the words leave my lips, I know they're nothing more than wishful thinking. I chew my bottom lip.

Disapproval covers the jokester's expression. He doesn't pull his punch when he says, "That kind of thinking will get you killed."

He's not wrong.

"What is your plan exactly?" I ask, finally turning my body towards him, away from the window. "You teach me new combat skills, and I suddenly become skilled enough to fight off any would-be attackers?"

He dips his chin. "It's a start."

An overwhelming desire to just sit in the chair and go back to staring at the weather consumes me, but the feeling is interrupted by The Darkness murmuring.

Grow in strength.

Learn to fight.

Become unstoppable.

The whispers give me pause. Why would The Darkness want me to learn to fight?

Sensing my question, I receive a reply.

Protect us.

Keep us with you always.

I shudder when a tendril of Darkness trails over the back of my neck.

Henry sees. "What is it?"

I shake my head. "Nothing. Just a chill." I'm not about to confess there are voices in my head. "Fine. I'll train with you. Can I at least go change first?"

Henry rises. Gone is his serious demeanor, replaced by a flirtatious grin. "Absolutely. Would you like company?"

I roll my eyes. "No, thank you."

"Your loss," he calls after me as I duck out of the parlor.

I will never admit it to him, but his teasing taunt pulls a small smile from my lips.

———

"Lift your back hand. Keep it close to your head. You need to make sure the side of your face is shielded from any stray punches."

I heed Henry's instruction and raise my gloved hand. I'd met my newest trainer in the palace's state of the art gym nearly an hour ago. After fifteen minutes of thorough warmup exercises, he'd tossed thin, padded gloves onto my lap and told me to get ready to spar.

I'm not completely unaware of how to fight in hand-to-hand combat, but the majority of my training in Seelie had consisted of using weapons both offensively and defensively. My muscles had grown strong in the weeks I'd trained, but the new style of fighting is starting to make them burn.

"Good. Now, strike my palm, then follow with a left jab."

I take a breath and execute the order. Only, I don't pull back fast enough.

Henry's palm slaps the left side of my head where I let my guard down. The hit isn't hard, but the failure stings.

"I told you to keep your face shielded," he chastises. "Do it again. This time, pull back to protect your vulnerability."

Gritting my teeth, I comply. This time, when Henry moves to slap me, my hand blocks him.

"Good. Now, advance with all you've got. Push me back. Take over the fight."

The frustration brewing in my belly bubbles with renewed fervor. He's given the same instruction three times now, and I've yet to be able to push him back. I'm exhausted. Henry is taller, broader, and stronger. The only way I'll drive him back is if he lets me. Which I don't see him doing anytime soon.

Shaking my head, I drop my hands and say, "I need a break."

Henry's normally playful eyes harden. "You'll get a break when I say you get a break." He's every bit the drill sergeant.

"No." I pull the Velcro strap from the gloves and yank them off my sweaty hands. Without another word, I toss the gloves on the mat and move towards the modern water fountain installed at the back of the gym.

I make it three steps before my feet are swiped out from under me, and I land painfully on my left hip.

I roll over and shout, "What the hell was that?"

Henry stands over me with crossed arms. "It's not time for a break."

Anger ignites, and I shove myself to my feet. "I'm *tired*. A quick break isn't going to ruin this riveting training session."

I pivot to continue on my way to the fountain, seeing Henry's lightning fast arm snap out from the corner of my eye.

I spin and grab his wrist, twisting until the limb is pinned behind his back.

He winces when I tug tighter. I lean in and growl into his ear, "I said, I'm *tired*."

A haze has descended over my eyes. The world is tinged in red, and I feel the beginning loss of control. I tell myself to take it easy. Henry's not my enemy.

But my temper doesn't see reason.

And unfortunately, Henry isn't deterred by my aggressive maneuver. If anything, his maniacal grin screams entertainment.

One moment, I have the upper hand. In the blink of an eye, Henry has thrown his weight, creating slack and unwinding himself from my twisted hold.

He doesn't hold back.

I dodge and weave, avoiding his on-target swipes. Every fiber of my body is taunt and ready. We move as if in a dance—an aggressive and tight dance. There's little room for error where I'm concerned. One misplaced step and I will meet the end of Henry's padded fist.

Suddenly, fire flares in my chest. I'm not weak. I don't need to avoid his attacks. I need to throw some of my own.

Invigorated by the thought, I halt. Instead of leaning away from Henry's next strike, I slap it away with my left hand, then follow it with a forceful right punch.

His eyes brighten with approval as he barely manages to turn his chin and avoid the hit. Then, it's on.

He strikes, I dodge.

I strike, and he ducks.

We go back and forth with frenzied effort. With half a thought, I acknowledge I shouldn't be able to move this fast. My arm blurs in front of me, and my reflexes are quicker than I've ever experienced. But Henry takes my speed in stride. He manages to keep himself out of range.

He steps to the side, jabbing towards my head. I'm so focused on avoiding the hit, I don't see his left leg swing out in a graceful swipe.

Once again, I hit the ground hard. This time, though, I'm not mad. It was a good hit, and one that I should've seen coming. My chest rises and falls rapidly as I try to catch my breath.

"Good work." Henry reaches out a hand. "You even tapped into your Fae speed."

I grab onto him, and he helps me to my feet. "Yeah... I noticed," I pant.

"You're pretty fast," he continues, sounding completely

normal. Henry must have some serious cardiovascular health to
not be out of breath.

"Not fast enough," I huff in reply, angry at myself for
forgetting to watch for an attack from below. Frederick had
often drilled the importance of keeping your attention on all
parts of your opponent, at all times. He'd be disappointed by my
error.

Henry only smiles, completely unbothered by my failure. He
winks, and I know he's back to his flirty self. "Feel free to take
that water break if you want."

"Don't mind if I do." I shuffle away, rubbing a sore spot on
my back where I'd hit the mat.

As I lean down to drink from the fountain, I hear the doors to
the gym open. A tingle of awareness zips down my spine, and
I'm pretty sure I know who's just walked in.

I keep my eyes on the arc of water, leaning down until my
lips can drink in the refreshing liquid, but I mentally toss my
hearing across the gym. Strong, purposeful steps fill my ears. I
pick up the sound of Henry pulling the Velcro off his gloves.

Then, Henry confirms I was right about who walked in when
he says, "Your Majesty."

Bass grumbles, "You know better than to call me that when
we're alone."

"But we aren't alone," Henry counters. For a second, I feel
both of their gazes turn toward me. My cheeks heat when I think
of Bass looking at my backside.

"I see." Bass clears his throat and pitches is voice lower.
"How'd it go?"

"Better than I'd hoped. She tapped into her speed."

"But no Darkness?"

"None."

"Good."

I stand from the fountain, wiping the moisture from my mouth before I turn around.

"Have the scouts reported back on movement in Seelie?" Henry's words come out in a rush, and they almost make me stumble.

I see Bass give Henry a harsh, silencing look before he turns his purple irises on me. He lifts a hand. "Hello, Sera."

"Hey," I return, taking care to act like I hadn't been listening to them this entire time. My mind races with what Henry's question meant. Was Bass spying on Seelie? If so, why? Was it to monitor if Dark Fae attack, or something more nefarious?

I close the distance until I'm back on the mat, facing Henry.

He gives me a flirty wink. "Back for more?"

I tilt my head. "What do you have in mind?" The question escapes before I have the chance to process its implication. Again, my cheeks heat. That is *so* not what I meant.

Henry's eyes sparkle with mischief. He opens his mouth to respond, but Bass interrupts before he gets the chance.

"I think that's enough for today." An aggressive tremor accompanies the words. My gaze snaps to him. My eyebrows raise in question.

If Bass sees, he ignores it. "George is waiting for you in the library."

"Me?" I blink.

"Yes," he says. "For your history lesson."

"Oh."

Silence descends on the gym, and there's no hiding the odd tension suddenly twisting its way among the three of us. Henry shifts uncomfortably, avoiding my gaze, while Bass is as rigid as a stone statue.

"Well…" I trail off, looking between them. "I guess I'll go to the library."

"Do you remember the way?" Henry finally looks at me. "I can take you there if you don't."

"She's fine," Bass growls, the warning clear.

Henry's eyes swiftly abandon mine, suddenly finding the mat beneath his feet riveting.

What the heck is going on?

Without another word, I turn away from and swiftly exit the gym. The tension billows and rolls in my wake, lingering among the guys I've left behind.

In the time it takes for me to find the library, which is longer than it should be because I definitely don't know the layout of the palace after only one full day in it, I've yet to find an excuse for Bass's frustrated and antagonistic behavior.

It couldn't be because of Henry's flirtatious behavior. Surely, he knows it was just a joke.

Right?

CHAPTER SEVENTEEN

The flowers blooming in the night are stunning. I wander through the garden, my fingertips trailing over the silky petals, enjoying their soft caress. It's quiet, and I'm finally able to find peace in this chaotic court. Smiling and scraping into low curtsies to appease His Majesty and his friends is exhausting. King Uri is determined to show off for the Unseelie visitors, which means I'm paraded around like the prized possession I am. I won't have an evening to myself until the members of the rival court leave. But even then, I'm not sure King Uri will leave me on my own. He's become overly attached the past few days, and I fear he somehow knows about my condition.

A pale hand settles low on my stomach. A chortle of laughter trails on the Seelie breeze, revealing the celebrations are still in full swing, with no sign of slowing down any time soon.

Wait... I'm not in Seelie...

The thoughts winding through my mind are not my own. When I try and fail to control the pale hand resting against the stomach, I know I'm in another one of the strange visions I'd experienced since arriving in the Fae Realm. Or maybe I'm just dreaming.

I want to believe this is nothing more than an illusion created by my tired mind, but I can't deny how *real* everything feels. I feel the breeze blowing around me, and the cool night air kisses my cheeks.

The scene tugs on my attention as the body I'm in continues to walk through the stunning landscape. I try to hold on to my consciousness, but I'm swept away by whatever magic fuels this memory or potential dream. I become one with the strange young woman with the pale, delicate hands.

A cobblestone dislodges from the path under my feet, and my ankle rolls slightly. I hiss and stumble to right myself before I fall on my face.

"Careful," a smooth, tenor calls out. The sound of footsteps accompanies the voice. "King Uri won't be happy if his favorite toy is damaged."

I recognize the intruder and his unsavory sense of humor. With calm I don't feel, I turn around and dip into a well-prac-ticed curtsy. "Your Highness."

Prince Sebastian steps off the adjacent path. His hands are tucked in his trouser pockets, and a strand of black hair falls over his forehead. Not for the first time, I acknowledge how incredibly handsome the Unseelie prince is. More so than ordi-nary Fae, which is saying something. All Fae are attractive, but the prince... he takes it to another level.

"Kristianna."

"Just Kristy," I remind him. The prince and I have met several times since we were first introduced. Sometimes in public, and sometimes not.

King Uri takes pride in seeing his favorite lover coveted by other males, especially the powerful ones. He enjoys when others want what they can't have—what he *has.*

While in public, the prince and I converse politely. He does his part to play an eager male, strategically admiring my appearance when others are in earshot. And I do my part to play the loyal pet of His Majesty. I accept the prince's attentions, but my eyes always find their way back to my master, seeking his devotion and approval. It's all an act, and it makes me sick.

Rumors have spread like wildfire through the Seelie castle. I've always been the subject of gossip, but they've reached new heights with the perceived romantic attentions of the Unseelie prince. I cannot go anywhere, not even deep in the kitchens where no Fae stray, without being the subject of fervent whispers and incredulous stares.

Thank the Fae gods that I've had years of pretending to make this well-choreographed dance believable. Otherwise, our plans would be ruined before we even had the chance to give them a try.

Prince Sebastian steps closer and holds out an arm. I take it, and we proceed to stroll through the gardens. I don't know how he manages it, but the prince always finds the most opportune times to meet in private. This is when our conversations are not scripted or fake. This is when we plan.

As if reading my mind, the prince asks quietly, "Are you ready for tomorrow night?"

If anyone was close enough to hear us, they might interpret his question to be sexual in nature. His smooth voice can make anything sound like a proposition. But despite the image we project for Court, the prince and I are not romantic in the slightest.

"Yes," I breathe, still barely able to hope that this is really going to happen.

Days ago, on the prince's first visit to Seelie, we'd been intro-duced. And within seconds of meeting, Prince Sebastian knew my secret. A secret even I hadn't known at the time.

I'm pregnant, and it's King Uri's child.

And if anyone finds out, my child will be ripped from my womb, and it's very likely I'll be put to death too.

In spite of how free Fae are with taking their human servants as lovers, halflings are not permitted to exist in Seelie. The posi-tion is incredibly cruel and disgustingly two-faced, but it is the rule. And I, as a meager human abducted from my home realm at the age of ten, have absolutely no say in anything.

"I wish I could take you to Unseelie," Prince Sebastian says, staring at my still-flat stomach with a worried brow. "It feels wrong to send you out on your own... especially in your condition."

His concern is genuine. That truth is still difficult for me to accept without suspicion, but I've known Unseelie Court is not the same as the one I live in.

After speaking with the prince, and even venturing to ques-tion his guards when I happen upon them in the castle, I under-stand the rumors are true. Unseelie is better place to live. Sure, halflings still aren't accepted, but at least Unseelie Fae don't abduct humans and force them to work in their Court without pay.

"I'll be fine," I tell him, both to reassure him and to reassure myself. The prince has vowed to do everything in his power to protect me and my unborn child. I'm still not sure why, but I certainly don't begrudge having his support at a time like this. There's no way I'd be able to escape Seelie on my own. But with the Unseelie prince's help, I just might have a chance.

"But my people aren't evil swine," he continues, glancing between me, my stomach, and our surroundings. He's flustered

and frustrated. He wants to do more, but we both know he can't. It would only be a matter of time before King Uri found out Prince Sebastian took me to Unseelie, and he would mark it as a traitorous act. Prince Sebastian's father would be forced to return me, and I'd be back to square one.

No. The only option for me is to leave the Fae Realm entirely. I'll return to Earth. Hopefully, I'll be able to find my parents. If not, I still like my chances of staying hidden once I'm no longer in the same realm as the powerful creatures. It will be harder for Fae to find me once I'm concealed among thousands of other humans.

"Sebastian." I lift my free hand and place it on his shoulder. We stop walking.

The prince turns to me, and I see the turmoil swirling in his lovely purple eyes. I have a strong desire to allay his fears. I've never seen a Fae so worried before. Certainly, not about me.

*I take a breath. "The plan will work. You and your guards have thought through every possibility. I'll be able to escape to the Human Realm, and I'll be safe." When his eyes, once again, flick to my stomach, I add, "**We** will be safe."*

He sighs, dropping the arm which holds mine. He runs a hand through his hair. The gesture is so normal, I momentarily forget he's a prince. To me, he's just a good guy trying to save the life of a woman and her unborn child. Prince Sebastian is one of the good ones, and I thank my lucky stars that I ran into him. I hope to be able to return the favor one day.

My last thought reminds me of something I'd overheard in the castle. "Sebastian, is everything all right between Seelie and Unseelie?"

His eyes snap up to mine. A hint of wariness enters his gaze. "Why do you ask?"

"I overheard some soldiers speaking to His Majesty," I confess.

"Oh?"

I nod. "They didn't outright say the king gave them orders regarding Unseelie, but I saw one soldier looking oddly at you and your guards on your first night at Court. His name is Yuri. I-I can't really explain it, but I just got a bad feeling. Almost like they were planning something."

To my surprise, a smirk pulls the corner of Prince Sebastian's lips. I think he's going to mock me for my concern, but instead he says, "You have impressive instincts, Kristianna."

"Kristy," I correct again, then ask, "Are you saying I'm right? Is there conflict brewing between the Courts?" If so, it's even more imperative I get out of Seelie, pregnant or not.

I've heard horrible stories of the The Great War just before The Divide occurred between Seelie and Unseelie. Countless Fae had lost their lives. That, coupled with the low birth rate of Fae, is what triggered the superior race to begin abducting humans in the first place. They needed laborers, and weak humans without the magical ability to fight back were the perfect recruits.

"I'm saying King Uri is bold," the prince tells me. "He knows my father is nearing his end, and he's positioning his sentries to assess Unseelie's defenses once my father is gone. But have no fear, no war will manifest from his antagonizing prods. Unseelie is untouchable, and that will remain true no matter who oversees the court."

His candidness catches me off guard. I'm used to Fae speaking in code or half-truths when I'm around. The prince doesn't seem to share the same need for secrecy. He must really believe in his Court's defenses.

"I'm glad to hear it," I offer lamely. I can't think of anything else to say.

"Kristianna?" A new voice fills the night, and fear courses through my body when I identify it as Lord Tarkin's.

The formidable Seelie sentry is cruel and malicious. Just thinking his name reminds me of the lashes he'd bestowed upon me when I hadn't maintained a stoic demeanor in public. How could I? The sight of the executioner would make anyone tremble with fear.

But my human emotions were not excused. I'd embarrassed the king. And while King Uri might have ordered the punishment, the sentry enjoyed doling it out too much for my comfort.

Prince Sebastian stares into my eyes, and I know he's reading my mind. It's one of his many gifts. Understanding darkens his eyes as he realizes who is searching for me. He puts his finger to his lips. The shadows seem to shift, welcoming him into their embrace as he backs into the dark.

Not two seconds after the prince has disappeared, Lord Tarkin arrives.

The tall, broad sentry doesn't look at me as he assesses the surroundings. His hand rests lightly on the sword on his hip, ready to use the weapon at the slightest provocation.

"Lord Tarkin," I greet, feeling proud for not sounding as terrified as I feel. I don't know if the prince has left, or if he watches in the shadows. Either way, I face the sentry on my own.

His hard gaze finally lands on me. "Where have you been?" He demands, not bothering with pleasantries.

I wave my arm towards the lush garden. "Enjoying the flowers." My heart beats rapidly, and I pray Tarkin is too distracted to hear it.

He growls something under his breath. Not for the first time, I wish I could hear as well as Fae. It doesn't take a genius to know his words weren't pleasant.

"King Uri is looking for you," he snarls.

The news surprises me. The last I saw the king, he had Rachel and Holly draped over his lap, taunting them by dangling sweet fruit over their mouths while they opened wide.

"I see." I straighten my shoulders and flare out the skirt of my dress. "I'll go to him at once."

I make it one step past Tarkin when his hand snaps out and grabs onto my upper arm.

A fresh wave of terror washes over me, but I do my best to hide the emotion from my face.

The sentry leans close and breathes deeply. He stiffens, and his eyes widen ever so slightly.

"You weren't alone."

Crap.

Do I dare lie? Or will Tarkin be able to smell the deceit?

I opt for honesty, praying it isn't a mistake. "Prince Sebastian found me a while ago. We walked together for a bit, but then he left to return to the party." The words come out effortlessly. Once again, I'm thankful life in Seelie forced me to develop this impeccable ability to conceal my true feelings. I wouldn't survive without it.

"I see." Mistrust flashes across the sentry's expression, but he doesn't call me out on the lie. "Come. I shall escort you to His Majesty." Tarkin's grip on my arm tightens as he begins to pull me through the garden. I go without a fight. There'd be no point. I would immediately lose if I tried.

Right before we step out of the gardens, I feel as someone slips a piece of paper into my left hand. The sleight of hand is impressive. Tarkin's pace doesn't slow for even a moment.

I tighten my grip on the note and keep my head high as I'm escorted back to take my turn as the king's plaything. When I'm sure no one is looking, I lean down and slip the paper into my slipper. The king won't bother with my feet when he decides to grope me later. It's the only place on my body that is safe from his eager hands.

It isn't until many hours into the night, after the king has had his fill of me, that I sneak into my private rooms and retrieve the note. With shaky hands, I unfold the paper and read.

"Tarkin is suspicious," handwriting which can only belong to Prince Sebastian scrolls elegantly across the paper, belying the urgency of the information. "The plan has changed. You leave tonight. Get ready."

CHAPTER EIGHTEEN

I WAKE UP GASPING FOR BREATH. I THROW MYSELF INTO A sitting position and dig my hands into the semi-familiar comforter covering my legs. Convincing myself I'm back in my own body and in control of my own thoughts is a struggle. Sweat beads on my forehead, and my silk nightgown sticks to my body. I lift my hand and sigh with relief when I see my skin, not the pale tone of the woman in my mind.

The limb falls to my side and I attempt to calm my racing heart.

What did I just see?

A door crashes open in the main room. Heavy, purposeful footsteps boom against the floor as they head straight for my room. Fear courses through my veins.

The door flies inward, and my wide eyes drink in the sight of Bass standing there. All my fear dissipates.

He pants for breath, like he's just finished a run, and sweat trickles down his naked torso. My jaw unhinges as I take in his chiseled abdomen and muscular pecs. Every muscle is flexed and ready for a fight. His eyes glow purple as he scans the room, swiveling his neck to peer at every nook and cranny of the spacious bedroom. His muscles don't relax until he's convinced I'm the only one in the room. Even then, he's still tense.

The unnerving vision replays in my mind, and I can't help but note the differences between the Fae before me and the one I'd seen in my mind. His hair is a little shorter now. The style is more human than the long, loose look he'd sported in the gardens.

My eyes travel lower, lingering longer than they should on his torso as I continue to admire his figure. I clear my throat and move on, noting his pajamas. I blink, surprised to see they are the green, plaid pajamas I'd gotten him for Christmas two years ago. The pants had come with a matching top, but I can't say I'm disappointed to see he's forsaken the second item.

When Bass's attention finally lands on me, I feel the full weight of his concern.

"Sera," he exhales my name like it's a balm to his frantic nerves. "Are you all right?" He draws closer until his legs are pressed up against the footboard of the bed.

"I'm fine."

Bass bobs his head, but my words don't stop him from searching me for injuries. I try not to fidget. I'm too aware of how the nightgown clings to my skin. It leaves little to the imagination.

I clear my throat and ask, "What are you doing here?"

"I—" Bass closes his mouth, running a hand down his face, then shakes his head. "I-I don't know. I was dreaming, and then I felt your panic. I thought... I thought the Dark Fae had reached you." He shudders.

"What was your dream about?"

He closes his eyes and takes a steadying breath. "It doesn't matter. I'm just glad you're unharmed."

"It does matter." I sit up straighter. "What was your dream?"

Bass eyes me curiously. "Just a memory from my past."

Oh my god.

The possibility makes my blood pump with adrenaline. "What about your past?"

Now, Bass avoids my gaze. He's trying to put on a mask. It's not going to work.

"Let me tell you about my dream." I move until I'm leaning forward on my knees, putting myself at his eye level. There's three feet of air between us. Bass's eyes flicker down to my chest before quickly refocusing on my face.

I take a breath. "I dreamed about a woman. She was in the Seelie garden, walking alone, and then you showed up."

Bass doesn't move. He doesn't even blink. I have his complete and undivided attention.

I continue, "I've had several dreams about her. But they aren't really dreams, are they? Memories would be a more accurate word."

A bead of sweat trickles down the column of Bass's throat, but he says nothing.

"In these visions, I can see and hear everything the woman experiences," I tell him. "I hear her thoughts. I know what she thinks. She loathes how she's treated. She despises Seelie Fae. And yet... she didn't despise you."

Bass's eyes close. "*Sera...*" He doesn't continue. He's at a loss for words.

"Be honest with me, Bass," I demand quietly. "Was that your dream tonight?"

His head falls forward. "Yes."

How is that possible?

My hands begin to tremble. My mind finally begins to connect the dots of what I've seen and heard these past weeks. "Explain."

Bass lifts his gaze. "Explain, what?"

"Everything," I breathe. "I'm tired of vague excuses and confusing explanations. I want you to tell me what's going on. Why did we have the same dream? Why could you feel my panic? And most importantly…" I trail off, needing to swallow the nervous lump building in my throat before I can continue, "Is that woman my m-mother?"

Unlike the other times I fell into the woman's memories, this is the first time I've heard anyone say her name. But I need Bass's confirmation before I will let myself believe it.

A host of emotions flicker across Bass's face. He's no longer able to keep them at bay. "Sera," he reaches out to grab my hand, pulling me a little closer to the edge of the bed. I'm so nervous that I let him. His fingers tighten when they feel my trembling. "This isn't the time for this conversation. You should sleep. We can speak in the morning."

So he can spend the next few days avoiding me? Absolutely not.

"No. Tell me now… *please.*"

It's the "please" that does him in.

Bass groans. "There is so much to explain."

"I've got time."

He releases a half-hearted chuckle. "You've always been obstinate."

I don't know about that. I feel like I'm reserved and happy to go with the flow. Pascale is the one who can be pushy.

"Don't do that," Bass chastises softly.

I frown. "Do what?"

"Compare yourself to others." He shakes his head. "I've always hated when you do that."

I gape at him. My hands grow clammy. "D-did you just read my mind?" I remember the woman's thoughts… Bass had read her mind too.

"Not on purpose. You tend to project your thoughts. It's hard not to hear them."

Mortification floods my body. I try to pull my hand away, but Bass holds on tight.

I stammer, "D-do you read my mind often?"

"Not on purpose."

"Do you do it to anyone else?" It's wrong, but I'll feel less violated if I know I'm not the sole victim of this invasion of privacy.

"Yes."

"Why?"

Bass shrugs. "It's my power. I only intentionally use it when doing so is a benefit to protecting my court." I want to accuse him of deceit, but he can't lie. He's telling the truth.

I shake my head, unable to believe the turn this conversation has taken. "I can't believe this…"

"It's a rare ability. You don't need to worry about anyone else invading your privacy."

That's not what I'm worried about.

"You never answered my questions."

The small smile disappears from Bass's lips. "Which one do you want me to answer first?"

All of them.

"Is that woman my mother?"

His eyes dip down as he nods. "Yes."

"*Oh my god.*" I close my eyes, and emotion threatens to clog my throat. "Does that mean my father is…"

"King Uri?" Bass finishes for me. I open my eyes and see the hatred brewing in his eyes, and I know the emotion is not directed at me. "Yes. He was Kristianna's master."

The trembles pick up again. And, again, Bass's grip tightens. When the shakes travel to my legs, Bass shifts his hold until his hands are wrapped around my shoulders, helping hold me up.

"W-why didn't you tell me?" Bass knew the truth. We've talked about my mother before. Why would he not tell me who my father is?

His mouth is grim. "You had enough going on without me dropping that bombshell on you."

"That wasn't your call," I tell him.

His nostrils flare. He doesn't defend himself, but he doesn't agree with me either. That spikes my anger.

"Do you think you were right?" I ask, my voice rising. "Did you ever stop to consider how keeping the truth from me would make *me* feel? Do you even care?"

I snort derisively, not giving him the chance to respond. "Of course not. You only think about your motives, and how keeping secrets affects *you*. I'm a second thought. I've been trying to forgive you for not telling me I'm half-Fae. I've tried to overlook the fact you and Pascale have hidden your true identities from me, but I'm done. I'm done with being the last to know *everything*. This isn't right. It's not fair."

I've forgotten Bass holds me so tightly. Anger distracts me. I don't feel his fingers dig into my flesh until he gives me a firm shake.

"*Fair?*" Bass growls. I have enough common sense to grow wary when I hear the deadly note in his voice. "You think what I've done has been unfair to *you?*" His laugh is not amused. It's a forced and dangerous sound.

"Everything I've done has been to protect you. To keep you

from feeling fear or unease about the past. You grew up in the mortal realm. You had a normal life. All thanks to the efforts of those who care about you. You have no idea what's been done to keep you safe."

"So tell me," I growl back. "Just… freaking tell me what I don't know."

I see a flicker of self-control spark in his eyes, and I know I need to keep his temper roused if I have any hope of getting the truth from him.

"Why did you help my mother escape Seelie? Are you afraid to tell me it was just to stick it to your rival court?" I sharpen my words so they cut like a knife. "I heard you speaking with Henry in the gym. You're spying on Seelie. Is this entire situation just a charade to you? Is keeping me in Unseelie just a way to make Camden mad—to rile up Seelie Court?"

The Darkness had remained silent during our exchange thus far, but my rant triggered it.

Careful, dear one, it whispers in my ear. The warning comes too late.

"Do you want to know why we have the same dream?" Bass leans forward, getting in my personal space. The heated intensity in his eyes makes me question if I should've pushed so hard. "You want to know why I can feel your every emotion? Why I can't keep my eyes off of you?"

I gasp, taken aback by the desperate feeling Bass puts into the last question.

"Because we were never just friends, Sera," Bass continues. He shakes his head like he's trying to clear away a thought, but he doesn't succeed. "From the moment I first felt your life stirring in your mother's womb, I knew exactly who you are to me."

My heart hits my sternum painfully. At the same time, tingling butterflies take flight in my stomach. I don't know what to make of the conflicting emotions. Am I excited, terrified, or weirded out?

A flash of desire scorches my blood when Bass pulls me closer. Only inches separate us now. His eyes trail over my face, then dip lower, locking onto my heaving chest. This time, he doesn't immediately look away.

Heat blooms in my face, and my voice comes out huskier than I intend when I ask, "Bass? What are you doing?"

A deep, predatory growl rumbles in his chest. "Something I should've done a long time ago."

Then, his lips crash into mine, and I am lost.

CHAPTER NINETEEN

Two Summers Ago

The standing speaker beside me booms with the latest song the DJ's selected. I rub my temples, trying to ignore the irritating vibrations as they assault my skin. Normally, I wouldn't be bothered by the sound waves, but today is a bad day. I had the late shift at the diner last night, learned I failed my anatomy exam, and Greg Donahue, arguably the most dateable guy at school, had asked me on a date. The last bit might not seem like a bad thing. Most girls at my high school would die to have the chance to date the star lacrosse player. But not me.

I'd turned Greg down. Partly because I thought it was some kind of elaborate prank, and partly because I wasn't interested. That'd been less than three hours ago, and already I'm being blasted on social media for being a snobby bitch. Both terms couldn't be farther from the truth, but there's no point in trying to argue with the social media mob. I've insulted our school's golden boy, and they are out for vengeance.

Whatever.

"Care to share what ails you?" A familiar voice practically shouts in my ear.

And just like that, by bad mood lifts. I turn around with a wide smile and greet my crush, "Hey, Bass."

My best guy friend returns my smile, leaning against the wall of the offending speaker and eyeing me up and down appreciatively. "Nice outfit."

"Thanks." I resist the urge to pull down on the leather mini-skirt. The black ensemble was Pascale's idea. She thought the daring outfit would distract me from the mean comments currently being posted under my yearbook photo; one of our classmates had uploaded it to her page.

"Where's Pascale?" Bass asks.

"Getting water. I'm holding our spot for your band's set."

His teeth gleam in the strobe lights. "You know you don't have to do that. I can get you guys backstage passes."

I shrug, trying to pretend like my poor pulse isn't racing. Bass is so freaking hot. No matter how often we hang out, I'm always a little nervous when I'm around him. "Pascale prefers to watch from the crowd."

"Ah, yes. And you're too nice to tell Pascale she's ridiculous." Bass reaches out and tucks a stray piece of hair behind my ear, leaving my mouth dry. He's not normally one for physical contact, and his touch thrills me.

His hand falls away, looking at me expectantly. I have to clear my throat several times before I can speak. "Well... you know Pascale. She's persuasive."

Bass laughs.

The music lulls.

"How did your anatomy test go?" he asks with genuine interest. He knows I've been freaking out about the assessment this past week.

Sometimes, it baffles me that such an interesting and cool guy is my friend, but he is. Not to mention, he's the best-looking guy I've ever seen in my life.

Even now, the girls around us are eyeing me with assessing glares, trying to figure out how an ordinary girl like me could catch the attention of such a magnificent male specimen. If they knew we were only friends, they wouldn't look so jealous. But I'm not about to do anything to reveal we aren't the item they believe us to be.

"I failed," I admit on a disappointed sigh.

"Ah." Sympathy fills his gaze. "Sorry to hear that."

"It's all right." I try to feign indifference, but Bass knows me too well to buy it.

"You'll ace the next one," he tells me. "Maybe you should work less hours at the diner. Staying up so late can't be good for your academic performance."

He's not wrong, but his concern makes me chuckle. For a local rockstar, Bass can act like a really mature guy. He's not what I expected a free-spirited musician to be.

Bass sees my amusement. "What's funny?"

"Nothing." I continue to smile. "Excited for your set?" I gesture towards the stage. The DJ acts as his band's opener. They have about another half-hour before it's their turn to take the stage.

"Sure," he replies. "But I'm looking forward to catching up after the concert. It's been too long."

His comment sends my soul flying. We haven't hung out in a few days. I've missed our time together, and I'm thrilled to know he misses me, too.

"Are we going to the diner?" I ask. "Pascale hasn't told me the plan."

"I don't think there's an official plan, but we don't have to go to the diner. Is there somewhere else you'd want to go?"

"N-not really." I want to kick myself for stuttering. Why am I so nervous? It's not like Bass is asking me on a date. We *always* hang out after his concerts.

"Do you like Chinese food?" he asks out of the blue. The intensity of his gaze continues to make my heart race.

"Yeah."

"There's a great Chinese place about two blocks away. We should go there once the concert's over. You know... to switch up the pattern." He smiles again, and I'm mesmerized.

"That sounds great," I reply, practically breathless.

"Great!" Bass tucks his hands in his pockets, then turns towards the stage. "Well, I should probably go warm up with the guys in the back."

I bob my head. "Yeah. Of course. I'll see you later."

He grins, then shoots me a wink. "Count on it." The crowd parts for Bass. Women and men ogle him as he passes. Like me, they've never seen someone look so perfect. I'm giddy after our conversation, and I can't wait for the concert to be over so we can hang out.

"Excuse me. Out of my way big guy," Pascale's voice precedes her as she shoves her way through the crowd, carrying two sloshing cups of water. She holds one out to me. "Here ya go!"

"Thanks." Still smiling, I take a sip of water and some of it spills down my chin.

Smooth, Sera. Really smooth.

"What's got you so happy?" Pascale looks at the crowd around us. "Is there a hottie in here or something?"

"No," I continue to grin. "Bass was just here."

"Oh." Understanding dawns. Pascale knows about my crush.

Heck, anyone with two eyes and common sense would know how much I like Bass. And it isn't just because of his looks.

Bass is funny and kind, and he's got an intelligent sense of humor. He's fun to be around. But it definitely doesn't hurt that he's mighty nice to look at.

"Are we still on for a late dinner after the show?" she asks between sips of water.

I nod. "Bass thinks we should try a Chinese place that's close by. What do you think?"

"I'm game." Her answer isn't surprising. Pascale's not a picky eater, and she's willing to try almost anything. Suddenly, my friend's eyes grow wide and she mumbles, "Shit."

"What?" I turn around to follow her stare, but Pascale grabs my arm and begins tugging me away from our coveted spot beside the stage.

"Nothing," she says quickly. "It's hot in here. Let's go outside."

I resist her pull. "What are you talking about? The show will start soon."

Before she can reply, a tall, slender figure steps into view. I recognize her immediately.

Emily Perkins, the most popular girl at our high school, stands in front of our path. Her arms are crossed, and her three-inch stilettos are propped in a wide stance. She looks stunning with long, blonde hair and a killer body.

Over her shoulder, I'm able to make out at least three other girls from our school. They're all part of Emily's mean girl group. And, currently, their hateful glares are focused on me.

"Uh... hi, Emily," I semi-shout to be heard over the music.

"Don't 'hi' me," she snaps back. Her malice is at its peak level tonight. "Just who do you think you are, Sera?"

"Um..." I'm totally confused. I look between all of the girls, but I can't glean a reason for their abrasive behavior.

"Look, Emily, just get out of our way," Pascale practically growls, doing her best to seem threatening despite her tiny stature.

Emily and her posse laugh cruelly. "And what if I don't?" Hatred sparks when she looks back at me.

"Then I'm going to kick your ass into next week," Pascale replies. Emily and her friends can't see, but magic begins to gather around Pascale's body. Her powers are amping up, preparing for a fight. I don't think Pascale is foolish enough to actually use her pixie magic on the group of rude girls, but you can never be too careful.

I place a staying hand on Pascale's arm. "Calm down," I mutter so only she can hear.

Pascale's fists clench, but the power around her starts to deflate.

"Oh look," Emily taunts with a mean smile, "little miss goody two shoes is telling the munchkin to calm down."

"What's your problem?" I ask.

Emily's expression hardens. "My *problem* is you. You think you're better than everyone."

I frown. "What are you talking about? No I don't."

Emily continues like she didn't hear me, but I get the answer I'm looking for when she says, "Who do you think you are, turning down Greg Donahue? You're not better than any of us. You're not better than him. Someone needs to knock you off your high horse."

I rear back, totally shocked. It's one thing for people to say such things online. It takes zero balls to talk shit about someone behind the safety of a keyboard, but to say it to my face... wow.

Just... *wow.*

"I never said I was better than him," I reply calmly, hoping to diffuse this situation before it gets any worse. Already, we've caught the attention of the people immediately around us. I'm not interested in being anyone's entertainment.

"Please," a different girl, Molly, hisses from behind Emily. "You're so stuck up. Why else would you turn him down when he asked you out?"

Bass's face flashes in my mind.

"Because I don't like him."

"Pft. Whatever. You don't like him because you think you're so great. You don't talk to anyone. Not since we started school in kindergarten. I, for one, am so sick of seeing you walk around like we're all beneath you."

"Where is this even coming from?" I exclaim, too shocked to maintain my false sense of calm anymore. I don't act like I'm better than anyone. I avoid talking to other people because I don't want them to think I'm crazy. I see magical creatures crawling through our city. Most of the time, it's hard to hide my reactions whenever I cross paths with them.

"Everything all right over here?"

Oh no. Kill me now.

I peer over my shoulder and see Bass standing behind me. His arms are crossed, highlighting his muscular biceps, and he wears an angry frown.

I give him a look, begging for him not to get involved. He's not even supposed to be here. He should be warming up with the band.

Bass doesn't so much as glance my way. His hard eyes are locked on the mean girls.

When I turn back around, I see Emily eye Bass with appreciation. But residual anger forces her to use Bass's arrival as another means of insulting me.

"Oh, I get it. This no-name guitar player is the reason you

turned down Greg. You prefer to be some guy's side piece. I had no idea you were such a whore, Sera."

I gasp as the insult slaps me across the face. On its own, I wouldn't really be that bothered, but the fact Bass is here to witness my humiliation makes it so much worse.

Suddenly, the temperature in the room drops. My wide eyes snap to Pascale, silently begging her to get ahold of her power. But she's not looking at me. Pascale stares at Bass, and she looks terrified. I don't understand her expression. Bass looks totally calm. Except for the muscle ticking in his jaw, that is.

"What did you just call her?" he asks Emily, and there's no missing the threat in his tone.

Emily has the good sense to not answer. Instead, she shakes her head and rolls her eyes. "Come on girls, let's leave Sera to her lowlife boyfriend." Then, she spins on her heels and strides away. She doesn't make it three feet before a cup of cold ice water hits her back.

Emily squeals and jumps around, trying to dislodge the chunks of ice sliding down her shirt.

I whirl on Bass and see the satisfied smirk pulling on his lips.

Grabbing onto Bass's arm, I maneuver us through the crowd to avoid Emily's impending wrath when she realizes who threw the cup. I keep walking once we exit the club, and I don't stop until we are a block away. I drop his arm and whirl on him.

"What the hell was that?"

Bass blinks, looking bored. "What?"

"You know what." I fling my arm wide. "What the heck were you thinking? You can't just throw ice water at people."

"Normally, I'd agree with you, but a little ice water is mild compared to what that girl deserved."

And to think, I thought he was mature...

Not once in the months I've known Bass have I ever seen him act so petty.

What is going on?

"Yes, Emily's mean, but who cares? You should've just let it go. That's what I was going to do." I rub my temples, unable to believe I'm having this conversation right now.

"Seriously, Bass. Do you know how hard high school already is for me? If Emily finds out you're the one who threw water at her, she's going to have it in for me more than she already does." I'd expected the Greg fiasco to die down soon, but this latest development might land me as the mean girl's enemy list for the rest of the year. Great. Just how I wanted my senior year to end.

"I care." Bass's nostrils flare.

His sudden intensity gives me pause, and makes my heart beat a little faster. "W-what?"

"I said," Bass prowls a little closer. "I care."

He looks at me like I'm a meal he can't wait to devour, and my poor love-struck soul doesn't know what to make of his behavior. My heart is officially hammering in my chest.

"Bass?" I take a step back. Coarse brick snags my thin blouse as I collide with the building behind me.

"Don't do that," he growls disapprovingly.

My eyes widen. "Do what?"

"Move away from me like you're scared of me." Bass continues to draw near. He props both arms on either side of my face, and I'm trapped.

I swallow the lump in my throat. Again, I seek an explanation. "What's going on Bass?" My question is breathless. "What are you doing?"

My friend's brown eyes seem to glow. I think I imagine a flash of purple just before his head dips lower.

Oh my god...

He's going to kiss me!

How we'd gone from talking about Emily to this is beyond me, but a thrill races through my body as I watch Bass look at me like I'm the air he needs to breath.

I've had feelings for him from the moment we met. I can't really explain it. Being around Bass has always felt so ... *right*. Like he and I were meant to be together or something. I know that sounds ridiculous, but it's the truth.

I've wanted something to happen between us for so long. I often fanaticize about how I'd confess my feelings, and Bass would break into a wide grin and reveal he feels the same.

And now... I think it's about to happen.

I must be dreaming.

But no.

The scratchy brick reveals this situation is very much real. Anticipation builds in my stomach, and I can hardly breathe. I suck in a quick breath, and it sounds like a tiny, eager gasp.

The noise distracts Bass, and I'm devastated when whatever spell he's under dissipates into the night air.

One moment, Bass is closing the distance between us. The next, he shoves away from me, spinning and stomping down the alley with a frustrated growl.

I'm dumbfounded. All I can do is stare at his muscular back as the tension rolls over him, all the while feeling like my heart is shattering.

Bass stops walking, clutching a hand to his chest like he's been punched.

Then, he glances back at me.

I don't know what he sees in my expression, but his lips set in a determined line just before he pivots and returns to me. "Screw it. I'm tired of waiting."

Three long, purposeful steps are all it takes for him to reach me. Then, without warning, Bass's hands frame my face. He stares into my eyes with so much emotion, it makes my soul sing.

Then, he presses his lips against mine and we create the most blissful, but also devastating, memory of my adolescent life.

CHAPTER TWENTY

I'd like to say the kiss I'd waited so long for didn't create a rift in our friendship, but that would be a lie.

For a few blissful moments, my heart and soul had taken flight in that dirty alley. Kissing Bass was everything I'd imagined it to be and more. He was my first kiss, and as far as I was concerned, I'd be happy for him to be my last.

But that wasn't what Fate had planned.

Shortly after Bass's lips collided against mine and my hands found their way up his shirt to trace his chiseled torso, the passion which had overtaken my friend expired from him like the air from a punctured balloon.

I'll never be able to forget the horrified and shameful expression on Bass's face when he broke away from the kiss. With a stuttering excuse, he'd left me standing with my back flush against the wall, and an unsatisfied fire ignited in my stomach.

The next day, Bass and his band went on tour, and the only communication I received from my friend were sporadic texts or emails. All of them platonic. Not one referenced the impassioned moment we'd shared.

I'd convinced myself what happened was a regrettable mistake. Bass hadn't really wanted to kiss me, no matter what his behavior suggested. There must've been some weird energy that night, and we'd both succumbed to its control without thinking about the consequences.

But right now, with Bass pushing me back until I lie flat on the bed and covering me with the length of his body as he deepens our kiss… I can't help but wonder if I'd been wrong.

A fervor consumes Bass. His hands dig into my hair, then they travel all over my body. His fingers scorch a delightfully painful path over my skin, trailing up my legs, settling on my hips. His thumb brushes against the edge of my underwear, sending waves of heat to my core.

I'm not much better. Once the initial shock wore off, my hands press against his rippling back muscles, groping and squeezing with reckless abandon. Bass growls approvingly in his throat, and his tongue dives past my lips, tangling with my own for a toe-curling moment.

"Sera," Bass breathes into my mouth, leaning back to look at me with wild, lustful eyes.

The haze of desire lies heavy on both of us, and neither of us are ready for it to lift. "Yes?"

His hand cups my cheek. "You're so goddamn beautiful." This time, his kiss is brief and gentle. He draws back, content to gaze at me with so much emotion, I don't know what to make of him.

My legs have tangled themselves around his lower back. I brush away a stray strand of inky black hair. I've imagined doing that so many times.

"And you're the most handsome man I've ever seen," I reply,

too caught up in the moment to feel embarrassed by the declaration.

His lips twitch in a cheeky grin. "Man?"

I return his smile with a shy one of my own. "Man. Fae. You know you're the best looking of them all." I don't know what confident woman has taken control of my mouth, but I admit my thoughts without any sort of hesitation.

He growls approvingly, then dips down for another lingering kiss. This time, when he pulls back, he twists so he lies on his side. His arms tighten, pressing me against his body. His fingers trail over my face like I'm an exquisite piece of art to be admired.

My body is on fire, and desire courses through my veins, but I'm scared to say or do anything to ruin this moment. I've wanted this for so long. I can't believe it's happening.

A smile pulls at Bass's lips. "I've wanted this for even longer than you," he tells me.

I mock frown. "Don't read my mind."

"Again, it's not on purpose." His fingers trail down my neck and over my shoulder. I arch into the delectable sensations.

"I'm pleased my touch causes this reaction."

I meet his heated gaze. "What did you mean when you said you've wanted this longer?" Unless Bass liked me before we met, there's no way he's right.

Bass chuckles. "From the moment you met me, huh?"

I slap his chest. "Stop it."

He continues to laugh, but the sound is silenced when he kisses me. I have half a mind to break away and insist he answer my question, but then his tongue finds its way back into my mouth, and lust takes over.

I roll until I'm above Bass, straddling him as I sit up. He follows, keeping our chests pressed together, and his hands dive into my hair, holding me close as his lips devour me passionately.

I'm lost in a sea of sensations. My heart has wings. Here I am, making out with the guy I've dreamed about since I was sixteen. I don't spare a thought for all that's happened recently— all the revelations and truths shoved on me after years of secrecy. None of that matters. Bass and I... this is what matters. *We* matter.

My legs tighten and I feel evidence of Bass's arousal under me. My nerves go haywire, and I release an impassioned moan, wanting nothing more than to do away with the clothes between us. I've never gone that far before, but I'll be damned if that isn't exactly what I want to do at this moment. Sharing that with Bass... drowning in ecstasy by his hands... I want it. I want it bad.

Suddenly, Bass breaks our kiss. I'm flipped over. My pulse spikes, thinking I'm about to get what I want, only to be disappointed when Bass flings himself off the bed. He backs away until he's across the room, as far from me as he can get.

"Bass?" The word comes out husky with desire. My heart is racing, and lustful heat consumes me, desperate to be released. "What's wrong?"

"Nothing," he says in a strained voice. Matching heat is in his expression. I can see he wants me. But his hands hold onto the wall behind him, as if to hold himself back from pouncing on me. But that's exactly what I want him to do.

Bass releases an anguished groan. "Gods' mercy, Sera, stop throwing your thoughts at me."

The desperate note in his voice is like a bucket of ice water on my hormones. Suddenly, I'm all too aware of how disheveled I am. My nightgown is bunched at my hips, showing off the black underwear underneath. I grab the comforter and yank it in front of my body.

I can't believe I did it again. I let myself believe there was something happening between me and Bass. I'm such an idiot.

"No." Bass is shaking his head, still catching his breath. "I'm the idiot, not you."

"Stop reading my mind!" I shout. This is so mortifying. I wish Bass would just leave and spare me this awkward rejection.

Bass winces, running a hand through his disheveled hair. I did that. Seconds ago, my hands were all over him, and his were all over me. And yet... here we are.

I'm that hopeless seventeen-year-old all over again. Only this time, I don't think Bass can afford to disappear on me for months at a time. Not with the looming threat of the Dark Fae. I bet he's cursing himself for inviting me to Unseelie and agreeing to keep me safe.

"You can't seriously believe any of that's true."

"Ugh!" I throw my hands up in the air before realizing doing so leaves my half-naked torso in plain view. I quickly retrieve the comforter, clutching it like a shield. "Seriously, Bass. Just leave."

"Not until you let me explain."

Explain what? How sorry he is for giving me a kiss I won't be able to forget the rest of my life? No thanks.

"I already know what you're going to say," I tell him. "And I'd like to spare us the humiliation. Please, just go."

Bass straightens, and his fists clench at his side. "If you knew what I plan to say, you wouldn't be asking me to leave."

I seriously doubt that.

I shake my head and my shoulders roll forward. "Bass... I'm tired. Can you please just go. We can talk in the morning."

"It is the morning."

I glance at the clock on the bedside table and see he's right. It's early, but it's still morning.

"I mean later in the morning," I reply.

He frowns and takes one step forward before he remembers he's so disgusted by what he's done that he needs to keep his distance.

A growl escapes his throat. "Sera. Stop it. Let me speak."

I close my eyes and take a deep breath. If he's determined to make me suffer, there's not much I can do about it. "Fine. What?"

Now that he has my attention, Bass looks uncharacteristically nervous. He shifts his stance, chewing on his bottom lip. I try not to think of how sexy the gesture is, but I can't help it.

Oh, well. It's not like Bass doesn't know I find him attractive at this point. Might as well just own it.

"You asked me to tell you what you don't know... you want answers."

He waits for my response. I nod. "Yes, answers would be nice."

Bass breaks eye contact, and he begins to pace along the wall, but he doesn't close the distance between us.

"I met your mother when she was pregnant with you. It was at Seelie Court. I'd heard King Uri liked to dangle his favorite lover in the faces of other males, trying to elicit desire and envy in them. I was prepared for the tactic, and I had no intention of falling for the trick."

He pauses, closing his eyes briefly. "There I was, standing there, wishing my father had never sent me on the pointless diplomatic mission. Seelie Fae have always behaved like drunken fools during festivities, but I'd never seen such blatant debauchery by so many powerful and influential Fae. The entire scene was sickening. I'd been in the middle of planning my grand escape when King Uri made his move, introducing me to Kristianna."

I'm holding my breath. Part of me dreads hearing what he plans to say, and the other part of me can't wait to finally have the veil of ignorance lifted from my eyes.

"I knew within five seconds of speaking to Kristianna that she was with child."

"How?" I can't help but ask.

Bass gives me a small smile. "Your mother once asked me the same question."

I watch him, waiting for him to explain.

I don't have to wait long.

"I sensed your mother was pregnant because I could sense *you*."

My eyes widen.

Bass continues, "Your power signature was faint but detectable, nonetheless. At first, I'd tried to convince myself I could sense your power because it rivaled my own. As the offspring of the Seelie King, you were bound to be a worthy magical opponent. But it wasn't long before I realized that wasn't the case at all…" he trails off, staring at the plush carpet before finally lifting his chin and meeting my gaze.

I find my voice. "Then what was it?" I ask. "How could you sense me when my mother didn't even know she was pregnant?"

He meets my gaze. "Because you weren't my magical opposite, Sera. You're my magical *match*."

"What?" My forehead furrows. "What do you mean?"

He sighs. Once again, running a hand through his hair. It's his go-to move when he's nervous, I realize.

"This isn't how I wanted to have this conversation," he mutters, almost under his breath. Lucky for me, I've become pretty adept at using my enhanced Fae hearing.

"What conversation?" I sit up. "Just say it, Bass. What do you mean when you say I'm your match?"

"I mean exactly what it sounds like, Sera." His purple irises flare. "Did you think it was a coincidence that I befriended your mother? That I helped her escape Seelie? I know you want to think that I did it because I'm a good guy, but that's not true. Assisting Kristianna would be the equivalent of declaring war if I'd been caught."

Now, my heart is racing for a reason the exact opposite of desire. Fear and anticipation build in my chest. Bass can't be saying what I think he's saying...

"I risked the safety of my court to help Kristianna escape, but it wasn't because I'm a good guy with a conscience," Bass tells me grimly. "Everything I did... it was all to save *your* life. For you, Serafina Richards, I would risk one thousand battles and hundreds of years of bloodshed. Since the day I sensed your soul, I knew I would do absolutely anything to protect you, and I don't give a damn how that makes me look. You're my number one priority, Sera. And you have been for almost twenty years now."

The bedroom threatens to spin. My knuckles turn white from my tight grip on the comforter, grounding my mind. Bass's words should terrify me. Risking war to protect me? That's crazy!

But I can't deny they have the exact opposite effect of terror. I hate to admit it, but everything Bass says just sounds so... *right*. Like they've been the weight that's held me down for years, and now that I'm finally free of their burden, I can breathe for the first time in my life.

Bass abandons his position near the wall and, once again, draws close to the bed. He watches me like I'm a skittish cat about to bolt. I have no doubt that's exactly how I look. My eyes are wide, and I feel my pulse flickering in my neck.

He stops walking when his thighs press against the mattress. He gazes down at me with determination. He's not running, but I can't help but wonder how long that will last.

"I've never run from you, Sera," he tells me. "I've only run to escape my weakness. I told myself I wouldn't do this until you were older—until you had the chance to live a normal life.

"If you met a mortal and decided to be with him, I would've stepped back. I would've waited for the relationship to run its course. As morbid and pathetic as it might sound, I knew if you chose to be with another, he would eventually die as a result of his mortality. You're half-Fae. I convinced myself we had several human lifetimes to find a way to be together. I didn't want to force it on you. I've never wanted to force this on you."

"What is 'this' Bass? Be specific. What are you talking about?"

This time, Bass doesn't deflect or change the subject. "I was made for you, Sera. I was made to help you thrive, to protect you, and to love you. Humans call it soulmates, to Fae it's just called mates."

CHAPTER TWENTY-ONE

Now, the room is officially spinning. I have to close my eyes to clear away the nausea. But it's not a bad kind of nausea… more like a *"I can't believe my wildest dreams might be happening"* nausea. You know… the excited kind of nausea.

"Say that again?" I can't afford to let myself believe this yet. I need him to tell me again. I need to hear it again.

"I'm your mate, Sera. It's the reason behind everything I've done, and everything I will do."

This feels so surreal. I open my eyes and look at Bass. He's nervous and wary. He's uncertain of how I will react.

"The nymphs at the welcoming ceremony?" The question flows past my lips without much thought.

A nervous smirk tugs his lips. "Not my doing, just two of my subjects who'd learned of my fascination with the Seelie Prince's fiancée and drew their own conclusions. Hara and Jilla are known for their love of stirring up trouble."

"How is this possible?" I breathe. "You're—you're a king."

His bloodline is one of the most powerful in all Fae Realm. I'm only half-Fae. How can I be his match?

Bass gazes down at me like I'm the most amazing thing he's ever seen. "Everything I am, finds its perfect complement in you, Sera. No one knows how the gods choose who to link together. Some believe it's the product of wanting to produce the most powerful offspring, while others think it has more to do with fortune and souls aligning harmoniously."

From an evolutionary standpoint, the powerful offspring idea makes the most sense. But again, I'm half Fae. Even if Bass and I were to have kids... they'd be a quarter human. Not exactly the best recipe for powerful Fae.

The thought of children makes my face heat, and my core tighten.

A knock sounds in the distance, followed by someone opening a door. I vaguely hear Vagar's deep growl as he greets the visitor. I wonder who would be visiting at this hour. My first thought is Henry or George. Not that either Fae would visit me this early, but maybe they're looking for Bass.

I don't think about it for long. Bass continues to stare at me with unveiled adoration, and I struggle against hoping this isn't some kind of cruel trick and that he won't immediately regret this moment once he comes to his senses.

"Sera," he exhales my name, and there's such *feeling* in his voice. My breath catches in my throat. "This isn't a trick. I—"

What he's about to say is interrupted when the bedroom door swings open.

Our attention turns to the doorway and the rigid Fae standing in front of it.

I blink several times, not believing who I'm seeing.

"Camden?"

————

Sure enough, the prince of Seelie is standing in my bedroom… *in Unseelie Court.*

Immediately, I'm on high alert. Something must've happened to cause him to travel here.

Before I can ask what's wrong, Camden snarls, "What's going on here?"

I stiffen, all too aware of how close Bass stands to my bed, and how flushed and invigorated I must look. I glance at Bass. To his credit, he looks normal. The admiration and affection are gone from his expression, and he wears the careful mask of the aloof and condescending Unseelie King.

"I believe that is my question," Bass replies calmly. "What are you doing in my court?" His voice holds the hint of a challenge. Visiting Court without an invitation can be seen as an act of aggression in the Fae Realm.

"The better question is what you're doing in my fiancée's bedchamber?" Camden snaps back. His normally serene green eyes are blazing with suspicion and anger.

I try to come up with a lie, but I'm at a loss for words. Camden has every right to be suspicious about Bass's presence in my room, half dressed, at such an inappropriate hour. And whatever he's thinking is probably not far from the truth of what's happened between us tonight.

Guilt and its gut-wrenching grip grab ahold of me, keeping me silent.

"I sensed Serafina was having a nightmare," Bass replies in a bored tone, as if explaining the situation is beneath him. "I came to check if she was all right."

Technically, that's true.

Camden must realize that, but his eyes remain narrowed in

suspicion. "How could you sense it?"

I hold my breath, praying Bass won't be so crass as to admit our connection at this moment. Not in front of the guy who is still technically my fiancé.

Instead, Bass deflects with a strategically vague reply, "Not much goes on in my court without my knowledge."

For a moment, Camden looks like he doesn't know what to say to that. Then, he nods as if he's had a revelation. "Your mind reading ability."

What? How did Camden know about that and not tell me?

"Precisely." Bass says, tucking his hands behind his back, looking regal despite his naked torso and pajama pants. "Now, if you'll answer my question: why have you come to my court unannounced?"

Camden glances my way. His eyes lock on my flimsy night-gown, and his face flushes.

"Perhaps we should speak in the main room." Camden turns like he's about to walk out of the room, but he stills when he sees Bass doesn't move to follow.

Bass crosses his arms. "We will speak here."

Camden frowns, but he stays. It's his turn to cross his arms. "Surely, you already know why I'm here, what with the spies you've positioned at Seelie borders."

It takes every ounce of strength not to react. I don't know if Bass plans to deny Camden's claim, but I'm deter-mined not to let my behavior reveal anything one way or another.

"They are there to monitor Dark Fae's movements," he replies calmly. "Nothing more."

Camden doesn't believe him, but he has no proof to prove otherwise. "Convenient."

"I suppose so."

"What is going on?" I interject before they continue to throw short, pointless responses back and forth. "What's happened?"

Camden looks at me, but quickly averts his gaze. He clears his throat. "Do you have a robe, Sera?"

"I—" I look around. There might be a robe in the bathroom. I get up to look, but all it takes is one snap of Bass's fingers and the robe drops into my hands out of thin air.

"Thanks." I peer up and find him smirking at me, but there's playful heat in his eyes, telling me he's thinking about our makeout session prior to Camden's arrival.

I duck my head and quickly slip on the robe, tying the sash tightly around my waist, and pretending like every fiber of my being isn't thrumming with lust.

Thank goodness Camden had averted his gaze to give me a semblance of privacy. Otherwise, there's no way he would've missed that something has happened between me and Bass. Heck, I'm surprised he can't smell the pheromones I'm sure are floating off my body.

I clear my throat. Camden looks up and relaxes when he sees I'm covered.

I shift my stance, awkwardly looking between the two Fae. "Maybe we should go into the parlor," I say. There's no way I'll be able to focus with Bass and my bed in the same room. And it's obvious Camden has major news to share. There's no other reason he'd show up in Unseelie.

"Very well." Bass swings his arm towards the door and tells Camden, "After you."

The Seelie prince doesn't hesitate. He strides out of the room with purpose. I go to follow, but I collide with an invisible force-field, blocking my way.

I look closer and see the shimmering purple surface, and immediately recognize it as Bass's handiwork.

I meet his gaze. "What are you doing?"

"Giving us a moment of privacy before we go out there." He says. "I'm sure I don't need to say this, but you cannot share what I've told you tonight with anyone."

"Okay..." I don't know if he's talking about how he helped my mother escape Seelie, or how we're mates. Either way, his words sting. Not wanting him to hear my pathetic thoughts, I do my best to not have any. When that doesn't work, I imagine a concrete wall at the forefront of my mind. I picture its durable surface and tell myself it is strong enough to hold my thoughts inside. Bass can't access them while the wall is up.

"I mean it, Sera. There are people who would use you against me if they found out what you mean to me."

"Oh." My heart clenches, but not in pain. The feeling is more like happiness.

"Yeah." Bass tilts his head and wears a small smile. "*Oh.*"

I avert my gaze, feeling the burning of a blush coming on. "S-should we go out there?" Before the guy I'm engaged to wonders what's taking us so long?

Bass nods, then makes his way to the door. I follow.

It hits me that I'm going to have to have the breakup conversation with Camden sooner rather than later. I mean... I've always planned to do it. But now that I've kissed Bass and everything... I don't know.

The engagement wasn't my idea and I never planned to go through with it, but I had started to develop feelings for the guy. He's kind, smart, and sweet. Not to mention, I pretty much led him on right before leaving Seelie.

I feel awful.

What happened tonight feels like I'm cheating on him, and that's not right. He deserves better.

Just as I am about to pass Bass and walk out of the room, I

feel his fingers brush against mine. The simple touch sends the butterflies flying, and I know I wear a silly grin as I step into the parlor.

The smile immediately dies my eyes land on the scene before me. Frederick, Morty, Jordan and Zander stand there. Vagar is in the background, glaring menacingly at the Seelie intruders, but not making a move against them.

I take in the group's disheveled appearance, noting the angry red marks on their arms and faces, as well as the bright scratch running down Jordan's cheek.

I suck in a breath. My attention bounces over the group. When I look back at Camden, I finally notice his torn shirt and wrinkled trousers. I'd been too distracted to notice he's obviously been in a fight.

It's Bass who breaks the tense silence. "So, my scouts were right." He states as a matter-of-fact. There's no inflection in his words, and he doesn't say anything to help me deduce what the heck is going on.

Camden scowls at his rival. "That depends. If your scouts reported that Dark Fae have infiltrated and taken control of Seelie Court, then yes. Your scouts were right."

CHAPTER TWENTY-TWO

PASCALE, RICHIE, AND I SIT AT THE BREAKFAST NOOK TUCKED IN the corner of the apartment's kitchen space. Vagar, as usual, stands guard in the nearest shadow. I push the scrambled eggs around my plate, trying to convince myself to take a bite, but I just can't find my appetite. Camden's reveal in the early hours of the morning have haunted me every moment since, and I still can't come to grips with the reality that Seelie Court is now in the hands of the Fae who want me dead. All so they can take back the power contained within the diadem.

Don't let them take us.

Use us. We can protect you.

I close my eyes and imagine shoving away the shadowy voices. It takes some effort, but they eventually grow silent. Vibrations travel from the diadem to my scalp, but that eventually stops too.

"What do you think they're talking about?" Pascale asks.

I open my eyes. "I don't know."

Bass, Camden, Henry, George, Frederick, Morty, Zander,

and a whole host of Unseelie soldiers had locked themselves in a meeting two hours ago, shortly after the grand reveal that Seelie had fallen into Dark Fae's control. I imagine Camden and the other Seelie are debriefing the others about the details of what transpired. I'd only heard bits and pieces before Bass insisted the rest of the story be heard by his generals. It didn't take a genius to know Bass had war on his mind, and the thought has created a pit in my stomach that grows with every passing minute.

Feeling someone's gaze, I turn and see Vagar staring at me with a worried frown. I blink. "What is it, Vagar?"

My bodyguard hesitates, then shakes his head, grumbling, "Nothing."

"I'm sure we'll find out soon," Richie speaks, drawing my attention from my guard's unusual behavior. "No doubt, King Sebastian will tell you everything." There's implication in the words, and I'm suddenly hit with a realization.

"You know, don't you?"

"Know what?" Richie tries to look confused. I'm not buying it.

"You know what," I tell him. I think back to the night I first met Pascale's friends. They'd all known Bass protected me, and I am willing to bet the diadem on my head that they know why the king of Unseelie would bother with a measly human in the first place.

"I don't know what you're talking about—"

"Save it, Richie," Pascale sighs. "I know that look. Bass must've told her."

"Ah." Richie looks relieved. "Well… uh. I've had the integrity of my manhood threatened if I spill the beans so…"

"How long?" I direct the question to Pascale.

My best friend chews the inside of her cheek. "Since the

night of the last concert we went to... before Bass's band went on tour."

The same night he'd kissed me and then disappeared...

Of course.

I guess I'm glad Pascale hadn't known the truth our entire friendship, but that doesn't mean I'm overjoyed to learn she'd kept the secret from me for as long as she did.

"Let me guess," my voice is dry, "Bass told you not to tell me, and you agreed?"

This time, Pascale doesn't look away. She feels no guilt. "It wasn't my place to tell you."

I take a breath, trying to calm down. I don't want to get angry and risk The Darkness rearing up again. "You'd acted surprised when the nymphs told Camden I'm Bass's m-mate." The word threatens to stick in my throat. It's so weird to say out loud, and part of me struggles to believe it.

I cough and continue, "You pretended like you didn't know." Pascale hadn't lied, but her deception came close.

"I was surprised the nymphs knew," Pascale replies. "Bass doesn't go around telling everyone about you. He has enemies who would use you against him."

Bass had said the same thing. I try to imagine who might want to hurt Bass, but I draw a blank. Other than Seelie Fae, who would want to act against the Unseelie king?

"Well, how does Richie know?" I throw my intense stare to the mysterious Fae.

"It wasn't hard to figure out," he replies. "There's only so many reasons King Sebastian would concern himself with the welfare of a mortal. Or, someone I thought to be mortal."

My eyes narrow. Does Richie know I'm half-Fae? It certainly sounds like it.

The door opens, interrupting us.

Jordan enters. She'd gone to clean up and change, and I guess she'd fallen asleep, delaying her arrival. But she's here now, and I've never been so relieved to see someone in my life.

I'm immediately on my feet. I cross the room and throw my arms around my friend, holding her tight. The last I'd seen her, she was still lying in the healing ward, recovering from the injuries she'd sustained in Queen Aria's competition.

Now, aside from her latest scratch, she looks good as new. There's no sign of the stab wound that had nearly killed her.

Jordan and I had a plan during the queen's contest. We would reach the Cursed Cavern, but let another contestant go forward and claim the diadem. Neither of us wanted the "honor" of a forced betrothal to the prince. But that plan changed when Trish dealt Jordan a vicious blow, just after the mountain began to shake from an earthquake.

I'd raced through that cavern in order to save her. I hadn't thought twice about what winning would mean for me. All I'd cared about was ending the contest so my friend could get the help she so desperately needed.

Seeing her whole and holding her against me, I know I wouldn't hesitate to do it all over again. Consequences be damned.

I lean back, still holding onto her arms. "You've lost weight." Her cheek bones are sharper than when I last saw her.

Jordan cracks a smile. "Yeah, being unconscious for weeks can do that to you."

My arms fall to my sides. "I'm sorry I wasn't there when you woke up. I wish I had the chance to see you before I left Seelie."

"Please, you don't need to apologize. I should be thanking you. If it weren't for what you did, I wouldn't be here right now." Jordan swallows the lump in her throat, then looks at the top of my head. "I-I know the sacrifice you made to help me out. I don't think I'll ever be able to repay you."

It's my turn to swallow. "You would've done the same for me."

Jordan reaches out and squeezes my hand.

Someone coughs behind us.

Both Jordan and I turn and see that Pascale and Richie are watching our exchange.

I make introductions. "Jordan, this is my best friend, Pascale. And this is Richie. They're both Unseelie." I walk back to the table. Jordan follows with wide eyes.

"Your best friend is Fae? Girl... I think you left out some information when we gossiped in the barracks."

I smirk. "Maybe a little."

"Nice to meet both of you," she shakes their hands.

I sit and gesture for Jordan to do the same. "Are you hungry? We have extra food."

"No, I'm good. Morty's been stuffing me with food, telling me I need it to keep up my strength." She rolls her eyes and puffs out her cheeks, pretending she might vomit.

"Is that the hunky guard who hovered over you in our rooms?" Pascale asks, waggling her eyebrows.

"Yes." Jordan smiles.

"Things must be going well between you?"

When Jordan first told me about her relationship with Morty, I wasn't very supportive. But after seeing the sentry care for her while she healed from her injuries, I can't deny the truth. Morty truly cares for my friend. And that's great... as long as Jordan still wants to be with him.

Part of me hopes Jordan will change her mind and go back to a normal life on Earth, but the other part of me selfishly wants her to stay in the Fae Realm with me.

"Things are good," Jordan replies with a knowing smile.

"You and the sentry are a couple?" Richie asks, sounding surprised.

"Yes."

"In Seelie?" His eyes widen. "That must be a challenge."

Jordan shrugs. "I've been pretending to be Sera almost since the moment I woke up. So Morty and I haven't really had the chance to announce our relationship to the court, not that we really planned on doing that anyway."

I frown. Is their plan to keep their relationship a secret? That doesn't seem feasible. Eventually, someone will figure out the truth.

"Did anyone suspect you weren't really me?" I ask, deciding to avoid discussing my friend's relationship. It has the potential to become an argument, and that's the last thing I want to do after not speaking with her for so long.

"Not that I'm aware," she says, then shoots me a teasing grin. "It helps that you weren't exactly known as a social butterfly. None of the nobles or servants thought twice about my desire to spend the majority of the day in my rooms."

"That's good," Pascale chimes in. "What about Camden? Was he able to act normal?"

"Uh, not really. He pretty much avoided being seen with me. I think he assumed he wouldn't be able to hold up the facade. Either that, or he wanted to remain loyal."

Her words, though said with absolutely zero accusation, pierce me with guilt. Not four hours ago, I was making out with Bass, who Camden views as his rival.

"Is there anything else you can tell us about the attack on Seelie?" Richie questions Jordan.

I lean forward, just as eager to hear more information. We'd gotten the basics in the parlor, but we were missing out on the finer details. Those were being shared in the meeting we weren't invited to.

Jordan shakes her head. "No, sorry. I was sleeping when the bulk of the attack happened. Morty woke me up, and then we had to fight our way out of the castle's borders in order to transport to safety."

Now I understand why they were such a mess when they first arrived.

"Any idea why the prince brought you all here?" Pascale questions. "Why not take you somewhere in Seelie?"

"No clue," says Jordan.

"Is he planning on a counterattack to re-take Court?"

Again, Jordan says, "I don't know."

I purse my lips, wondering why Pascale is practically interrogating Jordan. Her behavior is a far cry from the laid-back and fun-loving pixie I've always known.

"Maybe we should wait for Bass to tell us what's going on," I say out loud, giving Pascale a pointed look. Understanding fills her gaze. She knows I'm telling her to back off.

"Bass?" Jordan frowns, confused.

"King Sebastian," I modify quickly, but it's too late. A host of questions flicker across Jordan's expression. But before she can ask any of them, the door opens and in walks Morty, Frederick, and Zander.

My muscles tense when I see the last sentry. Zander did everything he could to make my life hell while I trained for the contest in Seelie. He's always been an ass, and I can't help but wish he'd been left back in Seelie.

Vagar shifts forward, placing himself between me and the newcomers. The sentries stop their approach, eyeing the Dark Fae warily.

Fighting the urge to smile, I tell Vagar, "It's okay. I know them."

My bodyguard doesn't immediately back down, leveling a bone-chilling glare upon the sentries before he heeds my words and resumes his position against the wall.

Morty's eyes find Jordan's, and I see instant relief. Cautious not to draw too close to me and elicit Vagar's ire, Morty walks wide as he approaches his girlfriend. "How are you feeling?" The concern in his expression is touching.

"I'm fine," Jordan replies with another playful eye roll. "Just as I was when you left for the meeting."

"Forgive me for worrying." Morty picks up her hand and kisses her fingers. "But can you blame me?"

Jordan's gaze softens, and I know my friend's got it bad. "No, I guess not."

Again, Morty kisses her hand. This time, his lips linger.

"Ugh. More of this?" Zander groans. I'm not the only one uncomfortable watching the loving scene. "Why don't you two excuse yourselves from society while you moon over one another? Not everyone wants to see this."

In no rush, Morty releases Jordan's hand, but not before she gives him a reassuring squeeze as they share a small smile.

"Thank the gods," Zander mumbles, then turns to me. "So, you left Seelie? Can't say I'm surprised. I knew there was something more pleasant about Court these past few days."

His insult doesn't even come close to landing its mark. Still, Vagar growls, and I have the satisfaction of seeing Zander flinch.

"Nice to know you missed me," I reply.

Zander grumbles something, but he's wise enough not to articulate it and risk pissing off my guard.

I look at Frederick. Camden's personal guard stands quietly, observing the room. Feeling my attention, his eyes shift to meet mine.

"Nice to see you're okay, Frederick." He and I haven't always seen eye to eye, but Frederick was good to me during my training. He'd helped me catch up to the other women who'd had longer to prepare for the contest, and he also kept my secret about my power. He might be a hardass, but he's a loyal one. Even if I don't think he trusts me anymore.

"Thank you." He dips his chin, but anger is set in the lines around his mouth. "I hope your time in Unseelie hasn't been too much of a burden." He eyes me up and down pointedly.

For a moment, I'm confused. Then it hits me how horrible I must've looked in Seelie. I rarely ate, and sleep hadn't come easy to me. The trauma from the contest and the revelations about my past had affected me both physically and mentally.

But here in Unseelie, I haven't struggled with those things as much. Sure, my emotions run high at times and I'm terrified about what is to come, but I've felt more relaxed here.

Without warning, the feel of Bass pressed on top of me, devouring my mouth, assaults my memory.

Geez... is there anything else I can think about besides Bass kissing me?

It takes all of my control to keep a straight face. "Unseelie is not as unpleasant as I'd been led to believe."

"I'm glad to hear it." He tells me, though his grim expression says otherwise.

Morty clears his throat. "We should go to our rooms and rest more," he tells Jordan. "King Sebastian has invited us to dine with his Court this evening, and I'm sure it's going to be a busy night."

The news takes me by surprise. I haven't even been invited to Court dinner yet. I take my meals with Pascale and her crew.

Even George and Henry have made appearances since I arrived in Unseelie. Bass has been notably absent. I'd chalked it up to him being busy, but now I'm wondering if he's been entertaining his court while making sure I was kept at a distance.

The thought darkens my mood. The Darkness buzzes in the diadem, but I force the shadows to stay back.

Jordan eyes me, chewing her lip with indecision.

I force myself to don a smile. "That's actually not a bad idea," I say. "We can catch up this evening after you're recovered."

I see Jordan wants to object, but I subtly jerk my chin. She picks up the silent cue. There's a question in her gaze, but she doesn't argue with Morty.

"Of course." She pushes back her chair, looking at me. "I'm really glad we talked. Promise to find me this evening?"

"I promise."

After exchanging polite goodbyes with the table, Morty and Jordan duck out of the apartment. To my distaste, Zander takes it upon himself to settle in the chair Jordan's abandoned. He reaches out and helps himself to three slices of toasted bread. He steals the knife beside my plate, using it to scoop butter and spread it on the toast.

I watch him with narrowed eyes. "Hey, Zander, would you like to join us for breakfast?"

"Yes, thank you. I'm starving. Fighting makes me hungry." He totally misses the sarcasm in my question, shoving the bread into his mouth.

Across the table, Pascale shakes her head, barely containing a smirk. I've told her all about Zander, and she knows how much I dislike him. The fact she finds this funny is a serious mark against her best friend loyalty.

The door bursts open again. My heart leaps into my throat as

I turn, fully expecting either Bass or Camden. I'm disappointed when I see Aerie.

The stunning siren glides into the room like she owns the place. Her confidence is unlike any I've ever seen, and I have to admit I'm a little envious.

"Why the long faces?" She moves next to Richie, eyeing the table.

Beside me, Zander drops the toast. One glance confirms he's taken by Aerie's impressive presence. So... the High Fae sentry isn't above lusting after Unseelie sirens... good to know.

"Where have you been?" Richie asks. "Tonk is looking for you."

"In bed," she replies.

Richie counters, "No, we checked your rooms."

Aerie releases an exasperated sigh. "I didn't say *my* bed." She sees Zander's jaw drop, and the siren pounces like a cat on an unsuspecting mouse. "What is it, sentry? Not used to females who aren't meek, submissive creatures like the ones in Seelie."

Zander flounders for a response. While he gapes like a fish, I consider Aerie's taunt and realize what she's said is true. Seelie noble ladies never speak their mind or do much of anything without the escort of some male, whether it's a family member or significant other.

How had I not noticed the inequality before?

Finally, Zander finds his voice. "My name is Zander. And to answer your question, no. I've never seen a lady behave so brazenly."

"I'm not a lady," she replies with a shrug, unbothered by the distinction.

"Clearly." Zander's tone is cool, but there's undeniable heat in his eyes. He's attracted to Aerie, even if he doesn't want to be.

Richie exhales. It's a tired sound. Almost like he's seen this exact scene before, and it bores him. "Do you have news for us Aerie?"

The siren gives Zander one last taunting smirk before she snaps her fingers and says, "Oh… yes. Her ladyship's presence is requested in the throne room."

I shake my head as I stand, choosing not to address the teasing title. I ignore Zander's gaze.

"Do you want me to come with you?" Pascale asks.

"Better not," Aerie chirps, already sliding into the seat I'm still hovering near, forcing me to step away from the table. "His Highness, the prince of Seelie, seems adamant about meeting her alone."

My stomach plummets to the floor. I'd thought Aerie's message came from Bass. I'd been eager to meet with him and learn what's happened in Seelie, but now that I know it's Camden who's called me… I'm wishing I never forfeited my seat at the breakfast table.

My cheek tingles. I turn and see Frederick stares at me, and I know there's no way he missed my reaction. I'm wary to speak with Camden, and Frederick knows it.

I avert my gaze, glancing briefly at the others in the room. "Well… I guess I better go."

Pascale gives me an encouraging nod. "Find me if you need anything. I'm not leaving the palace today." I doubt any of us are.

"Okay." I lift a hand. "See you guys later." Without looking back, I duck out of the room. Once in the hall, I lean against the wall and take a steadying breath.

My nerves unravel. I'm about to see Camden again. It's only been a little over a week, but so much has changed. I'm talking to The Darkness, I'm accessing the power, and… oh yeah… I made out with the Unseelie King.

My conscious demands I come clean to the guy who is still under the impression we will be married, but the coward in me wants to delay the uncomfortable conversation for as long as possible. We have huge problems right now. The Dark Fae conquered Seelie Court. Ending our engagement is going to cause unnecessary drama, and I'm second guessing if it's a good idea.

My head falls forward.

Vagar appears. Seeing me leaning against the wall, he quickly scans the hall for any threat. Seeing we're alone, he does something surprising when he reaches out and squeezes my arm reassuringly.

My entire body relaxes, and I'm amazed such a simple gesture can have such an effect.

"It will be fine," he tells me in his scratchy, growly voice.

I dip my chin. "Thanks."

He returns the gesture, then waves his hand down the hallway. "To the throne room?"

I push off the wall and roll my shoulders back as I prepare myself for what's to come. "Yeah. Let's go."

CHAPTER TWENTY-THREE

VAGAR IS TWO STEPS BEHIND ME AS I MAKE MY WAY TO THE Unseelie throne room. My ballet flats are nearly soundless as I walk across the smooth marble floor, periodically cushioned by carpet as we travel from room to room. I gnaw the inside of my cheek, wondering what I'm going to say when I see Camden. I imagine he's going to update me on the finer details of what's happened in Seelie, and I hope that's the extent of our conversation.

We arrive.

I face Vagar, blocking the path to the room. "I'll go alone."

My guard grumbles, but I hold up a hand. "I'll be fine. You can stand here and watch from a distance if you want, but I'd like to speak with Camden by myself."

Unnerving understanding reveals itself on Vagar's expression. Not for the first time, I acknowledge the Dark Fae has an uncanny ability to read me and my emotions. I wonder if he had this kind of connection with Queen Lani, or if I'm just super easy to read.

The throne room is quiet. Camden stands beside a portrait on the west wall, facing away from the door. I approach, my eyes lift and land on the image of a male who looks like he could be Bass's older brother. He's dressed in formal military regalia. Beside him is a stunning young female. Her eyes are bright purple, and the painter caught their happy shine. She's wearing a breathtaking silver gown, overlaid with lace and pearls. It I'm not mistaken, it's a wedding portrait.

I clear my throat. Camden whirls around with wide eyes. "Sera! I didn't hear you." His eyes scan the space behind me.

"Sorry." If I had to guess, I've tapped into Fae stealth without meaning to. I make a note to practice the handy skill later. It could be useful.

"It's fine." Camden steps forward and reaches for my hand. I let him take it, seeing no reason not to. It's an innocent enough gesture, as long as he doesn't take it any further.

"It's strange to see your hair like this," he says out of the blue. For a moment, I'm surprised he cannot see through Bass's glamour. But then I realize Camden is a prince, while Bass is a crowned king. I wonder if the two will be equal in power when Camden ascends the throne, but part of me suspects Bass might always have the advantage.

"Oh, yeah." I run my free hand over a strand of hair. "It's definitely different."

"It's still lovely," he says kindly.

I blush.

Camden squeezes my fingers. "I'm so glad you're unharmed, Sera. I can't tell you how worried I've been."

"Me? I'm not the one who was just attacked." A quick scan confirms the scratches I'd seen on him have healed with the help of Fae magic. He's changed clothes, and I notice the casual look is Unseelie style, but it's still fine quality. He must've borrowed clothes from some noble or Bass himself.

"I'm talking about all this time you've been in Unseelie," Camden explains. His thumb brushes over the back of my hand. "Barely a minute passed when I wasn't worried something horrible was happening to you. I nearly went mad with exhaustion until Frederick forced me to start taking sleeping potions."

The extent of his worry confuses me. "King Sebastian promised to protect me. And Unseelie is not a horrible place."

In fact, Unseelie exceeds Seelie for being a welcoming and peaceful Court. But I'm not going to tell him that. Camden has his prejudices about the opposing court, and nothing I say right now will sway his opinion.

"I'm relieved to hear it," Camden says, ever the diplomat. "And I'm glad the ruse with Jordan worked for as long as it did. I'd much rather Dark Fae attack Seelie and come out empty handed than come here and get their hands on you."

His words make me shift uncomfortably. My life is not worth anyone else's, and I don't like that he thinks otherwise.

I pull my hand out of his, then fold my hands to keep him from grabbing me again.

Swallowing the lump in my throat, I ask, "How bad was it?"

His lips turn down and his eyes dim. "Many sentries lost their lives. Once it was clear Dark Fae had taken hold of the castle, Queen Aria demanded the rest stand down."

My eyes widen. "The queen surrendered?"

"Yes." Camden rubs his eyes. "And while I loathe the idea of my homeland being controlled by those monsters, I can't say I disagree with her decision. Every sentry and court member would've been slaughtered otherwise, and there's no telling what they would've done to the townsfolk and humans next."

Begrudgingly, I, too, find myself agreeing with the queen's decision. "How did you guys escape?"

"Our plan was always to get Jordan out if Dark Fae attacked," he tells me.

I'm thankful for the consideration for my friend's safety, but his next words reveal the decision wasn't totally unselfish, "If the Dark Fae got a hold of her, they'd know right away that she really wasn't you. And then they'd come for you. Keeping her safe helps keep you safe."

I frown, not liking the reasoning in the slightest. "Jordan's also an innocent human," I point out. "You should protect her for that reason alone."

Camden detects my underlying frustration. "Of course, you're right." He attempts to placate me. "All I meant was it was also strategic to get her out of Seelie. I'm glad we did. Both for her sake and yours."

I avert my gaze, and turmoil still churns in my stomach. I can't get over his motivation for saving my friend, and I'm close to losing my temper.

Do it, The Darkness whispers. Shadowy tendrils curl around my wrists.

Teach the princeling a lesson.

I press my eyelids together, willing the taunting shadows to disappear.

"Sera?"

I open my eyes. Thankfully, the shadows are gone. I exhale a relieved sigh. I'm getting better at controlling them. Now, if I can just get them to stay dormant in the diadem, that will be ideal.

Seeing Camden's concern, I say, "I'm fine," then change the subject. "So, what's the plan? What did you discuss in the meeting?"

I'm still bitter I wasn't allowed to attend, but the argument had been I wasn't a trained soldier, nor was I Fae.

Both Camden, Bass, and Frederick had kept their mouths shut when the Unseelie General made that statement. They knew it wasn't true, but they weren't going to reveal my secret for the small chance I'd be welcomed in the strategy room.

"Nothing was decided," Camden tells me, sounding exhausted. "Several options were presented, but we couldn't agree on how to proceed. Should we attempt to take Seelie back? Or focus on neutralizing the enemy first, then take the Court back after we succeed?"

"I don't get it. Wouldn't the Dark Fae all be in Seelie?" Neutralizing the enemy and taking Seelie should be the same thing.

"No. Only the solders," he tells me. "The leaders remain in their territory, and we have no knowledge of their numbers. We could take Seelie back, killing all of the Dark Fae there, only to be overrun by another army the next day."

Shit. I had no idea Dark Fae were so numerous. I'd imagined they were a fringe group in the Fae Realm, not some ominous massive force of foes.

"And even if there aren't many more," Camden continues, "Their battle skills are savage and effective. We can't meet them in combat until we have a better grasp on how to fight them. Not if we want to win the battle."

I gnaw on my lip. What the heck are we supposed to do?

Countless Fae have been killed and injured, all to protect me and the stupid diadem on my head. It's not worth it. There has to be a way to resolve this conflict peacefully.

"The Dark Fae only want the diadem," I say aloud. "What if we can find a way to get it off my head and hand it over to them? But only if they agree to peace once they get what they want?"

Camden shakes his head. "For one, none of us knows how to unbind the diadem from you. And two, the power contained in the relic is far too strong to give to an enemy."

That is vastly different from what Camden had said to me on my last night in Seelie. He'd told me he'd gladly give up the diadem to keep me safe. What's changed?

"But Fae can't lie. If they agree to a peace treaty and vow to uphold it, we will be safe."

"Sera," Camden sighs. "Your optimism is a credit to you, but there is much you don't know about being Fae. Vows are carefully constructed to be broken. No Fae willingly makes a promise they can't find a way out of."

"It sounds like Fae are a bunch of lying backstabbers, then." I snap.

Camden's expression darkens. "You forget, you are speaking about yourself, too, now."

The word stills, and my breath accelerates.

This is it.

Camden's broached the subject of my heritage. This is the perfect time to tell him what I've learned. King Uri is my father. My mother was his servant, and apparently his favorite. Camden and I are related. This is the perfect time to tell him and get out of our engagement.

So why can't I find the words?

I know Bass asked me not to say anything… but that was just about us being mates.

By telling Camden I'm the illegitimate daughter of his uncle, I can finally find my way out of the engagement. I'll be able to break it off without hurting Camden's feelings.

The truth is right on the tip of my tongue, but I just can't let them fall…

Why can't I do it?

Unaware of my internal debate, Camden continues, "There's no negotiating with the Dark Fae. They've proved that with their unprovoked attacks."

"I just…" I shake my head. "I just don't like this. This situation wouldn't be happening if it weren't for me."

"You can't think like that, Sera." Camden steps close and manages to, once again, slip my hand into his. "Fate would have dictated this come to pass with or without your involvement. But, for what it's worth, and despite how selfish this sounds, I'm glad Fate chose to involve you in this. I'm glad you came into my life. No matter what comes, I'll always think that."

He won't think that once he finds out about me and Bass…

I take a breath and pull away, stepping back so I'm not in reach. "Thank you for the update. It's… it's a lot to take in." I might not be able to admit the truth to him yet, but the least I can do is not lead him on.

He frowns, not sure what to make of my behavior, but he doesn't address my separation. "Of course. This must be overwhelming. Perhaps you should rest in your rooms before dinner."

I bite my cheek. Once again, I'm not the one who had to fight her way out of Seelie. I'm not a weakling. I can handle bad news. Especially when it involves me. But I don't say any of that. Instead, I take his out for what it's worth: a way to exit this uncomfortable situation.

"That's probably not a bad idea." I give him a small smile. "I'll see you later?"

Camden bows his head. "You will. Enjoy your day, Sera."

"You too, Camden."

With restraint, I take my time turning around and exiting the throne room. Camden would ask questions if I ran out of there like a bat out of hell.

I exhale deeply when I'm out sight. That had to be the most

awkward conversation the prince and I ever had. I'm sure he suspects something isn't right, but he can't possibly know what it is.

The truth is just too crazy to imagine.

I'm walking down the hall, wondering how this evening is going to go with Seelie and Unseelie sitting together during this time of turmoil, when a hand reaches out from nowhere and grabs my wrist.

CHAPTER TWENTY-FOUR

STRONG FINGERS WRAP AROUND MY WRIST AND TUG ME INTO AN adjacent room before I have the chance to react. Fear spikes and my powers flare to life in my hand, but my panic fades when I smell sandalwood and night lilies.

"Bass?" I hiss, looking over my shoulder to see if anyone saw me and is coming to investigate my sudden disappearance. I'm shocked when Vagar shoots me a conspiratorial wink, then shuts the door.

What the heck?

I didn't even know Vagar knew how to wink!

Bass pulls me deeper into the room. "How'd your meeting go?"

"Fine." I shiver when Bass's hands travel from my wrist to the small of my back, drawing me closer.

"Just fine?" He leans forward and presses a tender kiss on my temple.

My thoughts are fuzzy as desire clouds my mind. "Bass? What are you doing?"

"Making sure you remember who I am, and how much you like me." His fingers sneak under my shirt and trace small circles against my back. I arch into him.

Despite my obvious attraction, I reply, "What makes you think I like you?"

I feel his grin against the side of my head. "Years of experience."

Bass's lips press into mine, and I'm swept away by their heady sensation. My arms snake around his neck like we've been doing this for years. I still can't believe this is real, but there's no denying it when I'm pressed up against him like this.

Bass likes me. Actually, I'm pretty sure he more than likes me.

He breaks away and leans back, content to stare at me like I'm the most enticing creature in the world. My soul sings with happiness.

"Why did you really pull me in here?" I ask, sounding a little out of breath.

"To make sure your conversation didn't upset you," he replies, followed by a quick peck. "And to make sure you didn't reveal our connection."

I frown a little. "I told you I wouldn't."

"And I believe you," Bass replies smoothly. "But Pascale's told me how torn you've been about wanting to break your engagement with Camden. I wasn't sure if you'd feel tempted to use our... *relationship* as an excuse."

The thrill of hearing him refer to us as having a relationship is overshadowed by the reminder of my best friend's secrets. "Is there anything Pascale *doesn't* tell you?"

Bass's face grows somber. "It may be difficult to believe, but I swear your friendship with Pascale was not my scheme."

Seeing my skeptical expression, he continues, "I mean it,

Sera. You and Pascale were friendly for months before I enlisted her to help keep you out of danger."

I stare at the skin at the base of his throat, avoiding his penetrating eyes. I want to believe him, and I want to believe Pascale. And I do. I think…

It's just embarrassing to wonder what all Pascale has told him throughout the years. And it's annoying to be the only one out of the loop.

Bass hooks his finger under my chin. "Don't be upset," he pleads. "Not after what happened last night. I need you to know… I've been waiting for that for a long time." He doesn't need to specify he's thinking about our make out session. The lust and desire rolling off him says it all.

Suddenly, I feel shy. My cheeks turn pink. "Me too," I murmur.

His expression lightens, and I don't think I've ever seen him look so happy.

My hands trail down his arms, resting just above his elbow. "I wanted to tell Camden about my mother," I confess. "And the identity of my father. I thought telling him we're related would make him call off the engagement, saving me the trouble."

"But you didn't?"

I shake my head. "No. I—I haven't had the chance to digest the news myself. Admitting the truth to him just felt… wrong. It wasn't the right time. Does that make sense?"

Bass gently twirls loose strands of hair around his finger. "It does. It's a lot to process."

His lack of judgement means the world to me.

My head sways closer to him, longing to lose myself in another soul-satisfying kiss.

But before I can make contact, Bass interrupts, "I need to talk to you about dinner."

I blink away my lust and see he looks nervous.

"Dinner?" I parrot back. "You mean tonight?"

"Yes." He frees my hair and loosens his grip on my back to allow more space between us.

"What about it?"

He takes a breath. "You know Seelie will be joining us, as well as my generals?"

"Yes."

"We will also have other noble Seelie in attendance."

Before I can ask who, he says, "Those who don't live in the Seelie castle have heard about the Dark Fae attack. Some have traveled here as political refugees. I gave permission for them to cross my borders and stay here until the problem in Seelie can be resolved."

I bob my head, agreeing with the humanitarian act. "I'm glad."

There's no telling what the Dark Fae will do next. They could destroy Seelie searching for me. I can only hope they're stopped before that happens.

"Is there anyone in particular you're trying to warn me about?" I say it as a joke, but when Bass doesn't so much as crack a smile, I have a feeling I've hit the nail on the head.

"Oh god," I exhale. Dread fills me. "Who is it?"

Once again, Bass takes a preparatory breath. "Camden's sister. The Lady of Meadowbrook."

"Oh." *Yikes*. That has the potential to be awkward, but it's no more awkward than having to interact with Camden, himself.

He clears his throat, and it's his turn to avoid my gaze. "The lady and I are well acquainted and... well... I suppose I wanted to warn you that I will need to act friendly towards her to not raise suspicion."

I don't get it at first, but then Bass's guilty expression registers.

I release his arms and step back. Bass doesn't try to stop me. He watches me intently, waiting for my reaction.

It takes a second before I'm able to mutter, "When you say you're well acquainted… are you saying you two dated?"

"Nothing that official," Bass replies.

That's not a no…

"But you're Unseelie," I fumble for an appropriate response. My mind is spinning. I can't figure out what Bass is trying to tell me. "She's Seelie. How could you two be anything?"

"We aren't anything."

"Then why mention it?" I counter, feeling my pulse begin to accelerate.

I expected this, didn't I? I knew last night had been too good to be true. Something was bound to come between us, and it looks like I've finally discovered what that something is.

"Sera," Bass growls, reading my thoughts. "Relax. It's not what you think."

"Then explain," I snap back, irritated that he has the nerve to sound annoyed. "Stop being coy and just say what you need to say."

I cross my arms angrily, erecting a barrier around my mind and my heart. Whatever he's going to say, I won't let it affect me. I'm not weak. I'm strong. And it's going to take more than disappointment to damage me.

Bass's nostrils flare. "I mention it because I will need to be overly friendly with her," he repeats his earlier explanation.

"What does that even mean?" Overly friendly? Like, flirting?

I successfully push away the stab of pain trying to prick my chest. I refuse to let it through my barricade.

"It means she will have my attention tonight." Bass runs a

hand through his hair. "And for the sake of keeping up pretenses, I think you should do the same with Camden."

"What?" I gasp. "You can't be serious."

He frowns, looking anything but happy, but he's definitely serious. "As I said, we can't let anyone know about our connection. People will use it against both of us."

"Pascale knows," I point out.

"Yes, but she's loyal," Bass states. "As are George and Henry and a few others. But everyone else is a wild card. We don't know how the information will affect Camden or his behavior. He's young for a Fae. He hasn't learned how to keep his emotions from affecting his decisions. The last thing we want is for him to do something stupid like pick a fight with my court. Or, worse, refuse Unseelie help in retaking his court out of pride."

"Camden wouldn't do that," I argue. Camden is levelheaded and fair. He wouldn't sacrifice the safety of his people in order to spite Bass.

"No offense, Sera, but you don't exactly have first hand experience with how males behave when they're rejected by the object of their affection."

I flinch. His words are a barb under my skin, using my inexperience as a tool to make his point.

Almost immediately, Bass realizes what he's said, and how he said it. "That's not what I meant—"

I slash my hand in the air. "It's fine." I shake my head, chastising myself for letting my emotion crack through my barrier. "Whatever. Let's do it. You flirt with the princess, and I'll let Camden hang all over me." It's a petty remark, but I'm perversely satisfied when I see pain flicker across Bass's face.

Good. He should know how it feels.

I pull myself together and find the strength to walk to the

door, feeling my poor, sappy heart aching with sadness. "I'll see you later Bass. I need to rest before dinner if I'm expected to put on a show."

"Sera. Wait—"

I don't.

I slip out of the room. I'm done waiting, and I'm not doing it anymore.

CHAPTER TWENTY-FIVE

"YOU LOOK WELL," CAMDEN TELLS ME CAUTIOUSLY. HE'S standing in the main room in my guest apartment. He's more reserved than normal, and I have the feeling he's remembering my snappy behavior from the throne room. In hindsight, he didn't deserve the attitude, and I regret it.

"Thank you." I offer him a smile. "You look handsome." And he does. His bright blond hair and green eyes shine. His borrowed formal wear fits him perfectly. He's every bit the prince, and it's still so crazy to believe he actually wants me to be a part of his life. Not only does he not know me well, but he can literally have his choice of future partners.

Camden returns the expression with a relieved smile. Then, he looks behind me. "Is Pascale joining us?"

"No. She's been out most of the day. I think her plan is to meet us there."

"Very well." Camden holds out his arm. "May I escort you?" He's wary. He doesn't know how I'll react.

Geez... was I really that bad?

I slip my hand into his elbow. "Sure."

His demeanor brightens, and I decide I'm going to make a point not to be snappy or mean tonight. My problems are my own, and Camden isn't my punching bag. This situation is as much my fault as his. Meaning, he's not responsible for my personal turmoil. He's as much a victim of these circumstances as I am.

Vagar, ever vigilant, detaches himself from the wall and joins us as we leave the apartment.

We remain silent as we walk through the palace until Camden coughs. "I have a surprise for you." He sounds nervous. A quick glance confirms it.

"A surprise?"

He nods. "I don't know if King Sebastian told you, but my sister has sought sanctuary in Unseelie."

"Oh?" I try to seem surprised.

"Yes," Camden nods. "And... I would love for you to meet her. Perhaps we can speak with her once dinner is finished? You can get to know one another."

My stomach clenches. There's nothing I want less than to meet the female who was involved with Bass, but I can't say that to Camden. I'm stuck.

The only response I can give is, "That sounds nice."

His responding smile is a bright beam of happiness. "Excellent. Iona and I were quite close growing up. I'm sure she's going to love you."

I nearly choke trying to hold back my scoff. I end up coughing.

Camden's eyes shine with concern. "Are you ill?"

"No," I cough again, then wave away the question and change the subject. "I-uh... don't ever think I asked you. How old are you?"

The only sign the question surprises him is his rapid blinking. "I'm turning eighty-four in a few months."

I stumble. Logically, I knew Fae aged well. But hearing Camden is nearly one century old stuns me. He looks no more than twenty-five, if that.

Camden reads my shock like a book. "Does that bother you? You grew up among humans... I'm sure you don't have a Fae's grasp on age."

I swallow the lump in my throat. "No, you're right. I don't."

I pick up the skirt of my gown as we begin to ascend the stairs to the second floor. The dining hall is located in this area, and already I can see the difference in decoration when compared to the living quarters. The latter is more relaxed and homey, while this area's opulence puts the rest of the palace to shame. It must be where Unseelie aim to impress guests.

"So... I'm guessing your sister is younger." I try to sound indifferent, and I hope Camden can't hear my heart pounding.

"She is. By nearly a decade."

I bob my head. "Sometimes I wish I'd had siblings." Uncle Eric and Aunt Julie did their best to entertain me in my childhood, but I was pretty much alone whenever they weren't around. I didn't have a real friend until Pascale.

Which begs the question, does my family know the truth of my heritage? Do they know who my father is?

"Well, technically, Iona will be your sister soon," Camden says, trying to be kind. "I'm sure you two will get along."

All I can do is offer a tense smile. If Camden notices my less-than-enthusiastic reaction, he's nice enough not to mention it.

Two wide doors are flung open, and the light from a shimmering chandelier shines into the hallway, beckoning us inside.

Immediately, I spot Jordan and Morty. My friend looks lovely in a purple evening gown, and Morty is handsome in his

borrowed finery. Zander and Frederick stand nearby. Camden
leads us their direction.

Seeing the prince, the males bow and Jordan dips into a
curtsy. "Your Highness," they chorus.

"Good evening, everyone."

They rise, then all but Zander greet me. The loathsome sentry
does dip his chin, though. I have no doubt the gesture is out of
respect for Camden's presence. Otherwise, I'm sure he would've
ignored me.

"How long have you been here?" I ask Jordan, glancing
around. My eyes land on the back of a Fae with long, curly
blonde hair. She's surrounded by two Fae males. Seelie by the
looks of them. My stomach clenches when I realize who she
must be.

"Not long," Jordan answers. Following my gaze, she adds,
"They were here before we arrived."

As if sensing we're talking about her, the female turns around
with unimaginable grace. Her gaze lands on the Fae holding my
arm, and her face breaks into a gorgeous smile.

"Cam!" She rushes across the floor. "Is this her?"

I stiffen, bracing myself to be knocked over, but she comes to
a halt before we collide. Again, the group bows and curtsies. I
wonder if I should curtsy too, but Camden's hold on my arm is
firm. I wouldn't be able to curtsy even if I wanted to.

Camden chuckles. "Iona, please allow me to introduce my
betrothed, Serafina Roberts. Sera, this is my sister, Iona, Princess
of Seelie and Lady of Meadowbrook."

Feeling just a bid intimidated, it takes me a second before I
can reply without my voice cracking. "It's nice to meet you,
Princess Iona."

"Oh my goodness, please, just call me Iona. It is so nice to meet you!" Her eyes shine with genuine enthusiasm. I wish she sounded insincere and fake. It would be easier to dislike her.

"Camden has told me so much about you. I wish I could've seen you compete in the queen's contest, but my brother was adamant I stay away from the castle."

"Oh?" I turn my curious glance to Camden.

He smiles at his sister, then answers my silent question. "The contest is brutal. I'd rather my sister's thoughts not be tainted by such violence."

I can't tell if that notion is considerate or controlling...

I think it's a little of both.

Iona huffs a charming sigh. "My brother is too protective," she tells me. "He should know by now, I'm not a fragile piece of glass that will shatter at the slightest discomfort."

"Forgive me for wanting to keep evil as far from you as I can," Camden retorts, but he doesn't sound mad. Clearly, Camden and his sister share a loving relationship. It's sweet to see their banter and the care behind their words and looks.

Footsteps signal the arrival of more dinner guests. I look over my shoulder and see Bass enter the room, flanked by an entourage of soldiers, as well as George, Henry, Pascale, Richie, Aerie and Tonk.

Weird.

I glance around the room, confirming there are no other Unseelie in attendance. I'd thought this meal was meant to occur in front of Court. But aside from the soldiers, I know all of the Unseelie in attendance.

Perhaps it's a safety measure to keep my identity a secret. That's the only logical explanation for why the royal Seelie guests aren't being shown every courtesy by the entire Unseelie Court.

My eyes widen and my heart gives a little leap as I take in the handsome figure Bass cuts in his formal dinner jacket and form-fitting trousers. His hair is styled messily, giving him a roguish look. Between his style, and the enticing gleam in his stunning eyes, he has completely caught my attention.

The group strides with confidence and power. Bass's presence travels to all corners of the massive hall. It's like he's unleashed the hold he uses to dampen his power. Now, it's on full display.

I'm in awe.

His eyes slide over our group. Do I imagine it, or does his gaze linger on me for an extra second? He moves on before I can confirm.

A smile which matches his rogue-look pulls at his lips as he locks eyes with someone over my shoulder.

I hear a longing sigh. Immediately, my blood runs cold.

Slowly, I turn around and confirm it's Iona who's captured Bass's attention. And it's Iona who gazes at him with undeniable desire.

Just like that, my mood plummets into a dark, bottomless abyss, of which I fear there will be no escape.

CHAPTER TWENTY-SIX

THE SOUND OF CUTLERY SCRAPING FINE CHINA REVERBERATES through the dining hall. Conversation has been minimal since the meal began, and I'm wondering if it's going to remain this way for all seven courses.

I'm sandwiched between Camden and Pascale. Normally, I'd be relieved to have my best friend's company, but she and the other Unseelie Fae are stoic and broody. Or at least that's how they're trying to appear to the Seelie guests.

Camden and Iona converse easily. Even Frederick who's normally silent engages the princess. He smiles fondly and looks at her with respect and affection. He's not the only one.

Bass sits at the head of the table. Iona's to his right, and one of his generals sits to his left. The king fawns over everything Iona says, and it's grating on my nerves. My grip on the fork tightens when I hear Iona's musical laugh, followed by Bass's deep chuckle. I spear the vegetables on my plate and shove them in my mouth before I snap.

"Sera? Are you all right?"

I swallow the lump of food. "I'm fine."

Camden looks at my tight grip on the fork. "Are you sure? You haven't said much this evening."

I want to point out no one is saying much except the royals at the end of the table, but I bite my tongue.

"I'm sure." I place a hand on his arm and lower my voice. "I promise. Thank you for caring enough to ask."

Camden smiles. "You never need to thank me for that." His hand covers mine, and I can feel the affection emanating from the simple touch.

A booming laugh startles me. I jerk back, and my eyes lift on their own accord, meeting Bass's fiery gaze. He speaks with Iona, but his heated stare remains on me. I force myself to look away. I have no interest in looking like a love-struck fool while he flirts with someone else.

Camden's attention has also swiveled to the end of the table. His touch disappears. "Iona, what are you saying that's so funny?"

The princess's beaming grin turns to her brother. "King Sebastian and I were remembering the time he visited us in Meadowbrook. Do you remember?"

Bass visited them in Seelie?

Jealousy, cruel and ugly, churns in my stomach.

"You mean the time you stole my finest horse and then lost it for hours in the woods?" Camden returns. "Yes, I remember."

Iona chuckles. "Oh, come on. You can't still be mad about that. We found the stallion before nightfall."

"No, *I* found him," Camden corrects.

"But I helped search!"

Bass lifts his goblet to his lips, watching the siblings banter with a grin. Though, the lighthearted expression doesn't reach his eyes. I sense his attention shift to me several times. I swear, I even feel pressure at the front of my mind, as if he's trying to breach my defenses and read my thoughts.

Taking a deep breath, I imagine placing my hands on Bass's chest and shoving him back, far away from my mind. I must succeed because the probing pressure disappears.

Camden looks at me, rolling his eyes dramatically. My lips twitch with a smile.

"Ugh. How do you deal with him, Serafina?" Iona asks with mock annoyance. "My brother is so serious and stubborn."

"I don't think so," I tell her. And I mean it. "Camden's pleasant to be around."

"Ha!" Iona looks at Bass, shaking her head. "Serafina's been tricked. No way my brother is pleasant. How did he do it?"

Bass lowers the goblet. "Well, the humans have a saying..." He trails off, baiting the princess.

Iona doesn't hesitate. She bites the hook. "What's the saying?"

He takes another sip. This time, I meet his gaze over the rim of his goblet. "We're all fools in love."

My eyes widen for a fraction of a second before I carefully school my features. Then, my face heats.

Iona claps her hands in victory. "You're right, Sebastian. Her poor judgement can only come from being hopelessly in love with my brother." She grins wildly, looking between me and Camden. "Tell us, Cam. How did you win Serafina's affection?"

Oh my god. Kill me now.

Pascale reaches over and squeezes my hand under the table. I don't look at her, but I appreciate the supportive gesture.

"Iona," Camden says in a warning tone. "Don't be rude."

"Rude?" She blinks, shocked. "How is that rude?"

"Inquiring about a lady's feelings in public is hardly polite," Camden retorts.

Horror seeps into Iona's gaze. "Oh, no." Her attention swings to me. "Did I offend you, Serafina? I am so sorry if I did. That certainly was not my intention."

I feel the weight of everyone's attention. I fight the urge to slide down my chair and hide under the table. "It's fine."

But Iona continues to feel bad. "I should've never broached the subject. Please forgive me."

"It's fine," I repeat, a little sharper this time. I just want her to drop it.

"Your Highnesses, how long do you think you will be staying in Unseelie?" I'm surprised when Aerie comes to my rescue. We aren't exactly friends, but I guess we aren't enemies either.

I'm even more surprised when I see Aerie give Camden a flirtatious smile. First it was Zander, now she trains her feminine whiles on Camden. "I'd love to show you around the city. It's quite breathtaking and there are many sights to see."

Camden takes a moment to reply. If he were anyone else, I bet he'd be stuttering for a response. Aerie's beautiful, and it can't be easy for a guy to keep his senses when subjected to her attention. But Camden is a prince, and he's been groomed to control his reactions. I wish I had that skill.

"Not long." His words are short and crisp, not at all encouraging of Aerie's enticing behavior.

His answer catches my attention. "Really?"

"Really." His eyes soften when he looks at me. His affection is on display for the room to see. It's the one emotion he doesn't try to hide. "I can't stay away and let Dark Fae think they've won. I must go back and fight."

Fear for Camden's safety rises in my throat. Before I can speak, another voices their objection.

"Don't be absurd, Cam," Iona frowns. "You can't go back there. You don't have an army."

"Your brother thinks he will take my army," Bass interrupts.

Iona glances between the two, confused. The rest of the table does the same.

A muscle ticks in Camden's jaw. "You gave your word that you would help us."

"Help you, yes. Allow you to rush my army into Seelie without the proper preparations, no." Bass leans back in his chair, once again sipping from his drink like he hasn't a care in the world. He's every part the indifferent and distant ruler he'd pretended to be during the Seelie queen's contest.

"I must return," Camden replies. "The king and queen are there. We must get them out at least."

Concern for Queen Aria doesn't seem believable, but I think Camden is genuinely worried for the king. He's his uncle, after all.

Should I be concerned over his wellbeing, too? He's my father...

But try as I might, I can't convince myself to feel more concern for my biological father than I would any other Fae in Seelie. We may share blood, but that is the extent of our connection.

I'm shocked when Bass releases a derisive scoff. "The king? Please. Even if you returned to Seelie, you have no idea where the king is. No one's seen him in years."

"Really?" The word escapes past my lips. I direct the question to Camden. "No one's seen the king?"

"No," Bass answers for the prince. "There are some who even doubt he still lives."

I chew my lip and watch Camden.

The prince's jaw is clenched, and his hands are pressed into fists on his lap. "If that is the case, then it is even more imperative we go back to the castle and figure out the truth, once and for all. If the king is gone, my aunt no longer rules court, and it will be up to me how we fight to reclaim our land from the Dark Fae."

"Is that what this is about? Are you trying to confirm the king is dead so you can take the throne?" Bass jumps to the conclusion without reservation, and he does it scornfully.

"I'm trying to save my court," Camden growls. "The queen is compromised while at the hands of the Dark Fae, and she's not even meant to rule without my uncle. I will do whatever it takes to get my court back."

"Whatever it takes?" Bass repeats, taunting the prince. "What would happen if you found King Uri alive? Would you throw him to the Dark Fae for them to destroy, or would you kill him yourself?"

I gasp, as does the whole table.

Camden is absolutely shaking with rage. "What did you just say?"

I feel intense power begin to gather around the dinner table. I reach out and place a calming hand on Camden's arm, but I don't think it does anything. The reign on his emotions is slipping. He needs to pull them back in before he does something stupid like attack Bass. Not that the jerk wouldn't have it coming, but fighting royals is hardly conducive to maintaining an alliance.

Bass must feel the tumultuous power growing around the prince, but he doesn't blink an eye. "I'm sure you know I've heard the rumors. Your father was intended to inherit the crown after Uri, but he never had the chance."

Tension escalates. Camden's arm vibrates with the promise of violence.

"Such a tragedy, for them to burn in that inferno at your family's estate," he continues with a solemn shake of his head. "But wait... weren't you there the day they died?"

Hot, angry flames blaze through the air. Bass deflects the attack with unfathomably fast reflexes and an icy breeze. The king laughs. "Ah, yes. Those flames are certainly powerful enough to burn even the most powerful Fae to a crisp. How did you do it? Were your parents tied to their bed? Or did you knock them unconscious. I can't believe they wouldn't have fought against the flames."

Camden roars and leaps out of his seat. Iona shoves herself forward as she tries to intercept her brother, but she's no match for his size or his fury.

The prince pushes his sister aside and collides with Bass. The pair fly backwards, hitting the ground in a loud crash. Chaos erupts around the table. Frederick and the Seelie sentries go to try and pull their prince away, but Henry, George, Pascale and the others get in their way. Shoves and angry words are exchanged. Then Zander decks George, and all hell breaks loose.

Henry grabs Zander by the shoulders and tosses him on the table. Plates and glasses crash to the floor. Morty shields Jordan while also deflecting swings from Aerie and Tonk. Their efforts look half-hearted at best, but they're still attacking.

Iona is huddled at the end of the table, watching on in horror.

Darkness buzzes with excitement in the back of my mind. It loves violence.

I push it back, then stomp over to where Camden and Bass are wrestling on the ground. Camden exerts all his effort into the fire balls he's lobbing at Bass between punches, but the Unseelie only laughs and easily deflects each attack. He's taunting Camden, and I can't understand why.

"What the hell is your problem?" I shout at both of them, but mostly Bass. He's the one who started this mess. "Stop fighting. Right now!"

Use us to stop them, Darkness whispers.

We can make them stop.

The words are accompanied by intense pressure in the base of my skull. I kneel over in pain. "Ah! Get out of my head!"

Darkness swirls through my thoughts, fueling them with vengeful fire. I lose my balance and fall on my side, writhing from agony.

Use us.

Use us.

USE US.

"Sera!" I can barely make out Bass's concerned cry over the shrills of the Darkness.

I scream and scream and scream.

"What's happening to her?"

"The diadem speaks to her," Bass pants in disbelief. He must have read the dark thoughts whispering in my mind. "The Darkness. It wants free. It's trying to take control."

Yessss.

"NO!" Bass barks, speaking directly to the hissing shadows. "Stand down and leave her be."

Too late.

Then, The Darkness overtakes my mind, and I'm at its mercy.

CHAPTER TWENTY-SEVEN

I wake in a bed I'm not familiar with. The silk green sheets glide against my skin, and I realize I wear a skimpy lace nightgown. I've never seen it before. Heat fills my cheeks as I wonder who dressed me in the outfit. Then, the bedroom door swings open.

A woman with a gorgeous shade of red hair walks into the room. She carries a tea tray, using her hips to prop open the door as she enters, then bumps her hip against the wood to make it shut again.

The stranger lifts her head, and the breath rushes out of my lungs like I've been kicked in the chest.

It can't be.

My head fills with pictures Uncle Eric showed me. Her red hair... her pale skin... those brown eyes.

This woman is Kristianna... she's my mother.

And she's looking right at me.

I lift my hands to my face, confirming I'm not having another out of body experience. I'm really here. The only question is: where is here?

Kristianna has stopped in her tracks, gazing at me with a mix of awe and fear. I'm sure my expression isn't much different. She stands by the door, frozen in place, but the tea saucers rattle on the tray as her hands tremble.

With a shaky breath, she finally asks, "What are you doing here?"

I open my mouth, but I can't speak. Words escape me. I'm too caught up trying to figure out if this is a dream or some weird twist of reality. Either way, I don't know how to handle it.

Kristianna shakes herself free from her frozen state, then walks over and places the tray on a nearby table. "You shouldn't be here. You need to leave."

She closes the distance between us, and now I'm able to see subtle signs of aging. Though, she doesn't look a day over thirty. I do the math, and realize she is forty, at least.

"D-do you know who I am?"

Her eyes glisten. "Of course, I do, Serafina. I'm going to assume you know who I am, too?"

I nod. "U-uncle Eric showed me pictures."

Her hand covers her heart. "Eric honored my request then? He raised you?"

Her eyes light up when she says my uncle's name. I'm struck with the realization there must've been something romantic between Kristianna and the man who raised me. Meaning... they're not really related.

I shouldn't be surprised by the discovery. So much of my life has been a façade, all meant to protect me. But that doesn't make it any less upsetting. How much did Uncle Eric know about the truth of my birth? Does he know I'm half-Fae? What about Aunt Julie?

I take a deep breath and tell myself to take it easy. All of these questions can wait. Right now, I'm standing in front of the woman who gave birth to me. The woman everyone thinks is dead.

"He did," I answer her question.

Unsettled by her intense emotions, as well as my own, I break eye contact and look around the room. It's an elegant bedroom with fancy furniture and expensive artwork covering the walls. I've definitely never been here before. "Where am I?"

"Somewhere you shouldn't be," she replies seriously. "Which is why I asked what you're doing here?" She puts her hands on her hips, leveling me with a serious and somewhat accusatory look. I'm starting to think this can't be a dream. I wouldn't picture myself in scandalous lingerie the first time I met my mother.

"I don't know," I say defensively. "The last I remember I was at the palace in Unseelie—"

"With Sebastian?" Kristianna interrupts, her eyes widening.

I nod. "Yes…"

"Oh my goodness." She stumbles to the bed and leans against it. I can see thoughts swirling behind her distant eyes. "I knew it. I knew they'd look out for you."

"Uncle Eric and Bass?"

Her eyes meet mine. "You call the king Bass?"

"Uh, yeah. That's how he introduced himself when we met. I-I didn't know he was the king at that point."

"I'm sure." She wears a knowing grin. "I bet you didn't even know about Fae. But if you're here, I'm sure that means you've had some shocking revelations." She is purposefully vague. It's almost like she's searching to see what I know before she says something she shouldn't.

This is so surreal. The fact my mother is alive and talking to me right now, and she seems to know more about me than I expected, catches me off guard.

"I knew about Fae," I tell her. "I've had Sight for as long as I can remember."

Her grin falls way. "Even as a child?"

"Yeah."

"That must've been frightening."

I shrug. "A little. But then I met Pascale and learned I'm not crazy. I'm one of the few humans who can see Fae creatures. But I guess that's not entirely true... considering I'm not human." The accusation hangs heavy in the air, and I wait for her reaction.

Kristianna's face pales and her gaze lowers with shame. "So, you know the truth?"

"That I'm half-Fae? Yeah... I know."

She swallows the lump in her throat. "And do you know who your father is?"

"King Uri of Seelie."

My mother's head falls forward as she shuts her eyes, as if she can hide from the horrible truth of what happened to her—or what it's meant for me and my life. "Sebastian told you?"

"He did."

"When?"

"Recently." I try not to think of what else he's told me. Namely, what I supposedly mean to him.

A lone tear escapes the corner of Kristianna's still-closed eyes. "I'd hoped you would escape this Fate."

My heart squeezes. Her pain fills the room, and I feel it as if it's my own. "What do you mean?"

She opens her sad eyes. "I'm sure you've heard how Sebastian helped me escape when I learned I was pregnant."

I nod.

She takes a steadying breath and relives the worst memory

any woman can have. "You were so powerful, Sera. Even in the womb. When I reached the late stages of pregnancy, your signature was already detectable to the outside world. I'd been living with Eric and Julie at the time, but Sebastian insisted I finish the rest of the pregnancy in the Fae Realm. Specifically, Unseelie, where he could conceal your signatures from Seelie sentries searching for me."

It's hard to believe what she's saying.

I didn't have powers until I was kidnapped and taken to the Fae Realm. But maybe that's what it took to trigger my Fae magic to activate?

I don't really know. Fae stuff is still very foreign to me.

"So, you agreed? I was born in Unseelie?"

"Yes," she confirms. "And Sebastian used all of his strength to conceal your signature during birth, but you were just too powerful."

My heart threatens to stop beating. "What do you mean?" I whisper, dread building in my chest. "What happened?"

Another tear escapes. "I later learned the spike in power was detected throughout all of the Fae Realm, but only by the most powerful Fae. King Uri sensed it and sent sentries to spy on Unseelie to figure out what caused the disturbance. I was spotted not long after that, but thankfully you weren't discovered. Sebastian had been adamant about enacting another Concealment over you within hours of your birth, and I'm thankful every day for his decision. That Concealment is what kept you safe when they came for me. And it's what's kept you hidden all these years. At least... until recently."

This is... *insanity.*

It's too much. Denial claws at my throat. "Y-you're saying Bass was present at my birth?"

She doesn't hesitate. "Not in the room, but you were born in one of his private hunting lodges. He'd insisted on being around in case you needed anything."

I don't let myself feel anything in response to that. Certainly not affection.

"So, what happened?" I clear my throat. "After the king realized where you were... how did it not start a war between Unseelie and Seelie?"

Kristianna sits onto the bed with a sigh. "When Uri found me in Unseelie, I'd expected him to be furious. I was his favorite, and I'd insulted him by escaping. But the complete opposite happened. Uri was... relieved. That's the only way I can describe it. He was just happy to have me back."

Well, that's not what I'd expected to hear.

She continues, "Sebastian can't lie, but he managed to convince Uri I ran from Seelie because I feared for my life. Queen Aria's wrath had been growing, and I'd escaped to save myself. And he wasn't lying. He just omitted the fact I also escaped to save your life. Once Uri was convinced nothing romantic had been going on with me and Sebastian, he let the matter rest. As long as I agreed to return to him, that is."

"And did you?" I ask, though I think I already know the answer to that question. Another glance around the room reveals its finery is fit for a king. Or perhaps his favorite mistress.

She dips her chin. "I did."

My heart breaks for her sacrifice. While, at the same time, I struggle to understand it.

How could she leave her child behind, only to return to her abuser? It doesn't make sense.

As if reading my mind, she murmurs, "It was the hardest decision I ever made, Serafina, but I would do it again knowing my decision kept you out of danger. From the moment I found out I was pregnant, that's all I ever wanted."

Conflicted, angry, and emotional tears burn the back of my eyes. "I spent my life thinking I was a freak," I choke out. Gradually, my feelings strengthen my voice. "I thought I was crazy. I didn't have a real friend until I was sixteen years old. I grew up loved by Uncle Eric and Aunt Julie, but I never knew who I really was.

"Then I was kidnapped and thrown into a deranged competition meant to murder me and dozens of other girls, all because we look like you, the woman who stole Queen Aria's husband from her." My temper is flaring, fueled by The Darkness and its violent inclinations. I tell myself to reign it in, but my anger continues to boil.

Kristianna flinches. "Queen Aria?" She chokes out. "You were a contestant?"

"You didn't know?"

She shakes her head. "For as much as he claims to care for me, King Uri doesn't keep me privy to current events."

"Wait." I still. "King Uri is alive?"

Her forehead furrows. "Of course."

"B-but no one in Seelie has seen him for years," I relay what I've heard of the king's absence. "The Seelie think he's sick."

"No, Uri abdicated almost twenty years ago." She looks just as shocked as I am. "That means—"

"Aria holds the throne under false pretenses."

Shit. All this time, Camden should've ascended to the throne. So many young women would've been saved from a cruel death had Queen Aria never stepped up to take her "sick husband's" place.

"Wait a moment," Kristianna's head snaps back to look at me. "You competed in her contest?" She asks again.

I nod slowly.

"Oh, gods no." She leaps towards me so quickly; I don't have time to react. She tries to grab one of my arms, but her fingers pass through me like I'm a ghost.

I shriek. "What the hell?"

Terror fills my mother's gaze. "You won the contest."

It's not a question, but I confirm, "Yes."

"You have Queen Lani's diadem?"

"Yes." I lift my fingers to touch the mentioned item, only to find the diadem isn't there. Shock ripples through me.

What in the world?

"Y-you have to get out of here!" Kristianna waves her arms frantically.

"W-why—"

"You're a projection," she answers in a rush. "This scene is real. Your body isn't here, but your mind and magic are."

"Where's here?"

"Dark Fae territory." My stomach hits the floor. "You need to leave before they sense you."

"*WHAT?*"

What the heck is my mother doing with Dark Fae?

A loud crash sounds in the distance, and I hear multiple voices yelling.

"They're coming!" She shouts. "Leave. NOW!"

She doesn't need to tell me twice. I close my eyes and wish myself out of the strange room. But when I open them, I'm still there.

"I-I can't." Panic threatens to choke me.

The sounds draw nearer, and my gut tells me they are coming for me. I don't know the first thing about mental projections, but my mother's fear tells me all I need to know. Dark Fae will be able to trap me if they find me. I need to get out of here. Now.

My mother reaches for her necklace, grips it tightly, and shouts, "SEBASTIAN!"

The door is kicked open. Four Dark Fae file into the room. One tackles Kristianna to the ground while another lunges for me just as the scene starts to fade.

The last thing I see are red triumphant eyes before they disappear as the projection ends.

CHAPTER TWENTY-EIGHT

My mind feels like it's trapped in the gusts of a tornado, flung around in a random, nonsensical, and violent path. Pain burns behind my eyes. I release a strangled cry of agony. My body thrashes and bucks, trying to free myself from the chaos.

"SERA!"

SMACK.

My head snaps to the side. My cheek stings, but the slap isn't nearly as painful as the torturous sensations within my own head.

"Sera, wake up. NOW!" Bass's command is followed by someone grabbing my shoulders and shaking me.

I cry out as the move rattles my aching head.

Holy shit…

What's wrong with me?

I feel the soft caress of Darkness seep into my thoughts, whispering nonsensical words, trying to soothe me. I sense it doesn't like seeing me in pain. Which is surprising. I didn't think it cared about anything but its own freedom.

"Stop. You're hurting her." Camden barks angrily.

The slim hands release my arms. Pascale snaps, "She's suffering. We need to wake her up!"

"Her hand twitched," Bass states, silencing the rest of the room. Relief is evident in his tone. "She'll be back with us soon." He speaks with confidence, and I remember my mother clutching her necklace and calling his name like she was calling for help.

Could Bass and my mother have a means of communication? And if so, how could he keep that from me?

The list of Bass's offenses gets longer every freaking day.

My fingers flex against the soft surface below me. I try, but fail, to grip the material. My face scrunches as I try to will away the pain. I'm unable to release the tension and open my eyes. I groan, frustrated.

"Sera?" The bed dips and I feel Camden's breath fanning over my face. "Can you hear me?"

I try to respond, but a fresh stab travels through my skull from one temple to the other. I release another anguished groan.

"What's happening to her?" Someone asks shakily. I don't recognize the owner of the feminine voice.

"The Darkness took control of her mind and now she's fighting to recover from its intrusion."

The Darkness shrivels in on itself, ashamed of the role it played in my current state of agony.

The female gasps.

"How do you know that?" Camden asks.

"Because it's happened before."

"What!" The prince shouts. "When?"

"A few days ago," Bass replies, sounding indifferent, but I know him well enough to hear the tension in his words. He's worried. "Though, The Darkness hadn't held on to Sera quite as long last time. Her recovery was much quicker."

"Why didn't you tell me this?"

"Because it's not your concern."

"Not my concern?" I can imagine Camden's furious glare. "Sera is *my* fiancée. Everything that happens to her is my concern."

BOOM!

The world shakes. At first, I can't tell if it's in my head or real. Then, I register the room's startled shouts and cries.

"What the hell was that?"

They're here.

What?

I try to speak to The Darkness, but it doesn't explain. It only whispers again. *They're here.*

Another explosion shakes the surface I'm on. I want to scream. I need to open my eyes.

"Are those bombs?" Pascale shouts.

"Sounds like it." Bass, as usual, sounds calm. "Henry. George. Will you go see what's going on?"

"Of course, Your Majesty." George plays the part of a loyal subject well.

"Shouldn't you go yourself?"

"No. I'll stay with Serafina."

"I can stay with my fiancée," Camden tells him. "She's my responsibility."

"She's in my realm. Therefore, her wellbeing is *my* responsibility."

Is this really happening? Are Camden and Bass having this petty fight in the middle of a potential attack while I'm unconscious?

Someone shares my thought. "Enough, Camden."

Now, I recognize the unfamiliar female voice belongs to Iona. "And you, Your Majesty. Stop arguing. It's not helping anything."

Brava.

I'm not Iona's number one fan, but she rises in my esteem for standing up to the bickering Fae.

I focus on my breathing, trying to will the lingering pain to disappear. The pressure lessens, and I think I'm succeeding.

With a groan, I give the pain in my head another push. I swear The Darkness throws its weight behind the attempt, and my eyes fly open.

"Sera!"

"Serafina!"

Both Bass and Camden speak at the same time. The two Fae hover over me on either side of a four-post bed. I look between them, uncomfortable with their overbearing proximity.

"Move!" Pascale shoves Camden to the side and pops up in front of me. "Oh my gods, thank goodness you're awake. You totally freaked me out." Pascale leaps on me, wrapping me in a tight hug. I can't help but cringe. My muscles are tender. It's like they've been squeezed and twisted into unnatural shapes."

"Relax, Pascale," Bass commands. "You're hurting her."

"Oh, sorry!" Pascale releases me and leans back. I see her watery eyes.

I don't respond to her. My eyes are trained on Bass, and all of my emotion is in my gaze. To his credit, he stands his ground while under my accusatory stare. But I detect a flicker of remorse cross his expression.

"M-my mother," I croak. "I spoke with her."

Bass is the only one who isn't surprised.

"What?" Pascale asks. "What are you talking about?"

I don't take my eyes off Bass. "The Darkness projected me there," I tell him, and it's like we are the only people in the room. I ignore everyone else's confused glances and probing questions. This is between me and Bass, and I'm determined to get answers.

"What happened when you were with her?" Bass asks. "What did you see?"

"Nothing. Just a room. And her." I take a shaky breath, but don't dare stop now. "She's alive, Bass. She's alive, and you didn't tell me."

His eyebrows lower with sadness. "I didn't know. I swear it. Not until I heard her shout my name."

My body tingles. "Th-that was real? She really called to you?"

"What the hell is going on?" Camden's brash question breaks through my focus. "What is she talking about, Sebastian?"

We both ignore him. From the corner of my eye, I see Iona place a staying hand on his shoulder, silently urging him not to interrupt.

Bass dips his chin and answers my question, "She did. I gave her a charmed necklace before she left Seelie. She's never used it before tonight."

"But how did you know what she needed?" I ask. She'd only said his name. How could he know that she needed him to bring my projection back to Unseelie?

Bass's eyes gleam with implication. "I trusted my instincts."

I duck my face just in case I'm blushing. I had no idea our connection could extend so far.

"Will one of you please explain what you are talking about?" Pascale snaps, glaring between me and Bass.

Bass nods subtly, and I take a steadying breath. "I met my mom."

"Where?"

"I don't know exactly," I reply, "but I know she's in Dark Fae territory."

Gasps fill the room.

"As a prisoner?" Pascale asks, looking horrified. Aside from

Bass, she's the only one who knows I've never met the woman before. She knows how huge this is for me.

"She didn't look like a prisoner." I picture my mother carrying the tea tray. "A servant, maybe. But not a prisoner."

Vagar bursts into the room, interrupting my explanation. My guard's wild, red eyes find mine. My blood runs cold. I've never seen my guard took afraid. This can't be good.

"My queen," he huffs, relieved I'm awake, but alarmed by the news he has to share. "They're here."

"Who?" Camden questions. "Who's here?"

Vagar doesn't answer. His focus remains on me. "My queen?"

All eyes turn to me.

The Darkness whispers in my mind, and I know what it says is true. I sit up, straightening my spine, and brace myself for what's to come.

"The Dark Fae," I tell the room, confident in what the shadows whisper to me. "The Dark Fae have come. They're here for me."

CHAPTER TWENTY-NINE

"SERAFINA NEEDS TO LEAVE UNSEELIE IMMEDIATELY," CAMDEN commands to no one in particular. Fear rolls off him, but he tries to hide it. Unfortunately for him, nothing is hidden from The Darkness. The voices continue to speak into my mind, telling me their thoughts and the thoughts of those around me. I try to ignore them for the most part, but some of what they say sticks.

"Sera can't leave," Vagar is the one who contradicts the prince.

"Yes, she can. It's not safe here." Camden motions toward the windows where the sound of fighting has started. Everyone but Camden, Vagar, and Bass has left the room either to assess the situation or take shelter. I've regained control of my body and most of the pain has disappeared. My head's still tender, but I have clear thoughts and walking doesn't make me want to cry.

"If anyone tries to use magic to leave, Dark Fae will detect it. I don't doubt that's exactly what they are waiting for."

"Then she leaves without magic. Either way she needs to get out of here."

I'm pacing the length of the room, but Camden's words bring me to a halt. "I'm not going anywhere."

Camden's gaze swings to me. "Be reasonable, Sera. They're here for you."

"They're here for the diadem."

"Which is attached to you." Camden's wide eyes implore me to not fight him. "Your safety is our number one priority."

"Well, it shouldn't be. There are innocent people out there, fighting off Dark Fae because they have the misfortune of being in the court where I'm hiding. It's my fault they're here. I want to stay and help." The door leading to my balcony is open. I can hear the shouts of fear and clash of power as Unseelie soldiers try to hold off the intruders.

"What can you do?" Camden returns with an edge. "The last I checked, you don't even have control over your powers. And you *just* fainted because The Darkness took control of your mind. Be serious, Sera. There's little you can do to fight this battle. You need to run."

I cross my arms, angry at him for his harsh words, and angry with myself for thinking he has a point. "Then I'll give myself up."

"Don't be ridiculous."

"I mean it. I'm not a martyr, but I can't just sit back and do nothing while Dark Fae attack Unseelie, all so they can get to *me*."

No!

You can't surrender.

They will abuse us. We want to stay with you.

I hiss and shut my eyes, rubbing my temples. The Darkness's pleas sound like shrills, and they're exacerbating my lingering head pain. I manage to crack my eyes open in spite of the discomfort.

"Sera?" Bass inches closer, concern floods his expression. "What is it?"

I wave him away. "Nothing. I'm fine."

Vagar watches me knowingly. "It's The Darkness," he reveals. "It doesn't want to be taken by Dark Fae. It's begging the queen not to surrender herself."

"What?" Camden spins toward my guard. "How do you know?"

"They speak to the queen," Vagar replies. "I can hear them."

"Y-you can?" I didn't see that coming.

"Yes. All Dark Fae can hear the will of The Darkness to some extent, but not as well as the one who controls them." Both Camden and Bass eye the guard curiously.

"But I don't control them." I point out. "This is the second time they've pushed me out of my own head and have done what they wanted."

"You have more control than you think." Vagar's massive arms cross his chest, and the muscles beneath his gray skin bulge with the movement. "The Darkness is an unruly child. You must treat it with a firm hand, and it will fall in line."

The whispers trail off as he speaks, almost like a petulant toddler who's been found out.

Bass and Camden stare at me in silence. I watch as the weight of the truth settles on each of them.

"How long?" Bass questions. He's asking how long I've been having conversations with the monsters trapped in the diadem.

"After I went into the city." And attacked the rude Unseelie Fae.

He nods. "The first loss of control. The Darkness started communicating with you after that?"

"Yes."

"Gods," Camden exhales, but he looks excited. "Do you know what this means? You are the true ruler of The Darkness."

I frown. This is hardly the time for him to look so gleeful. We're under attack, for goodness sake.

"Serafina became the true ruler the moment that diadem chose her," Bass growls.

"Yes, of course," Camden is quick to drop his smile. "I know that. It's just that… power over Darkness isn't a well understood phenomenon. Queen Lani disappeared and took her knowledge with her."

I bite my lip, hoping Bass doesn't reveal that I've actually seen the queen.

He doesn't.

"Now is not the time for such concerns," Bass tells the prince, mimicking my own thoughts. I wonder if he'd actually heard them from me…

Bass gives me a look, and I have my answer.

I sigh. I really need to get ahold of my thoughts. Once again, I erect the thick barrier in front of my mind.

"Vagar," Bass addresses the guard. "What are the enemy's numbers?"

The Dark Fae's back straightens like a soldier receiving orders on a battlefield. "Not enough to overtake the palace, but enough to attack on several fronts."

"I imagine they left the majority of their force back in Seelie," Bass murmurs, lost in thought. Then, he barks at the guard, "You were once part of their people. What do you think is their strategy?"

Vagar considers the question. "To cause a distraction."

"For?" he asks.

"The chance to get to the diadem when the queen is most vulnerable."

Three pairs of eyes swing to me. I will myself not to look afraid.

"Surely, they can't think to succeed," Camden remarks. "They'd know Serafina would be protected."

Vagar grunts. "Dark Fae are maniacal and crafty. I'm sure they have a plan to neutralize anything keeping them from the queen."

"You're right."

The hair on the back of my neck stands on end. I look toward the open door and gasp when I see a Dark Fae glaring down at us from the balcony railing with triumph.

Glass vials fly through into the room, shattering into pieces when they hit the ground. Smoke plumes into the air in gray and blue clouds.

"NO!" Bass shouts, but it's too late.

The potent smoke fills the room, impairing all of my senses. I cough, choking just before something hard collides with the back of my head.

CHAPTER THIRTY

As much as I wish otherwise, the blow doesn't knock me unconscious. I fall to the ground, stars shining in front of my eyes, as blood seeps out of the open wound on the back of my head.

"Grab her!" A Dark Fae hisses. The sound of a scuffle penetrates the ringing in my ears, and I know Camden, Bass, and Vagar are fighting for my life.

I scream as four sharp stabs penetrate my calf muscle.

"Got her," a different creature yells. I feel the familiar signs of transporting. "BASS!" I shout. I'm in no shape to fight my abductor. I try to call The Darkness forward, but the whispering power is strangely subdued. I can barely feel its presence.

The blurry room and vicious sounds disappear, as do I.

This can't be happening! No one's supposed to be able to transport directly out of the palace.

But maybe I'm wrong. Perhaps transport is only limited when entering the palace. My brain is a frazzled mess, distracted by pain. I can't think straight.

I arrive on a filthy stone floor, lying on my stomach. I try to move but the pain in my leg is unbearable. I turn around to see the damage just as my abductor withdraws his talons from my tender flesh. I let out a shriek, followed by a pathetic whimper. Blood gushes onto the floor. I try to draw the limb closer to staunch the flow before I pass out from blood loss.

Before I can, the Dark Fae waves a hand over my flesh and all traces of blood disappear as my skin is magically mended. The site is still tender, but at least I won't contract an infection having an open wound in this place.

Which reminds me...

"Where am I?" I ask my abductor, sounding more confident than I feel. I draw my leg towards my body and scoot away, leveling him with my best glare.

The monster doesn't answer. He crawls back and gets to his feet. That's when I see the thick metal bars behind him.

"Wait!" I call out just as he looks ready to disappear. "Don't leave me in here." It's a pointless plea, but I have to give it a shot.

I'm surprised when the Dark Fae doesn't immediately sneer at me or say something cruel. His eyes flicker to the diadem, and I swear I see a hint of hesitation.

I jump on the opportunity to reason with him. "I-I am the queen," I say with as much authority as I can muster while cowered on the ground in a dungeon cell. "You can't leave me in here."

"I have orders."

"Well, I'm the queen. My orders override all others you have."

The creature looks unsure. His horned head tilts to the side as he thinks. Hope flares in my chest.

"You're the queen of nothing."

I lose my chance to sway the creature to my side.

Slow, purposeful steps click against the cool stone. Queen Aria glides into view, wearing her golden crown and a slinky gold dress. Cold, cruel eyes meet mine, and her lips turn up with a sick sense of joy.

My blood runs cold.

"Serafina. My... I must say I'm surprised. I didn't think Dark Fae would actually be able to get you. They were hardly gone an hour. King Sebastian must be losing his edge."

My entire body is frozen with shock, but her words crack me right down the middle. "You... you're working with the Dark Fae."

She laughs. "You can go," she waves a dismissive hand at the Dark Fae. "The girl and I have much to discuss."

I lock eyes with the creature, begging him not to leave me alone with the crazed queen. I don't care that he stabbed me with his claws and took me from Unseelie. I'm more afraid of the insane female who'd taken over her husband's throne when he'd abdicated. I'm afraid of what she's capable of doing to ensure she keeps her power.

The Dark Fae sees my expression, and he doesn't leave.

The queen notices, and her eyes harden into an unforgiving glare. "I said, leave us," she hisses.

The Dark Fae hears the thinly veiled threat, and wisely decides to heed her command this time. I can't blame him. He walks through the cell's door, and the metal bars rattle when he slams it closed.

I stay on the floor, watching Queen Aria as she watches the Dark Fae's retreat with a displeased frown. "Imbecile," she mutters. "These creatures need to learn to respect their superiors."

I take a breath and try to reach out to The Darkness in the

diadem. Its voice is a slight purr, almost like it's waking from a long hibernation. The smoke must've done something to subdue its power, as well as my other Seelie-inherited powers. I try to call warmth into my hands, but my skin remains cool to the touch.

A distant door opens and closes. Finally, Queen Aria's attention returns to me.

"Alone at last."

I swallow back nausea caused by fear. "How long have you been working with Dark Fae?"

I think of the contest and all those innocent lives lost. Did Queen Aria do it so she could get the diadem for Dark Fae?

"Only for as long as necessary," she replies, contradicting my thoughts. "I wouldn't deal with the vermin if I could get the diadem on my own." Her eyes land on the coveted item, no longer concealed on top of my head. I venture a guess that the smoke also wiped out my glamour.

"But Dark Fae don't want to be subjected to High Fae anymore." That was the point of trying to steal the diadem from me in the first place. "Why would they help you?"

"Oh, dear. You are so ignorant about so many things." She frowns with mock sympathy. "Not all Dark Fae are a part of this rebellious group."

I try not to seem surprised, but I'm sure I fail.

"But those that are were more than happy to ally themselves with me when I promised to give them information to help them find you."

"But why would you help them if they aren't going to give you the diadem?" None of this makes sense.

"I negotiated peace for Seelie Court, of course," Queen Aria says with an obvious tone.

There's no way Queen Aria will be happy with only that. The

Dark Fae are fools if they think the queen won't backstab them the moment she has the chance.

Indignation about being at the mercy of the vile queen's plan makes me mutter, "It's not even your court."

The temperature drops to a bone chilling degree.

Queen Aria's eyes are hard as ice, and her glare pierces my chest like an icicle. "What did you say?"

I refuse to be intimidated. Being angry helps, and I'm on the losing end of this situation anyway. Might as well go for broke, as they say.

I get to my feet, not breaking eye contact with the queen the entire time, ignoring the ghost of pain still lingering in my recently healed leg. "I know about King Uri, or should I say the old king."

"You dare speak about my husband?"

"King Uri abdicated his throne. My mother told me."

The queen laughs me off. "What would a mortal know about Seelie royalty? Whatever web you're trying to weave, please save us both the time and just stop. It's pointless. You are my prisoner. The Dark Fae will find some way to detach that diadem from your pretty little head, and then I will take my rightful place as the most powerful queen the Fae Realm has ever seen."

A vicious and excited gleam enters her eye, and I swear I've seen committed patients look more sane. She believes in her plan, and she believes she will succeed.

In the back of my mind, I feel The Darkness wake. It stretches and twists, and I get the sense its confused about what's happened.

"You have no claim to the Seelie throne. Camden knows," I lie. "He will take Seelie Court back from the Dark Fae. Even if you succeed in getting this tiara off my head, he and King Sebastian will work together and defeat you."

"You forget, I will have the powers of Darkness at my disposal. I will be unstoppable."

The Darkness hisses low, disgruntled by the queen's claim. I feel their cool tendrils coil around the base of my head, determined not to be separated from me. Warmth gathers in my hands, and I know I have The Darkness to thank for my return of power.

"The Darkness isn't loyal to you," I whisper quietly.

"What did you say?" Fury flashes across her face.

I straighten and let the shadows trail over my arms and legs, coating me like a loose second layer of clothing. The Darkness squeals in delight, ecstatic to be given free rein.

Queen Aria's eyes widen. She takes a step back, watching me with unbelieving eyes. She sees The Darkness. She knows it's free. And she knows what I'm about to do with it.

"I said," my voice is deep and almost unrecognizable. The Darkness has breached every corner of my psyche and physical body. We are one. My will is theirs, and they are more than eager to do my bidding. "The Darkness isn't loyal to you."

A midnight black spear flies from my palm. The queen deflects it with a shield of light, but the force of impact forces her to stumble until she hits the metal bars behind her.

I follow the initial attack with a warm ball of fire, inflating it until it's the size of a beach ball. The blaze soars and strikes another pathetic shield. The queen lowers her defending arms.

"How?" She cries. "How do you have Seelie power?" I've never seen the queen look anything but arrogant and cruel. Her fear thrills me, and I want to make it grow.

With a cold, calculating smile I emulate after the best I've seen of hers, I say, "Don't you know, Aria? I got it from my father."

The shadows swell around me, and I let them roll close enough to touch the metal bars. In a moment, I'll tell them to destroy the barrier between me and my freedom. But for now, I want to see the queen squirm.

I see the moment she connects what I've said with the truth. She tries to show no emotion, but I see her pupils constrict, and her small gasp might as well be hooked up to a microphone.

My senses are heightened with the power of The Darkness. I hear the tiny drip of water hitting the back of the cell from a leak in the ceiling. I can hear the breathing of the guard assigned at the end of the dungeon's hall. He's listening to our conversation, and I can practically taste his indecision on what to do.

"What's the matter Aria?" I tilt my head. "I thought this is what you wanted. You chose redheaded women for your contest. You liked seeing women who looked like my mother die at your bidding. Aren't you happy to learn you actually found her daughter?"

"I-it can't be," she stutters. Her face has grown pale. "Kristianna is gone. She disappeared years ago."

"About twenty years ago, I think."

Her hands begin to tremble. "No. Uri wouldn't be so careless. He's ended many pregnancies throughout the years. He wouldn't let a child live, no matter how much he favored Kristianna."

The easy manner which she discusses infanticide infuriates and horrifies me.

"Lucky for me he didn't know about me," I snap. The Darkness continues to distort my voice, wrapping around each word and making it sound more like a growl.

"You're an abomination," she says, a little bravery returning as she shoves off the bars. Now, I can't tell if she's shaking out of fear or the betrayal committed against her by her husband. The same husband who'd abdicated his throne and disappeared for almost twenty years.

Where was her anger then? Or did she not mind that he left

because she got to step into his royal shoes despite the fact she wasn't next to rule?

I shake my head. I'm done with Fae politics. I'm done being a pawn in these dangerous games.

"If you want this diadem," I lift my chin, letting The Darkness bend and disintegrate the bars behind the queen. "You're going to have to cut it off my head."

"That is easy enough." Fire sparks in her eyes, and I see the attack before it has the chance to leave her hands.

The Darkness rears high with a loud, soul-shattering cry of violence. Queen Aria cowers back, abandoning her plan, but it's too late. My shadows have marked her as enemy number one.

They surround her in a whirling tornado of black menace. She flails about, blasting weakened Seelie power at The Darkness to no avail. They continue to taunt her, striking out in sporadic swipes, and hissing in glee. This is what they've waited for: the chance to destroy at will.

There's just one thing they need from me before they can fulfill their deepest desire.

I step out of the cell, no longer impeded by metal bars. Queen Aria tries to grab onto me as I pass, but The Darkness whips out angrily, forcing her to pull back or risk losing her limb.

I walk down the cold, wet stone, feeling no emotion. I want justice, but I don't have it in me to feel anything but obligation. Queen Aria wants my Darkness. She wants to take what's mine, and she's not against killing me to get it.

I can't let her threaten me anymore. The Darkness is mine. I belong to the Darkness. We are one, and together we are unstoppable.

I reach the doorway. The guard's breathing is gone, meaning he's finally decided to go get help from his comrades.

Good. I'd rather they save me the effort. It'll make it easier to deal with them if they come to me.

Over my shoulder, I relay my command just before I leave the dungeon.

"Finish her."

I hear one loud scream, and then Queen Aria's life is snuffed out like the flicker of a match that's no longer useful.

I don't look back, focused instead on moving forward to face my next foe.

CHAPTER THIRTY-ONE

THE PATH OUT OF THE DUNGEON IS CLEAR. EITHER ALL THE guards have abandoned their posts, or it had really only been that one.

I'm in some sort of rundown fortress. Jagged stone walls line the halls, and hefty torches provide flickering light. The Darkness cushions my steps as I walk, billowing around me and assessing our surroundings. It's eager to exact more violence, and I'm likely to let it loose if anyone steps in our path and tries to stop my escape.

I walk for five minutes; I don't see one soul.

It's too quiet. Where is everyone?

Dark Fae wouldn't have brought me here and left me alone. They've gone through too much trouble trying to get the diadem to slack off now.

Something else is going on here. I bring Seelie fire to my palms, preparing myself for anything.

There!

Enemies ahead.

I stop and listen to The Darkness. With my enhanced sight and focus, I see a metal door with heavy bolts at the end of the hall. Beyond it, I hear the sound of shifting feet and a few pain-filled moans.

Release us.

Let us fight our enemy.

Not yet.

I silence The Darkness and force it into submission. The shadows bow low, but I can feel them vibrating with the need to fight.

I approach the door with confidence. I don't care what's on the other side. I'll be able to handle it. With The Darkness, I'm invincible.

It's funny to think of how worried everyone's been about me. Don't they realize how powerful I am?

Camden never should've sent me from Seelie. If I'd been there when Dark Fae attacked, I would've annihilated them all.

The thought sends a pleasurable shiver through my body. I grin.

A voice in the back of my mind cautions me not to be so cocky, but I shove away the weak thought. I'm Serafina Richards, daughter of King Uri, and mistress of The Darkness. No one can defeat me. Not anymore.

I place my blazing palm on the door's handle and pull. It swings open easily. I send The Darkness forward to intercept any incoming threat, then step inside the wide chamber.

I freeze as I take in the scene before me.

Dark Fae, dozens of them, are gathered in the room. A few lie on the floor, bleeding black blood. The light of life has left their red eyes, and their skin has a pale, sickly gray pallor. There's been a battle in here, and it looks recent.

I fist my hands and assess the other, living, Dark Fae in the room. They kneel on the glittering black tile. Their horned heads are lowered in reverence, and it takes me a moment to realize who they're revering.

Me...

My muscles are taunt, and Seelie power flares in my hands. I'm ready to fight. I sniff, trying to use The Darkness to scent out any plot against me, but my shadows detect nothing but devotion. These Dark Fae are not my enemy.

"What's going on here?" My voice is still low and scraggly. It barely sounds like me. "Who is your leader?"

"I am, Your Majesty." A lone figure rises from the ground. I immediately recognize his breathing pattern. He's the guard from the dungeon. He's the one who brought me here. "My name is Greck."

Anger spikes as I think about his talons stabbing my calf.

Growling, I ask, "What is the meaning of this? Why do you all kneel?" I may not be able to sense it, but I fear this is a trap.

"To show our loyalty, Your Majesty," Greck replies with zero hesitation.

I blink. "Loyalty?"

"To you." He dips his head, revealing two pairs of curved horns across the top of his head. "We are loyal servants of The Darkness and the one who controls it."

I frown. Once again, I try to detect the sign of the Dark Fae's true plan, but I cannot sense malice from anyone.

Our subjects, The Darkness purrs quietly. The sound is barely above a whisper. *They fought against the traitors.*

They mean us no harm.

Trust them.

Could it be?

I eye the group, intrigued. Could I have been abducted by Dark Fae loyal to the diadem?

But no. Greck had been there when Dark Fae attacked Unseelie. He's with the bad guys. At least, I think he is.

"If you are loyal, then why was I taken?" I address the male, recalling how hesitant he'd been to leave me in the cell with Queen Aria.

"We infiltrated the rebel group years ago at the behest of our comrade, Vagar de Draeton."

I stiffen with surprise. Vagar? As in… my bodyguard?

The Dark Fae continues, "We joined the rebel cause shortly before Queen Lani disappeared. We knew the power-hungry rebels would try to steal the queen's treasure, and we've spent decades immersing ourselves in their ranks so we would be in a position to thwart their plans before they could destroy the Fae Realm."

I see several in the crowd look up and nod, backing up the Dark Fae's claims.

I'm not sure what to think.

Could these Fae really be the good guys?

"But I'm not Queen Lani," I tell the crowd, waiting for one of them to rise up and try to steal my diadem. "I'm not your sovereign. Why would you help me rather than your brethren?" I motion towards the dead Dark Fae on the ground.

A different Dark Fae stands. This one is leaner than the first, and I'd guess he's years younger, too. There's deep emotion in his ruby red eyes as he says, "The Darkness has chosen you. You are our queen. We will always protect you. Any who act against you must die."

He says the words with such intensity—such promise. I'm freaked out by it. These Fae don't even know me. How can they be so blindly loyal? I could be a monster for all they know.

We wouldn't have chosen you if you were a monster. The Darkness wraps around my arms, almost like an embrace.

Several in the crowd gasp.

"The Darkness… did you hear it?"

"It speaks to her."

"She's truly our queen."

I avoid the rooms wide-eyed stares and half-open mouths. I focus on Greck. He, too, looks affected by what he's witnessed. But at least he has the decency not to gawk at me.

I clear my throat, continuing to ignore the room's excited whispers. "What exactly do you want from me?"

"It's not a matter of want," Greck replies seriously. "Dark Fae have a need."

I take a breath. "Then what is it you need from me?"

Greck's eyes shine, and his lips part to reveal a fanged, but no less beaming, smile. "We need you to be our queen, Serafina Richards from the Human Realm, and we need you to use The Darkness to restore balance in this world."

EPILOGUE

My heart pounds in my chest with dread and adrenaline. The Darkness swirls in ecstasy, overjoyed to hear Greck's response. I shove down The Darkness's emotions and order it back into the diadem. This is serious, and I can't afford to let The Darkness influence me.

"Sera?"

A host of growls fill the chamber as Dark Fae hear the intruder. I spin around and am shocked to see Bass standing on the other side of the metal door, flanked by Vagar. Both are disheveled from fighting, but they aren't fatigued. They survey the crowd of Dark Fae behind me, primed and ready to throw themselves in another battle to defend me.

But they aren't the only ones.

A blur dives, and I'm stunned to see Greck take a protective stance in front of me.

Bass narrows his glare on the Dark Fae, then lifts his hard gaze to mine. "Sera? Are you all right?"

"The queen is fine," Greck snaps. "Why are you in Dark Fae

territory, King Sebastian of Unseelie? You know traveling across borders uninvited incites violence."

The Darkness squeals with delight.

"I'm here for your queen," Bass replies with cool regality, unaffected by Greck's threat. He motions to the Dark Fae behind him. "I've been escorted by the queen's personal guard."

Greck's attention flicks to Vagar, and recognition widens his red eyes. "Vagar de Draeton?"

Vagar steps forward. "Well met, Brother Greck."

"Well met," Greck returns. "You have protected our queen?"

Vagar nods. "Since the moment Queen Lani passed her the diadem. May the gods bless her reign."

"Gods bless her reign," the room choruses back.

A chill travels down my spine. I glance over my shoulder. The crowd of Dark Fae watch me with eagerness and hope. I can feel their expectation pressing down on me, as well as their excitement.

"Why have you brought the Unseelie king to our lands, Vagar?" Greck questions.

"Because Sera is my responsibility," Bass answers for Vagar. "I will always protect her."

His eyes catch me in their snare, and I feel the depth of emotion behind his words. No matter if we have miles between us or if we don't see eye to eye, Bass will always protect me. He'll never leave me on my own. Not anymore.

My stomach clenches, but in a good way.

The crowd has a less than enthused reaction. They mumble and hiss, clearly displeased by Bass's declaration. I don't understand why until Greck responds.

"The queen belongs to no one," the Dark Fae spokesperson growls. "We are her subjects. We will keep her safe. Look around you. We have eliminated the rebels in our midst, and we will destroy the rest with time."

Bass's gaze travels over the fallen Fae. "You killed these Fae?"

Greck's shoulders roll back. "We did."

"And the rest?" Bass continues seamlessly. "The rebels in Seelie? And those who lie in the dark, waiting for the chance to strike. You think you can protect her from them?"

"We know we can. It is our sacred duty."

"Don't be foolish," Vagar reprimands. "King Sebastian has an army at his disposal. You have a fighting force filled with potential traitors. His Majesty can protect the queen better than we can on our own."

"The queen can protect herself. She defeated the Seelie queen. She can defeat the others."

Bass and Vagar wear matching expressions of surprise.

"Aria?" Bass looks at me, a question in his eye.

"Dead," I confirm. I feel no guilt when I think of how I ended the cruel queen's life. I don't know if I should be concerned by that or not.

A flicker of shock crosses his expression, then he dons a neutral mask. Once again, he looks at Greck. "Sera will be leaving with us."

"She's not going anywhere."

Billowing power rolls off Bass, filling the air with its potent signature and heavy weight. "You dare get between a male and his chosen mate?" The question comes out low and dangerous; an obvious threat.

You could hear a pin drop. Not one of the Dark Fae speaks or even breathes. They all wait to see how their representative will respond.

For my part, I'm shocked Bass revealed the truth to such a

large group of Fae. What happened to keeping it a secret so no one can use him against me?

"I—" Greck pauses. "I didn't know."

"Well, now you do."

Greck swallows nervously. He hears the irritation in Bass's voice. But he doesn't hesitate to risk his wrath when he turns to me, "Is this true my queen? Are you linked to the Unseelie king?"

Dozens of eyes land on me.

I glance at Bass.

His nod is subtle, but I understand. Now is not the time to keep the secret. These Fae won't use it against him, unlike others.

I breathe in through my nostrils, then exhale. "Yes. King Sebastian and I are mates." I don't think that will ever be normal to say.

Murmurs fill the air.

"The gods have blessed the queen's reign."

"With the king, we will be unstoppable."

"May their mating happen sooner rather than later."

My cheeks are burning. The Dark Fae wear beaming, sharp smiles. I look away from the crowd, embarrassed by their enthusiastic responses.

"What did you just say?"

Every neuron in my body short-circuits. For several seconds, I cannot move. My mind must be playing tricks on me. There is no way Camden is here. There's no way this is how he learns the truth of my relationship with Bass.

Please, I pray to whatever god is listening, *don't let this be real.*

No one speaks. All eyes rest on something behind me.

I hold my breath and slowly turn around.

I'm greeted by Camden's infuriated and pained glower.

Damnit.

The Darkness senses my distress and tries to cuddle in my chest to comfort me. I thank it for the kind thought, but usher it back into the diadem. I don't know how this conversation is going to go, and it is probably best not to have the volatile power within easy reach.

"Camden," Bass speaks, aiming for nonchalance. "Nice of you to join—"

"Don't you dare speak to me," Camden snarls. He's shaking with anger. I bite my lip, unsure how to fix this situation.

"Camden—" I take a step forward, but Bass holds out an arm and stops me.

Camden sees and shouts, "Don't touch her!"

Surprisingly, Bass drops his arm. He holds his hands up to show he's not a threat.

Camden's behaving like a wild animal, pinned in a zoo, eager to destroy those who've stolen his freedom.

I lick my lips. "Camden, please calm down. I can explain."

"Is it true?"

I nearly choke. "What?"

"Is it true?" he hisses between clenched teeth. "Are you mated?"

"No. I mean… there's been no ceremony or anything like that." I'm rambling, but I don't know how to stop myself. "But we have a connection. We have for a while now."

"How?" Camden's eyes shine with angry tears, and I hate myself for causing him pain. "How did the king seduce you? Was it during the contest? Was it before you were my fiancée?"

My own eyes begin to water. Even now, Camden wants to give me the benefit of the doubt. He wants Bass to be the evil one and for me to be an innocent victim.

But that's not reality.

"I've known Bass since I was sixteen," I murmur, wishing this conversation could be happening anywhere but here. Camden deserves privacy, not an audience.

"But our connection has existed from the moment she was conceived by her mother and your uncle, King Uri of Seelie." Bass steps so he's positioned between me and the volatile prince, ready to intercept his reaction, no matter what form it takes.

Camden sucks in a breath. So do many others in the room. I wish we could speak somewhere else, but I don't think that's a possibility in Camden's current state. He looks ready to explode at any minute.

"You lie."

"You know I cannot lie."

Camden's hands fist at his side, glowing with power. I hope he's not dumb enough to fire at Bass.

"So, this was all a ruse to play me for a fool," he states with no emotion. That's scarier than if he just yelled.

"No, Camden," my eyes plead for him to believe me. "No one tried to trick you. I didn't even know the truth until recently."

"Don't lie for him, Sera," Camden snaps.

"I'm not lying!"

Camden ignores me, too immersed in his own pain and anger to see reason. He points a shaking finger at Bass. "This is war, Sebastian. You better get ready, because I won't stop until I destroy your kingdom."

I gasp and reach out for Camden's arm, desperate. If I can just explain, he won't be so mad. I'm sure of it.

Camden's kind and fair. He's hurt, but he will understand if I have the chance to tell him everything. I just need him to listen to me.

But I'm too late.

My hand goes right through his arm as he blurs. A tear rolls down my cheek as I make eye contact with his disappearing form, followed by another when I register the anguish on Camden's expression.

"P-please," my voice cracks. "Wait."

He jerks his head once, then his form disappears.

And that's how the Second Great War begins.

***

To be continued in *Queen of Darkness*.

ABOUT THE AUTHOR

Samantha Britt is an avid reader and enthusiastic writer of new adult and young adult paranormal and fantasy novels. When not lost in the fictional world, you can find her in Texas. More often than not, she will be busy making memories with her precious family which includes Sam, her husband, Dan, and their mini-goldendoodles, Bailey and Bella.

ALSO BY SAMANTHA BRITT

Made in United States
North Haven, CT
08 August 2023

40083429R00168